WHATEVER IT TAKES

WHATEVER IT TAKES

Vonnie Bittner

XULON PRESS ELITE

Xulon Press Elite
2301 Lucien Way #415
Maitland, FL 32751
407.339.4217
www.xulonpress.com

Paperback ISBN-13: 978-1-6628-3045-7
Ebook ISBN-13: 978-1-6628-3046-4

Jezebel his wife came to him and said to him, "How is it that your spirit is so sullen that you are not eating food?" So King Ahab said to her, "It is because I was speaking to Naboth the Jezreelite and saying to him, "Give me your vineyard for money, or else, if it pleases you, I will give you a vineyard in place of it." But he said, "I will not give you my vineyard." Jezebel his wife said to him, "Do you not reign over Israel? Arise eat bread, and let your heart be joyful; I will give you the vineyard of Naboth the Jezreelite."

I KINGS 21: 5-7 NASB

Acknowledgements

I would like to thank the following people for helping me along this long journey. First is Professor Cynthia Wolford, Creative Writing Class ENG 340. Thank you for encouraging me to write this short story into a novel. My friends along the way like Jan Gidley, Julie Williams, Linda Murphy, Veronica Perlick, my coworkers at St. Michael's and my instructors in my criminal justice classes in Tampa, FL, and many, many others.
A very special thank you to my Illustrator, of the book cover, Joel Lazarus. Isabel Bachman - The Conjurer is truly a masterpiece and a work of art. Thank you for putting up with all the details as I was seeing this portrait to be.

I want to give a heartfelt thank you for Pastor Wayne Mitchell, my spiritual advisor, Kathy and Nancy, my intercessors and prayer warriors.

Dedicated:

To my family
for allowing me the time I needed
to write this book

Table of Contents

Introduction

The captain announces, "Mr. Ethan, the plane will land in approximately 30 minutes." Ethan closes his laptop and puts his paperwork back into his briefcase. He moves from the conference room and closes the secure door behind him. Moving to the traveling seat, he sits down and fastens his seatbelt. *The thought of going home is always such a bittersweet feeling to me, he thinks to himself. When Linda was alive, I couldn't wait to get home. Now, each time I come home, I realize how much I really miss her. Our home is now just a house. She made it a home.*

I love the business I do and I get to meet the most amazing people all over the world. Some of them I will see tonight at the annual Bachman Gala. Again, tonight will be another bittersweet situation. Without Linda with me, it's just a company event. She made these parties come alive. Sadness comes upon him and he allows it for a time. He loves thinking about her. *Linda's smile would light up a room. As his memories continue, they dance together in the moonlight and forget there are other people around them dancing as well. He smells her hair as she snuggles against him with her head on his shoulder. Ethan whispers in her ear, do you know just how much I love you?"* His eyes are closed as he dreams of days gone by. Suddenly the plane lands and he wakes back up into the reality she is gone and not coming back.

Andrew Bachman hesitates just a moment before knocking on the door to his wife's bedroom and opens it.

The room is one of the largest in the house with a fireplace and bookcases on one side. A warm glowing fire is blazing, penetrating throughout the depths of her suite. Antique bedroom furniture handmade from a master artisan centuries ago, a masterpiece of cherry wood carved with meticulous detail and care. The poster bed brings out the colors of around the room and curtains, which pools on the floor beneath the windows. His wife Isabel took great pride in creating her most personal sanctuary; Andrew enters and goes directly to the sitting room where Isabel is sitting in front of her mirror looking extraordinarily breathtaking as usual.

Speaking out loud, "I am so glad I added a sink in this room. It is very handy."

"Tonight will be as perfect as all the other events I've hosted in our home. I can't wait to see the look on Ethan's face when we finally reveal our news. I am still amazed he never found out anything. It will surprise him. As much as I hate him, maybe we can start burying the hatchet. Now is there anything which I've forgotten?"

Isabel is finishing up her last touches on her hair and makeup as her husband walks into the dressing room.

"Honey, can you fix my tie? I can never get it just right like you do," he exclaims.

As he winks at her, she replies, "Certainty, but you would think after all these years you could fix your tie yourself!" She smiles as she is fixing the tie she adds, "Why does your cousin Ethan always have to come to our parties? He is such a downer with his self-righteous attitude. Doesn't he know how much I loathe him?"

Andrew answers, "Oh, I'm sure he knows without a doubt in my mind. I think he comes just to taunt you."

"That makes me hate him even more. Can't you do something about him?" she asks.

"Honey, you know I can't. We might own just 1% more of the company stock than he does, but he owns enough to block certain deals. I might be the Chairman of the Board, but Ethan is the CEO. They must include him in the major decisions, hence he's also needs to be at our party tonight. It is after all a business party, including a wonderful tax write-off."

"Isabel, you know we have been through this conversation a thousand times. My Father and Uncle David set the board up that way and there is nothing legally we can break that agreement. Believe me; I've had my lawyers look it over with a fine toothcomb. The bylaws are irrevocable," he states.

"I just wish when he gets here tonight our security dogs would just tear him to piece, and it finishes him!" Isabel finished stated, smiling vehemently.

Andrew walks away, shaking his head.

Invitation Only

Doorbell rings and their seasoned butler, Austin, answer's the door in his formal attire. Guests greet Austin as the valets' park their cars. The evening events are beginning. Each invited guests arrive in their black ties and the women in their grand splendor. This is not just another dinner party; it's the who's who of the Bachman's empire. Flowing gowns are stunning. The colors of each gown are vibrant with sequins, giving the attire of a 3-dimensional aspect, making it come alive, creating an element of eloquence and poise. The dazzling display of diamonds and gems glistened in the crystal chandeliers, sending prisms dancing throughout the room.

Isabel would expect no less than perfection from her guests and for herself. Tonight, they would not disappoint her! The gentlemen are wearing their black tie tuxedos ranging from Kiton, Brioni, Gucci, Zenga, and Alexander McQueen to Armani Suits, depending, what country they are from.

As the house fills with their guests, Isabel stands up. She glances one more time into the full-length mirror framed in a gold inlay. *Yes, this is the most exquisite evening gown she has worn yet.* This is a stunning crimson red. She leaves one of her shoulders bare while she covers the other shoulder with magnificent beading and satin. The beading continued down her left side, past her hourglass waist to the top of her hip. It covers her right breast with crimson satin and beading, which was painstakingly hand sewn. Her gown flows to the floor in a satin pool around her Christian Louboutin Maralena Flame Sandals.

The designer of her specifically created gown, Erin Whitmoyer, designed the earrings and elaborate ring just for her. She composed the gown along with the jewelry of rubies, diamonds, and gold. All are masterpieces into themselves.

Delighted with her appearance; Isabel strolls through her doorway as she shuts the door louder than normal. Sweeping down the hall; knowing she is getting her guests' attention without looking. She is the Queen of the gala, and she knows it. She turns as she now stands at the top of the staircase. Ever so slowly, she descends to the landing. The florist placed Black Magic long stemmed red roses on each side of the stairs and 2 large rose bouquets on pedestals on the landing next to the huge stained-glass window. Above her is a massive chandelier, illuminating the scenery behind her. Those guests, who have been to these parties before, look past her and perplexed at the stained-glass scenery she chose. The dragons, witches, and fairies flying above a small-town setting are haunting. The executives who are experiencing the gala for the first time, they can't take their eyes off her. She is riveting.

Isabel glances at her guests as they all accumulate at the bottom of the stairs. She gazing around, smiling. Her guests are all admiring her. Her pride absorbs all the attention in, stroking her ego to new heights. She descends the stairs. They invite only the top executives and their spouse or significant other. As she looks around, she sees that all were present except for one so far.

Maybe her wish will come true tonight and HE won't be here. She smiles even brighter at the thought.

The Bachman Tool and Dye Corporation extend internationally. They expect all the top executives of each office to attend, and no one dares to disappoint Andrew and Isabel Bachman! Missing such an event as this one would promise to commit career suicide. As Andrew mingles around the guests, he notices how each year more of Eastern Europe is in attendance. This year's additions are India, Japan, and Saudi Arabia. He's pleased with how well diverse his company is becoming. Ethan is doing such a magnificent job with all of our new clients and the countries where they are from.

Everyone who has worked with Isabel and Andrew knows Isabel for being the driving force behind Andrew, yet he is also a force to be re-conned with. Andrew's first cousin, Ethan Bachman, is a powerful man and in time they have become opposites. He is a man of integrity and has no reservations about standing up to Andrew and Isabel when he knows the decisions they are proposing are unethical.

Andrew and Ethan's fathers were twin brothers. Omri[(1)] and David Bachman had taken their father's small neighborhood blacksmith business of developing new equipment for local businesses and farmers to neighboring communities.

Omri and David framed the first work order they received from Canada, their first International country.

Today their hard work, perseverance, and dedication to create products worthy of the Bachman name paid off financially to their families for generations to come. They developed a board of directors just before the brothers passed the business onto their sons, Andrew and Ethan. The entire board of directors would be here tonight, along with all the top executives throughout the world!

As the guests mingled, the surprise announcement brings excitement to the variety of small groups forming throughout the grounds. The Bachman estate is eloquent and vast for its location. With shrubbery manicured and they strategically placed the flowers throughout the property. Not a leaf is out of place. Perfection with Isabel's final approval!

Jezreel Mansion is in an exclusive section of Manhattan. Visitors, without certain prior permission, and undesirables discouraged from trying to venture into this area due to the private patrol cars and gated communities.

The grounds had a mini forest with wildlife everywhere scurrying about. Chipmunks, squirrels, and rabbits frolic daily. Patio and pool areas, with all its waterfalls, have lanterns flicker in the gentle breeze, setting the serene mood for the outdoors. Guests could talk out here and can hear each other speaking. The music played softly in the distance from the live orchestra performing in the courtyard. The scenery is perfect and with something in the air that holds a mystery to the evening adds to the excitement. Everyone is wondering what the announcement is and the expectations, which might come with it. The catering staff overhears the guests questioning if the announcement is a new takeover of another business, a new office in yet another foreign country like Dubai, or if management is being moved. It seemed to be one or the other for the parties held at Andrew and Isabel Bachman's each year. The guests who are staying indoors are also questioning each other about what the announcement is. Nobody seems to know anything. This year's news is top secret, some are saying with no leaks. Andrew and Isabel were mingling with the guests, laughing but not divulging any hints of what the news was. "Time will tell" is all they will say.

Brian Schmidt, Adam Dickson, and Julie Wagner, the semi-new executors, are standing by the fireplace and admiring the family portrait. Sandra Sved, one of the Vice Presidents, and Julie are quietly discussing the resemblance the daughter has to Isabel and how the boys look like Andrew, Brian and Adam commented. The two oldest children, Athaliah (Athea) and Johoram (Jo) are away at boarding school but the youngest son they knew nothing about and surprised to see him in the picture. A member of the board of directors, Kent Noble, is standing close by. He leans over and whispers, "The youngest son had died years ago in a terrible accident. Isabel and Andrew were so distraught they had a private ceremony and haven't spoken of him since. It would be best to move on," he states.

As Kent walks away, he notices Robert and Diana Hampton. He heads over to talk with them. Robert and Kent endeared friends, almost as close as Robert and Ethan are. Both had known Omri and David and enjoy the stories of Andrew and Ethan growing up in the company. They watched as the company grew to international proportions. Kent and Robert are the only ones besides Andrew and Isabel, which know the secrets of the night's events.

Just then, the doorbell rings again. In walks the most eligible bachelor at the party. Any woman would love holding onto his arm, but he always comes alone to their parties. He deliberately makes it a point to be the last one to arrive.

Although he does not intend it to be, he is the electricity, which sparks the events at the Bachman's grand galas! He is a tall man, muscular and possessed. Intellectually, he maintains a keen sense in business. He naturally possesses an uncanny ability to make the right business deals, which everyone benefits. The most important value he possesses is his powerful faith in God and a dedication, which would have made his father David proud. He is handsome and debonair, yet he never uses his appearance to "influence other decisions or impressions" as others do. He is a man of integrity and honesty, a hard combination to find in the elite of today's corporate world.

Ethan Bachman travels alone, or with his entrusted executive assistant Esther Yagel, since the death of his beloved wife Linda a few short years ago. Has it really been 10 years since she passed on, he silently remembers? Ethan has no desire to develop another relationship, nor does he want to take the time. He vowed never to hurt like that again. Linda was a vivacious woman. She made him feel complete. She herself was also a woman of integrity and was outspoken when she saw the under privileged being taken advantage of. Linda was kind to others and even though she could not bear children, both Ethan and she took great pride in taking their "little cousins" under their wings. Linda often commented to Ethan she believed it was their love for Athea and Jo, which sent them to boarding school. Isabel could not stand the closeness Linda and Ethan had for her children, which she didn't have with them herself. It had been a well-known fact that there was no love lost from Isabel Bachman when Linda died. She hated Linda even more than she does Ethan!

Isabel would complain to Andrew that Linda made her feel belittled and evil. Though Linda never intended to make Isabel feel that way, she knew it was because of some things that Isabel did.

Linda would not allow Isabel to behave poorly in her presence, nor would she allow her to be a part of the benefit charities it involved her in. It was all a moot point now since Linda's heart gave out too soon. She did not wake up from her sleep one morning while Ethan was away on business. He has never forgiven himself for not being there for her in her time of need. He missed her intensely, especially at events such as this one, as he reflected to a happier time in his life.

Upon Ethan's entrance, he catches a glance of Isabel. She seems to send daggers out of her eyes towards him. He laughs and approaches her.

"I see you have outdone yourself again this year. You look ravishing as usual, Isabel. That blood red gown is very becoming on you!" he compliments.

"You look debonair yourself and late like usual," she retorts.

With a flip of her hand, the staff directs everyone into the dining room. Isabel and Andrew are the last to be seated, and they took their places at the ends of the table. With chatter softening, the lobster bisque is being served and waiting for the guest to partake. Its tomato base is slightly spicy with whole lobster claw meat in the center with a slight parsley garnish floating on the top. Guests remark on the richness of the bisque and the best they have ever tasted. Isabel remarks they had brought in the bisque from one of her favorite restaurants in Boston. Staff removes the dishes as the second set of staff brings out the next course, a small salad with just a hint of raspberry balsamic vinaigrette. The salad cleans the palate for the next course, which comprises potatoes with parsley and butter, followed by a Cornish hen for everyone, roasted over an open fire slowly cooked to perfection. Tiramisu is the dessert for the evening, followed by coffee, tea, and some sipping wine. Usually, the wine's presented in the bottles, but not in this case. The serving staff asks each guest what color wine they want, and they serve the wine in their wine glasses. Ethan thought it was odd because they usually serve the wine by handing each guest with the wine of their choice in glasses which are brought around the table, but he said nothing.

The Bachman's have outdone themselves once again, Isabel could overhear the guest saying, which pleases her. As the chatter escalates, Andrew and Isabel stand up. Isabel taps the side of her wineglass. Everyone quiets down and waits in great anticipation for the announcement.

Andrew speaks up. "As you all know, I appreciate a fine glass of wine. Have you been enjoying the wine served tonight?"

They all agree they have been enjoying it. Those with the red wines admire the bouquet and body, and those with the white wine are enjoying the delicate exchange of semi-dry mixed with a variety of fruits. The chatter escalates again.

Andrew taps his glass; he speaks up again, "I'm glad you have been enjoying it because The Brotherhood Winery, [2] the oldest winery in the country, from upstate New York is now owned by the Bachman International Corporation"

"I love the new name!" Kent Noble shouts out.

As the applauding continues, Ethan slams his fist on the table and without a word spoken, storms out of the room. He is furious! As he slams the front door shut, he is so lost in thought he does not hear a woman scream, "ROBERT!!"

Corporate Boardroom

Ethan is pacing the floor as the board members slowly trickle in. He looks out the enormous windows overlooking NYC. *What a breathtaking view,* he thinks. *I have never grown tired of it, but today I have other matters to deal with.* Moving away from the window, feeling anxious, and faces the Board Members who have arrived. He scans the room to see if Andrew has arrived yet. He's not here. The other members are making their coffee or tea and take their assigned seats without saying a word. Tension is thick that morning, and those entering the room did not want to be there. The silence is deafening. Ethan called the meeting when he got home last night. He notified all the members by text and they knew he was angry.

The dinner party the night before did not last into the early hours of the morning as it had in previous years. Disaster had struck to which Ethan wasn't aware of yet. Everyone is waiting for Andrew to enter. Even Kent Nobel, the senior board member, didn't want to be the one to tell him about Robert. The other board members are waiting to talk with each other before entering the boardroom.

Everyone decides it is Andrew's place to tell Ethan. They know how close Robert and Ethan were. Ethan and Robert weren't just colleagues; they were best friends. From the expression on Ethan's face and his reaction last night, it would be a shock, which Ethan won't be prepared for.

The corporation now owns The Brotherhood Winery, and Ethan is not having it. Everyone in the boardroom is sure there would be an explosion between Andrew and Ethan. It was rare to see such emotions from Ethan, and he was showing it last night when he slammed Andrew's door shut on his way out.

Owning this winery had become an obsession with Andrew years ago when it was once up for sale. The owners refused to sell it to them because of something which happened between Isabel, Andrew and The Winery. Nobody is sure of what the problem was, but they knew it was huge.

Charley Barrows, nephew of the previous owner, bought the winery. The property has been in the family for as far back as the family could remember.

Isabel went to Charley to buy it from him. He turned her down. Everyone knew that and how it infuriated her. They all learned not too long after Andrew married Isabel that turning her down for something that she really wants is not a pleasurable experience. Charley, at one point, was so angry at Isabel that he refused to have anything to do with her. That was when Andrew worked with him, but that ended up even in a worse situation. Now the deal is complete. They all couldn't believe it. They talked about it last night after Ethan left. There were so many questions they asked about Andrew and Isabel, but nobody got any actual answers. They were so pleased with themselves that they finally made the purchase that all they wanted to talk about is what the future has in store for their new company.

Both Andrew and Isabel seemed genuinely surprised by Ethan's reaction. It didn't seem to concern them too much, though. They blew it off as one of his self-righteous attitudes. Now was the time to pay the piper, and all the board members are about to watch the fireworks whether or not they liked it. They all watch Ethan as he paces the room. Would Ethan be able to keep his normally calm demeanor?

As much as Isabel wanted to be there, this board meeting is off limits to her, per Ethan's directives. Ethan knew when he was out of town on business she attended the meetings, even though she could not vote on matters. She is Andrew's wife, and she is powerful. When she wants to, she has a very pleasant side of her when she wanted something from you or the situation. She could not manipulate Ethan, and that infuriated her.

Andrew finally wanders in, looking as if his head is pounding from a slight hangover. Ethan glares at him as he takes the chair at the head of the table.

Ethan addresses him, "I'm glad you could finally make it," sarcastically.

Andrew just smiles. Ethan cannot restrain himself any longer. Andrew responds, but Ethan cuts him off.

"What do you mean WE bought The Brotherhood Winery? Not one person has consulted me in this matter. I know Charley, the owner, and he told me he would never sell it to you. The winery is the oldest and most respected winery in the country. It survived prohibition by making altar wine for the churches and thrives on its own. How did you change Charley's mind? It wasn't another of your ruthless deals, was it because I will not have dishonesty and treachery as a part of this company! You might have the deciding vote in this company, but our stockholders and I will not tolerate it!" Ethan blasts.

"I am serious, Andrew! We will not tolerate any unethical business dealings and this one smells rotten!! I don't know how or when you did this, but we will cancel it!! This was all done behind my back too!! You knew I would have stopped it! Now I know why I was sent to set up an office in Dubai for the past six months. You wanted me out of the way, so you could do this behind my back. Now it's a clearer picture! How could you, Andrew! The Brotherhood Winery is a distinguished winery. We are a tool and machine company. I see no association between the two except for your own greed and desires. I know that you have wanted to buy this company for a very long time. Why, I do not understand, but it seems to have become an obsession with yours and now you have made our company a part of it. I will not tolerate this from you! DO YOU UNDERSTAND ME ANDREW!" Ethan rants, trying hard to regain his well-known composure in times like this.

Ethan never raises his voice, except a few times with Isabel. He knows he is losing control over his emotions and this was not like him. He isn't sure why he is so furious about this situation, but he is. For now, he has to get his composure back. He straightens up and unclenched his fists, which have been pounding on the boardroom table. He waits for Andrew's response.

Andrew is now defending the purchase by stating in a calm reserve tone; "I wanted to surprise you Ethan with such a Christian company joining our corporation. I thought you would be happy. I do, however, have grievous news for you. Charley died, a month or so ago, in a terrible accident. He was on his way to one of our meetings. The last I heard, the police said they stopped investigating the situation. The Medical Pathologist said he died of natural causes before the car collided with a stone pillar."

"You have been so busy with setting up the new office. We thought buying the winery would be a wonderful surprise for you when you came back for the party."

"Robert and I have been working on this deal for several months. You left last night as Robert collapsed. He was getting up to give more details about the merger. He suddenly seemed to become dizzy and grabbed at his heart. Without saying a word, he fell back down into his chair and onto his wife with his eyes wide opened, looking at her in great distress. I just got word he had a fatal heart attack. He died in the ambulance before getting to the hospital last night."

After several minutes of total silence, Ethan replies, "I'm sorry to hear that. He is one of the righteous guys! I can't imagine Robert going along with the takeover of 'The Brotherhood Winery"!

"That is exactly why he was chosen to be on the project, because he was a Christian man and could keep the negotiations legitimate for you," Andrew calmly replies.

"For the record, let it be known I don't like it, not one bit! Something is wrong here and I will find out what it is!" Ethan then left the boardroom.

As he turns the corner he literally runs into one Detective, which his Executive Administrative Assistant, Mrs. Esther Yagel, is directing to the boardroom.

Chapter 3

The Detective's Interview

"Excuse me," Ethan says as he looks over at Esther. "Mr. Ethan Bachman, I would like to introduce you to Detective Dan Gibbons and Detective John Rocco from the New York Homicide Division."

"The Homicide Division, who was murdered?" Ethan inquires.

"Is there a place where we can talk?" Detective Rocco questions, "We are here to look into the untimely death of Robert Hampton. We are just starting our investigation and we have some questions for you."

"The boardroom is just clearing out. We can talk in there for now." Ethan replies.

Ethan quickly thought, *humm if they murdered Robert than these are some people the detectives might want to meet.* As he opens the doors, he sees the questioning looks of those in the room. Ethan strolls in first as Detective Gibbons and Detective Rocco enter behind him. They notice a room full of potential suspects of the influential society variety. From first appearances, these people are among the elite of the New York City and the International business markets.

Andrew is the first one to speak up, looking at Ethan with questionable eyes. "Ethan; who are these gentlemen?" He looks at their overly worn cheap suits. These men were not the normal men brought into the boardroom for business meetings, Ethan thought to himself, *Andrew, when exactly did you become such a snob?*

Ethan replies, "My dear cousin, this is Detective John Rocco and his partner, Detective Dan Gibbons. They are here to investigate the death of our colleague Robert Hampton."

"I don't understand. I got a phone call from his wife last night. She is saying he had a fatal heart attack and died on the way to the hospital. Why are homicide detectives here," Andrew asks?

Detective Rocco speaks up as he reaches out his hand. "Andrew Bachman, I presume. We would like to talk to you shortly, but for now we would like to talk with Ethan Bachman alone. Are you going to be available after I am done talking with Ethan?"

"I am a very busy man. I will, however, make some time for you when you finish speaking with Ethan. I'll tell my Executive Administrative Assistant to let me know when you are ready." At that Andrew and the other board members leave, Ethan is wondering, *when is it going to be their turn? They were all there last night when Robert collapsed.*

"Don't let me forget to ask Ethan for all of their names and phone numbers," Rocco says to Gibbons.

"Now gentlemen, how can I help you," Ethan questions?

"Were you there when Robert Hampton had his heart attack?" Detective Rocco asks.

Ethan looks at the detectives and replies; "I had just left when apparently Robert fell back into his chair. He was a good, honest man. We will miss him. Why are you asking me about him? I was told he died of a heart attack. "

"Is there something else going on here?"

Detective Gibbons replies, "Sorry sir, we're just starting our investigation, so we are not at liberty to comment but we have some further questions for you."

"Were you involved in The Brotherhood Winery sale?"

"NO! Absolutely not! I would have stopped the sale had I known," retorts Ethan. "I'm not sure what happened there, but Charley told me he would never sell the business as long as Andrew and Isabel were a part of the Bachman Corporation. The sale seemed to happen quickly and usually these types of sales take many months, if not a year, to pull together. Are you also investigating the death of Charley?"

Detective Rocco replies, "Again, sir, we can't rely on an ongoing investigation. Thank you for your time, sir. We now need to speak with Andrew Bachman before he leaves. We'll be back to talk with you soon."

"Wait, before you go, how is it you are talking with me first before Andrew and Isabel? There has to be a reason for that and because you are even investigating a fatal heart attack which just happened last night." Ethan inquires.

"Mr. Bachman, we came to you first because Mrs. Hampton called the station and asked to talk to a Homicide Detective. Apparently, Mr. Hampton told his wife that if anything were to happen to him, even if it seems to be of a natural cause, to notify the police right away and to come and talk with you. So that is why we are here now."

Detective Rocco asks, "Ethan, can I just call you Ethan as to not get confused with Mr. Andrew Bachman?"

"Of course, Ethan is just fine."

"Great, Ethan. You said you would have stopped this merger had you known about it. Why?"

The Brotherhood Winery is the oldest winery in the country. They were first established in 1839 and survived prohibition because they make the wine for the churches for communion. The owner is Charley Barrow, and he is a Godly man. He did not like Andrew, and especially not his wife Isabel. I am not exactly sure what happened between them a few years ago but I do know that Charley went storming out of this very room and told for all to hear that as long as Andrew and Isabel Bachman were a part of this company he and his winery wouldn't have anything to do with 'The Bachman Corporation"!

"So, you can see detectives, why I personally am also concerned with Robert's heart attack, such a convenient coincidence, and also with Charley's tragic car accident. Something is very wrong, and I will make any resources available to your needs. Here is my private number. Please call me anytime. Oh, and please be careful with this number. Very few people have it, especially not Andrew and Isabel."

"Thank you, Ethan. We really appreciate it. We'll get back to you when it will be necessary."

"I must warn you, Isabel might play innocent and naïve but don't be fooled, she's as sly as a fox and just as cunning and dangerous as a badger!"

"Thanks again. We will keep that in mind," replies Detective Rocco.

As the Detectives leave the boardroom, they hear a woman's voice quite loud. They didn't quite hear what she was saying, but it seemed to put the office staff at attention as they all scurry to the desks and look hard at work. The detectives look at each other and in unison say, "Isabel!"

Ethan told the detectives which office was Andrew Bachman's but they would have guessed it. They look to the left at the end of the hall. Of course, the corner office with the double dark oak doors is Mr. Andrew Bachman's office. Outside of the doors shows a significant detail of a master artisan. Impressive gigantic doors are bold, and quite ornate. The detectives notice another thing, the cameras. Nobody enters without being noticed first. To some, it would have been intimidating, but not for these seasoned detectives.

The executive assistant must have seen the detectives' approach as the doors open before they have a chance to knock. As they step into the outer office, they hear a voice welcoming them to Mr. Andrew Bachman's office. They turned to see an older woman with a stern face looking back at them.

"You must be Detectives Gibbons and Rocco. Mr. Bachman is expecting you. He has an appointment shortly. He must leave for it in 15 minutes." Mrs. Siegel announces.

Looking at her name plaque on her desk, Detective Gibbons then, looking sternly into her eyes, he announces, "Hello Mrs. Effie Siegel. We will keep that in mind, but this will take as long as we need it to take! Oh, and please don't disturb us either!"

Suddenly another set of oak doors opens into a lush office. The panoramic view is breathtaking of New York

City. *One would never grow tired of gazing into the city day or night, thought the detectives.* Mr. Bachman stands and walks around his desk to shake the hands of the two detectives. Rocco and Gibbons introduce themselves again and comment on the stunning view and how they wouldn't mind coming to work every day to see the city the way he sees it. Mr. Bachman points to the leather wingback chairs and motions for them to have a seat. Andrew moves around the desk, which again is solid dark oak. Just as the doors to the office, the desk is a masterpiece. The office is organized, with one wall of books and tools of just about every shape and size as decorations. There is a table behind the detectives which has a product they had never seen before and made a mental note to ask about it later.

"Now, gentlemen, what can I do for you?" Mr. Bachman asks.

"Detective Rocco and I understand that Robert Hampton was working on a secret purchase of The Brotherhood Winery, which was announced at your dinner party last night. Is that correct, Mr. Bachman?"

"Yes, it is! Robert Hampton must have put too much stress on himself, and I am certainly to blame for that. I did rather push him hard about getting it done and keeping it under wraps until last night. Robert has been, or should I say, was with this company right out of college and promoted up quickly. I could see his talents and positive work ethics. We will miss him as one of our most valued employees. I am not sure I have anyone currently employed by us right now that could even fill his position. There are few people today that are as trustworthy as Robert was, except for Ethan, of course. Now he is a man of faith. He walks the walk; he talks to the point of being obnoxious. But trustworthy he is!"

Detective Rocco interrupts, "Mr. Bachman, why was it so important to keep this merger under wraps, as you say. Was there a problem with this merger or something unusual about this particular business adventure?"

"We wanted to keep it as a surprise for my cousin Ethan. I didn't quite expect the reaction he all gave us last night. I thought it would thrill him to have another, 'Christian company' under our corporation's umbrella."

"Ethan and I were very close growing up. Our fathers were twin brothers, and Grandfather had them working all the time. We would come to the factory with them and play when we were younger. As we became teenagers, we started working to learn the business from the ground floor up. I mean, we worked as sweeping the floor, delivering mail, and then working some machinery. We both went to different colleges. I earned my Master's Degree at Princeton for business management while Ethan studied International Business and spent a lot of time in Europe and Japan. We both changed in time. I am older and started working in the business before he did. I mostly worked in marketing, but it wasn't a good fit. When Ethan graduated, I was glad to hand him the marketing division. I on the other hand went into the corporate Financial and Administrative division."

Suddenly, the intercom sounded. Mrs. Siegel announces it is time for Mr. Bachman to leave for his appointment. He gets up to leave.

"I'm sorry, gentlemen, but I must leave. Please stop by and make an appointment with Mrs. Siegel and we can continue this later, but for now I must bid you ado." With that, he grabs his coat and exits the door.

Detective Gibbons and Rocco look at each other. *They realize Isabel Bachman was not the only one Ethan should have warned them about, being as sly as a fox!*

Mrs. Siegel tells the detectives which offices are Isabel's and a moment later they were talking with Mr. Hiram Haddad, her Executive Assistant. Mrs. Bachman's office is not as impressive as her husband's but holds an ambience of power and elegance. Detective Gibbons thought, *if her portrait is anything like her, then they must be careful. She is stunningly beautiful. Her eyes, even in the picture, are captivating and, in a moment, I will find out just how captivating they are.*

We heard almost immediately raised voices after entering Isabel's office. The staff knows Isabel for losing her temper, but this time she is out of control. Security officers escort the detectives out of the building immediately.

"Ethan wasn't kidding with Mrs. Bachman. There is something seriously wrong with that woman and I don't just mean her temper," Detective Gibbons comments.

"Rocco, can you imagine what it would be like to work for her? Her staff must be saints because she would be fire me within the hour of starting. Nobody deserves to be talked to the way she speaks to not just her staff but people in authority like us!"

Rocco responds, "Did you notice her eyes? We have seen angry and delusional tempers. We have seen psychopaths out of control. There's evilness there, like I've seen nowhere else. It's like Lucifer himself is dwelling inside her. You know, like a body snatcher."

Gibbons laughing, "Rocco, you need to lay off some of those Science Fiction movies you have been watching! Body Snatchers? Yeah right!!"

"Well, there is something really off about her and I know we will find out what that is in time!" Rocco pauses, deep in thought for a moment.

"I think this investigation will be more involved than we originally thought. How about Charley Barrows? I don't believe in coincidences and I know you don't either. I am sure there is more to that accident than the officers involved know. We can put that on hold for today. Let's get to the Pathologist's office and see for ourselves what the good Dr. has to say." Rocco responds.

Chapter 4

Ethan's Visit

Ethan leaves the office, still as mad as a hornet. He has never felt this mad and frustrated in his life. *Andrew has been the Chairman of the Board of this company for almost 22 years. How much damage did Isabel and Andrew do to our beloved company?*

Thinking out loud, "*How could I be so deceived? How did this happen without me even hearing a hint about it? This news about Robert is more than disturbing yet. How could he have kept this information from me? He knew how I felt about The Brotherhood Winery and why did Andrew and Isabel desires it so badly.*"

"*Oh Robert, you weren't just my favorite colleague, but my best friend. I am so sorry this has happened to you. It must devastate your family! I'll head over there and see how they are doing.*"

"The family must be here already. I'm not sure this would be the best time to come by. I need to sort this out and I need to start today," he proclaims to himself.

The doorbell rings, and Diana Hampton opens the door. "Oh, Ethan, I'm so glad you stopped by. I really need to talk to you. Robert was so upset with Andrew for making him promise not to tell you what was going on. I think the stress of it all is what gave him that heart attack. We are so sorry for deceiving you."

Ethan looks at her as she starts to sob. He wraps his arms around her and pulls her close to let her cry. He thinks to himself, *"This poor woman is worried about me and she's the one who just lost her husband. How could I possibly be angry with Robert right now?"*

Ethan's anger subsides, and compassion replaces it. Mrs. Hampton stops crying and apologizes for letting him stand at the door while she cries deeply.

"Come in; come in, how rude of me. Would like a cup of coffee? We just made a fresh pot. I'll have one too!" A few moments later Diana's brother, Mark, emerges out of the kitchen with 2 cups of coffee with just a smidge of creamer in each.

Pastor Francis stands up and shakes Ethan's hand. Ethan looks up as he sits next to Diana on the couch.

"Pastor, it's good to see you again. I'm sorry it's been so long this time since I've been to church." He nods as he sits back down again.

"I know how busy you are. What's really important is that you are here now."

Ethan directs his attention, "Hi Mark, its good seeing you again too even in this awful circumstance." Mark hands his sister and Ethan their coffees and sits down in an adjacent wing-backed chair.

"Hi Ethan, I am so glad you stopped by. You and Linda have always been such wonderful friends with our family. How long has it been since Linda went to be with the Lord? 7 years?" Mark asks.

"In some ways it seems like a lifetime ago, yet in other ways it was yesterday and it's been 10 years. I still miss that woman so much!" Ethan replies.

Ethan reaches over and gently puts Diana's hand into his and looks into her eyes. "Diana, I am so sorry for your loss. I loved Robert as if he were my brother in flesh and not just in the Lord. We will all dearly miss him. He wasn't just an employee, he was my best friend. I know he was the only person who I felt I could confide in within the company. He had excellent business sense and was honest beyond reproach. That is one question I have for you. Do you have any idea what transpired with The Company and The Brotherhood Winery?"

"I know what a good sounding board to my Linda was, as I'm sure you were for Robert. Oh, how rude of me. I'm sorry you are probably not up to such questions right now. I am deeply sorry for bringing this up right now."

"Oh Ethan, don't be. We wanted to talk to you about this for some time and now seem to be as good as any. Besides, I made no promise to Andrew to keep quiet about this. I need to get this off my chest before I have a heart attack too."

Diana sobs again. Diana quiets herself again and looks up at those compassionate eyes of Ethan's and starts by saying, "Ethan again, I want to apologize for Robert. There was a part of him, which really hated Andrew for making him promise such a thing, yet he was his direct boss and Robert felt cornered. He knew if they involved him at least he could keep it honest without deception, except from you, anyway. As far as I know he started about 6 months ago with Andrew aggressively pursuing Charley to sell. He was offering him the moon for the winery, and Charley stopped taking his calls. That is when he got Robert involved, from what I understand."

"As you already know, Robert and I had become close friends with Charley after you and Linda first introduced us to him so many years ago. Besides the times we would go with you and Linda, we would arrange a festive weekend in the fall each year. We would enjoy a glass of wine with our dinner most evenings and most often than not it was one of The Brotherhood Winery wines. Robert savored the reds while I preferred the whites." Diana is quiet for a bit as she remembers their meals together. Suddenly she realizes she they are waiting on her to speak again.

"I'm sorry," as she wipes away her tears.

"Anyway, as I was saying, Robert was summoned to Andrews's office one morning about six months ago. As Robert said, Andrew was unusually personable that day. It reminded him how he was when he first started working at Bachman's 22 years ago. I'm digressing again. At first when Andrew asked him to talk with Charley, Robert adamantly refused to even considerate but Andrew wore him down. Day after day Andrew would approach his with another offer, sweetening the pot. Finally, Andrew realized Robert couldn't be bought. So he tried another approach. This time Andrew told him, he was going to make this deal happen with or without him and it was going to be Andrew's way. Well, we all know what that means, and it was going to be unethical and someone would probably get hurt. Robert agreed to work with Charley but refused to anything unethical or to force Charley's hand in the matter. Andrew agreed but made him swear not to talk to anyone about this and especially not you."

"That again was about six months ago. At first Charley was upset with Robert for even suggesting that he sell his beloved winery, but after months of negotiating with Charley and his board of directors, it looked like the sale was at least a possibility. Charley was still in the holdout. Andrew offered to finance the start of a new winery at no interest. Through Robert, Andrew offered to purchase hundreds of acres of land in upstate New York for Charley. Andrew would purchase the equipment he needed to get started. It obsessed Andrew with owning that winery. Robert tried to talk him into buying a variety of different other wineries in the same area, but Andrew wouldn't hear of them. He demanded to own The Brotherhood Winery at all costs. Robert tried to talk Andrew into making the purchase under his own name and not make it a part of Bachman's, but Andrew and Isabel wouldn't hear of that either. Isabel herself went to The Brotherhood's Board of Directors and promised them they wouldn't change and in fact would get a sizable increase in stocks and benefits if they agreed to sell to them. The board agreed to their terms. Charley was still holding out until that awful car accident over a month ago."

Diana sighed, "I so loved Charley. He made us laugh. We trusted him, and of course we love his wines. I know they said it was an accident. The report his family told us stated he had a heart attack and was dead before he even hit that stone pillar, but I find it so hard to believe that it was an accident. I don't know how Isabel did it. In my heart of hearts I know she had something to do with it and now my Robert." Diana sobs so hard Ethan sat closer and just holds her.

After a time Diana sits up. She apologizes again, but Ethan put his finger to her lips.

"Shhhh, it's ok Diana. I want you to know if Andrew or anyone else associated with him or Isabel had anything to do with his death or Charley's. I will make sure you are taken care of. I don't just mean financially either. I'm not sure exactly what has happened yet, but I promise you the authorities and I will find out."

"Ethan, please let it be investigated by the Detectives. We can't lose you, too!" Diana pleads.

The door opens, and in bounces Brittney. "Mom, OMG, I leave for one night while you and Dad are at your annual dinner and this happens! I can't believe it. I just was with him in the garden yesterday morning. We were talking about your upcoming trip, too. Europe and how exciting he was to take you to some places he visited on his business trips," Brittney sobs.

Ethan stands up, and she runs into his arms, "Uncle Ethan, I'm going to miss him so much!!"

"I know you are! Listen, if you need anything or someone to talk to, you have my private number and call it anytime!! I love you Brittney and I'm here or just a phone call away. You take wonderful care of your mom and I'll see you tomorrow."

Ethan turns and gives Diana an enormous hug on her way to her daughter. "I must be going. Please keep me informed if you think of anything else or just to talk." He shakes Mark's hand and encourages him to walk with him outside.

"Mark, something isn't right here. I find it very convenient for Andrew and Isabel to have Robert out of their way of me finding out what is going on with the winery. I also can't believe that Charley is dead, and nobody told me," Ethan says.

Mark responds, "Ethan, I'm not sure what has exactly happened here, either. I didn't even know there was a problem until Diana called me last night at the hospital. She told me what she told you, so I know no more than you do. I'll stay close to her and if she remembers anything else, I'll make sure I let you know. I feel the same way you do about the situation. Something is wrong with Robert dying when he did. He was such a great upstanding guy. I will really miss him, too. We went fishing now and then just to get back to nature instead of the rat race we all have seemed to spend too much time in."

"Mark, I will find out what is happening if it's the last thing I do. If you guys need anything at all, please don't hesitate to ask me. I'll stop by tomorrow and hopefully I will at least have an answer: it involved the police or two or more questions than answers."

Diana spoke up suddenly. "Ethan, there's one more thing. There is another reason I know there is something wrong. Robert told me that some people who worked in the lab under Isabel would get fired by her and never arrive home. Their spouse would come in the next day and inquire where they were shown the video of them being escorted out of the building with their personal items. Robert didn't know what happened to them, but knew it involved the police. He didn't want me to worry, so he downplayed it, but I could see it in his eyes: there was more to the story than what he told me. We never really talked about it again."

Ethan inquired, "How long ago was that. Do you remember?"

Diana responded, "I think it was about 15-20 years ago. It's been a long time since I have thought about it. I'm surprised I even remembered it."

"Thank you, Diana. I'll see you tomorrow."

"Take care, my friends." Ethan gets into his car and speeds away.

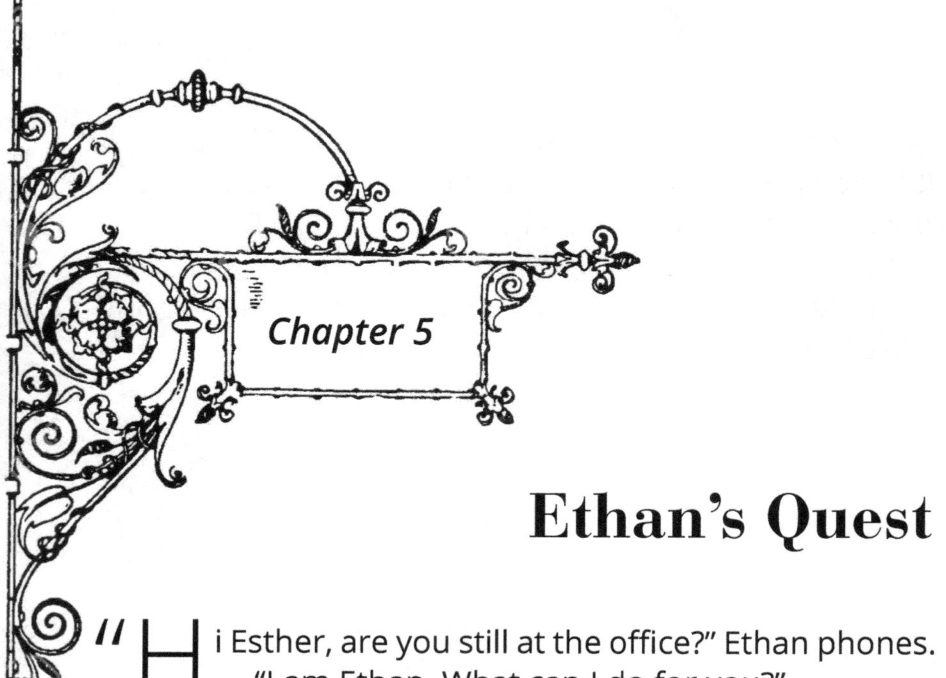

Ethan's Quest

"Hi Esther, are you still at the office?" Ethan phones.

"I am Ethan. What can I do for you?"

"I need you to cancel my appointments until further notice. I'm going to find out what is going on with The Brotherhood Winery take over and the death of Robert Hampton. If Isabel or Andrew inquire about me, just tell them to call me directly. Please don't indulge them with any information I will share with you."

"Ethan, isn't that the jobs of Detectives Gibbons and Rocco to do? You are too valuable to this company to have you die too! I'm really worried about what you are getting yourself into. You know how I feel about the other Bachman's. Nothing is beyond them to get what they want. Isabel would love to get rid of you from this business. Please don't give her or her hired hands the opportunity!"

"Thank you for your concern. I too know they will stop at no lengths to get what they want. I will be careful but know this, my Jesus is protecting me. He will lead me to the truth. I will do everything in my power to make this right for all involved!" Ethan states.

"Esther, how long have you been my Executive Assistant? 19-20 years?"

"Exactly 20 years next month. Why do you ask?"

"In all that time we have never really sat down and talked about things that need to be talked about. I know this is Saturday and your day off, but would you be so kind as to be my guest for an early lunch today? I have some paperwork I need to finish up with, so I'm coming back to the office. At 1:30 could you have the car brought around for us and make reservations at the Metropolitan Club."

"It will be my pleasure, Mr. Ethan!" Esther responds excitedly.

Esther has been waiting for this opportunity for a very long time. Rumors which circulated through the office were becoming more and more disturbing about Andrew and Isabel. She learned a long time ago to keep her ears open and her mouth shut. Esther knew of several times which Isabel had tested her in particular to see if she would go running off to Ethan about. Possessing a good instinct about such things is a lifesaving skill. Executive staff had heard of other staff members mysteriously being "fired" and never seen again by others in the office. There were even a few times when family members or friends would show up at the office looking for them. All were told they had been let go weeks ago, and they didn't know where they went once they left the office. The security guards would pull up surveillance tapes to show them leaving the building. Esther also knew it wasn't just Isabel's staff which walked on eggshells, especially when she was actually in the office. *All the staff did and I'm included. I know Ethan will protect me so she mostly leaves me alone, but I'm not taking any chances. I just will keep to myself.* The staff from the mail-room, just delivering the mail, is terrified of her, all except her own Executive Assistant, Mr. Hiram Haddad. Over the years Mrs. Bachman has only had one Executive Assistance but Mr. Haddad, as he preferred to be called by all staff, has been with her right from the beginning. Rumor has it they have been friends since college overseas. She tried to be friends with Mr. Haddad, but he maintained a distance from all the other employees unless he wanted information from them. Esther wonders if it was because Isabel asked him to or if he really was business only type of personality. Either way, there was no getting close to him. It seems to work for Isabel since she doesn't scream at him nearly as much as she does with the other office staff.

Esther wonders as she stares at the picture across from her desk. *The picture is of the ocean waves breaking on the rock in Vermont. She can almost hear the sound of the ocean, which quiets her spirit. Thinking about Mr. Haddad., it wasn't anything spoken, just a feeling she had about her that maybe they both had something on each other. She ponders about talking to Ethan about it and decides to let their conversation take its natural course and if the discussions lead that way, then maybe she would mention it to him.*

Esther finishes up some of her paperwork as the driver calls.

"Please tell Mr. Ethan his ride is available," Esther thanks him as she is pressing the intercom button.

"Perfect timing! I just finished what I had to do. Let's get out of here before something else pisses me off," Ethan states, only half joking!

The car ride is quiet. They only talk about general topics. Ethan did not trust the drivers. They all seemed nice enough, but he is also well aware the other Bachman's would pay a handsome price for information concerning Ethan and his involvement with various topics, including his very personal and private life.

Since the death of Linda, he has almost become paranoid about letting Andrew or Isabel get close to him. Isabel seems nicer to him after Linda's death, but it was like it wasn't genuine sympathy. He isn't sure why, but he instinctively knows keeping a distance from them was a deliberate decision he kept close to him.

They arrive at the restaurant. The décor is like stepping into an ocean front dock restaurant. Fish nets hang on the wall with plastic but realistic lobster, crabs, and fish. The hostess seats them in a secluded section. Their orders for lunch are made, bottled water and coffee all ready for consumption. Ethan looks over at Esther, thinking, *"Umm, you are a beautiful woman and have aged well. There is, however, such sadness in your eyes."*

"Esther, what is it that is troubling you? I can see it in your eyes and I'm sorry I didn't notice it before this." Ethan inquires.

"Ethan, you know I'm one you can always trust on keeping your most trusted secrets. I also keep others which are laying heavy on me and have for some time now. I haven't wanted to bother you with them, as you are always in a hurry to be somewhere. Did I understand you correctly that you will work in the area for a while?" She waits for him to answer as she sees him pondering her question.

"Yes, I'll be staying here until I get some answers about what is going on not just in the home office but with all aspects of the company. There is something rotten in Denmark, as the saying goes. I'm going to make sure its stench is sanitized, especially in the company."

"Please, Esther, start at the beginning and leave nothing out. Even the smallest of details might mean something important. I will record this, so I forget nothing and so later on what might not seem important now might end up very important."

"Ethan, I am so glad that we finally have the time to talk. When I first came to work for Bachman's, in the secretary pool, things were very different. People were joyful and shared their outside lives with each other. Today we all work on pins and needles. Isabel is on the warpath all the time. We all have experienced her wrath more than once. Ethan, many exceptionally skilled professional employees have left the company because they would no longer tolerate her abusive behavior towards them or others. I didn't tell you, but there was more than one time I felt the same way. If it wouldn't have been for my great respect for you and knowing you would someday take control over the situation has been what has kept me going."

Ethan, trying to maintain quiet while she talks, asks, "Will you give me an example of the employees which you feel should have benefitted our company which left and what has she done to you specifically?"

"Kristopher Lawrence is the first one which comes to mind. He was a genius at creating new designs for some of our clients. Isabel for whatever reason really hated him and poured her distaste for him whenever you and Andrew were out of town. She would verbally tear him to shreds in front of the other engineers. She would call him a buffoon and curse at him, which would make a sailor blush.

He wasn't the only one. Looking back at some employees you hired or recommended to see how many are still here. I have noticed a pattern. It will infuriate you, Ethan."

"I am not sure I can get more infuriated than I am right now. I remember Kristopher Lawrence. I believe he told me he was leaving to go back to his hometown to take care of his elderly parents."

"I think the Hamptons stayed in contact with him. Check with Mrs. Hampton as to his current situation."

"Ethan, each year it seems to get worse. The past 4 or 5 years there seems to be an ominous cloud over the offices. I can't really explain it. Principled people are leaving and some of them are missing. Their families have come looking for them and they are told they were let go weeks ago and don't know where they went after they left the building. Ethan: I'm scared and so is most of the other staff, too. I can see it in their eyes. We just keep our mouths shut, do the best job we can and leave as soon as we can."

"Esther, I am so sorry. I've been away too long. I didn't know it was so dysfunctional. Will you please make me a list of all the employees you know of without exposing yourself, which are missing or left because of Isabel and Andrew? Do not make this list on the company computers. You might be safer to write it by hand. Be very careful of anything you put on the company computers until I give you a head's up. There will come a time hopefully soon that we will bring others into this. I will bring the people whom you can really trust in the company up to speed soon enough. For now, this has to stay just between the two of us. Please, even be careful talking with the detectives. We don't know who has been paid off."

"Forgive me, Esther, for letting this situation get so far out of hand. I blame myself for not paying closer attention. It has removed the scales from my eyes. It's time to take back the company my family started so many generations ago. I want you to put on that list at the top of those employees which Isabel has singled out which still work here. Monday will be a fresh day at the corporate office. I want you to have some fun this weekend. Breathe deeply and know we will make this company an exceptional place to work at again."

"Thank you! I think I'll start breathing now." they both laugh. Lunch was incredible. Esther felt comfortable for the first time in years. *She now regrets not speaking up earlier. Would Robert be alive today if she had? Ethan seems to have read her mind, or maybe it is the look on her face.*

"Listen, what has happened has happened. We can't go backwards but we can look forwards. Don't blame yourself for any of this! We will start today to make the company great again, I promise you that," Ethan promises!

On the way back to the office, they talk of generalities and laugh as the atmosphere changes. Even the driver notices as they draw him into some conversations about The City and the weather has been so nice lately. Denzel is one of the few drivers who wouldn't take a bribe from anyone for any reason. He keeps to himself and maintains his employers at a professional arm's length. He didn't always like what he heard being said in the back seat, but it wasn't his business. Denzel prides himself on being known as one of the best drivers in the New York City by his colleagues and his employers. Secretly, he always has had the most respect for Mr. Ethan and makes himself available to him whenever he knows he is in town.

Blacksmith to International Corporation

The generations of Bachman men of the family were the blacksmiths in the towns they lived in. From a young age, the boys would learn about the family business. They became skilled at what they did and the importance of the reputation of the Bachman name. There were certain ethics, which were also passed down to their sons. First was the importance of honesty and integrity. If what they were making had the Bachman name, then a fair deal presented on the cost and the time it would take to make the product. They did everything to make that happen. The item also had to be the best quality product made. Many times the family would go to bed and the dad would still be hard at work when they woke up the next morning. After his son would grow up and became proficient at his skill, he would leave the family home and travel till he found a town, which needed a blacksmith, and settle down to start his own business and a family. The cycle would then start again.

Rarely would two brothers stick together. This was the case with Omri and David. They were twins. They like most twins did everything together. As they grew up and learn the blacksmith trade, their father knew instinctively they would be one of the rare cases. What one didn't think of the other one did in creating new tools and the best process for making them for their customers?

A farmer or business representative, usually the owner, would come in with a rough drawing of what they needed or sometimes just a description. The brothers would spend time on it to create tools and machinery for the need at hand. Omri was the most detailed and insisted on only using the best quality of raw materials. Business was expanding as more and more customers from neighboring communities brought requests for the boys to create tools and new machinery for them. Their dad enjoyed watching them work, and so did the customers. Their dad would step back and get to know their clients as they watched these two geniuses work.

Soon the reputation of The Bachman Tool and Dye Company became known as statewide for the best quality of tools on the market. David was the creative one and created the designs for Omri to develop.

They kept meticulous records, like their fathers before them, of all the tools and products they make for their customers. Their father advised the brothers early on to patent and copy-write all the tools they made and to keep a detailed written record of each tool or machine they developed. They would patent and copy write each item so only they could recreate the item, ensuring top quality work and return business. This decision proved brilliant and critical to the start of the financial empire it grew into today.

The tools and machinery they created made by their company and not duplicated without paying The Bachman Tool and Dye Company the right to do so. Within a few years the word had spread to Canada, Mexico and Europe, which if your company needed a tool created, The Bachman Tool and Dye Company were the ones to get it done with top quality and efficiency.

During WWI and WWII, the government even asked them to create products for them. Bachman Tool and Dye Company grew to become a corporation and hired more employees other than just family.

Instead of moving on, as most of their cousins and other relatives did, the brothers stayed with their father and built the family business. They didn't go on to college as most of their other friends did. The brothers started families and worked the business.

Omri was the first one to marry and to have a son. Andrew was his pride and joy. He brought him to work as much as he could, and the employees loved to watch him grow. Andrew was a delightful child and eager to learn whatever others will teach him. Math was his favorite subject in school. He was an excellent student in calculus, and solving problems seemed easy for him. He also clever and even could manipulate others to do things for him he wanted. His dad thought, someday he will bring this company to financial heights beyond his own imagination. Andrew will do well as an executive in this unfamiliar world.

David was more grounded ethically and had an eye for details. A client would come in and explain to him what needed to be created, and it was like David could see it in his mind and start sketching it out, as the client was explaining it. He made sure they always used the best quality of materials, as always. To David, customer satisfaction was always the most important detail.

A few years later David married, and a year later his son Ethan was born. It was exciting to have another baby coming into the office. Their grandfather was so proud of his sons and now to have his grandsons coming into the office, he knew it would only be a matter of time before they would also become part of the growing business. He would watch and wonder what the future would bring for these two small children. The business has changed so much since he was a small child and worked with his father as a blacksmith. The entire world has changed. It's becoming so fast-paced that one doesn't have time to sit back and just reflect on life. He felt himself very fortunate. His sons were taking over more of the business, so he could take time for his wife, which they so desperately needed. He knew she felt neglected and alone. She was a patient woman and understood the business. They're disciplined, and maybe even smarter than their dad. He accredited that to her. She taught their sons well; he thought. He loved her so much, and maybe it was time that he showed her. Smiling, and reached for her hand. "Have I told you lately just how much I love you?" With a slight squeeze and a twinkle in his eyes, he stared into her eyes. She could see the love he had for her, and knew he was up to something.

"Well, I thought that it's about time that I spend more time with you. Through all these years you have been so patient with me. With all the time I spent on the business that you should now be the center of my attention that the boys are old enough to take it over. Times are changing and I'm getting too old to change with it. The boys are embracing the change, so it's time for me to let them run with the business."

"Omri and David and I have been talking about how the world is getting more and more complicated. They are running the business now more than I am. I have the enjoyable part of visiting with our clients but alas it's time for the boys to get more of the pie so they can support their families, especially now they have sons on their own."

"I now understand more about how my dad felt when he watched me as a young man and seeing Omri and David as small children. With Andrew and Ethan now growing up in the business, the cycle of life is progressing on to the future. "

"Wow, I didn't even know you were thinking about retiring. What would you like to do first?" He could see the excitement in her eyes as she spoke.

"I need to go talk to that new lawyer, Kent Noble, which we hired I few years ago. He's sharp and will know how to make this transition work best for us all."

"The boys will be so excited! Maybe we can take our grandsons to that new place in California called Disneyland that just opened. What do you think?"

"Sounds like a superb place to start for our golden years, but for right now I can think of something else I would like to do with you first." Smiling and still holding her hand, he helps her up from breakfast table and leads her out of the kitchen.

Just before business closed at the end of the week, he called Omri into the conference room. Kent Noble and his old-time friend and senior lawyer Jack Kowlawski were already there waiting for the twin brothers.

Omri and David looked at each other as they saw the three of them in the conference room. Omri spoke up first.

"Hey Dad, what's up? I don't think I ever remember seeing the three of you together in the same place except at the company picnic or Christmas parties."

"Well, boys or I should say young men; I have some exciting news for you. I've been putting a package together with our lawyers, Kent and Jack, for my retirement. We expect you will stay together to run the business, especially since you have developed it beyond my wildest imagination. It's time for me to stop putting your mom second and the business first and give her the best of our golden years together."

"With families of your own now and the need for more financial income, I have split the profits of the company as follows: I will retain 20% of the business and stay on as the Chairman of the Board. I will in the most part just be here to help make final decisions on critical matters. You each, since you are twins, will each possess 40% of the business. You will make the everyday decisions in your departments, which you already manage. For the past year or so, my department has been meeting our clients and making sure it satisfied them with their products. I will still do this from time to time, but I won't be here daily anymore. You both are the apples of my eye and I'm so proud of the men, which you have become. You work well together as a finely greased machine. I know you will deal with more stress as our Tool and Dye Company increases. The tools and machinery which are needed in the future I can't even comprehend. Yet you both are all on top of what is coming next. I've watched as you anticipate, almost to the point of reading the minds of our clients, what they need. You both are amazing."

"Kent and Jack are working out the details of the agreements for my retirement, which will include the two of you setting up a board of directors. This doesn't have to be done right away, but we feel strongly that it will have to be done before we turn the business over to your sons. As you know, I love your wives as my own daughters. Times are changing and I see women will become more and more involved in corporate management. I welcome that with open arms. I, however, feel strongly that your wife and your son's wife are not to be involved with the decisions of this company. The reason for this is that you will both be so consumed with business I want your wives to be more involved with raising your children instead of nannies or boarding schools. Don't get me wrong; both your wives are very intelligent and wise women. An exemplary woman will make you a better man and will give you sound advice. I see a trend in today's world, since the end of WWII, where woman are choosing careers instead of the most important job of being there for their children instead of another adult to teach them your morals and the way of your parenting for them. Your daughters, if you have any in the future, may of course be a part of this wonderful company in whatever way you and her find to be the best position."

"You both have worked hard for ownership of our company. Omri, you will be the CEO and David will be the CFO and Marketing, sharing equally financially. I suspect that someday you both will do the same for Andrew and Ethan. Your mom and I wish the best for you and your families. Your health, wealth, and common sense are to lead this company and your families into this new world of great opportunities, respect and dedication. Stay grounded to what is important to your clients, great or small. Never lose sight of our company's humble beginnings and your clients are the most important part of our business and their satisfaction is your supreme goal "

"Now do either of you have any questions?" Omri was the first to speak up,

"Dad, you are such an intricate part of this business I don't think you realize how important you still are to the daily operations."

David then chimed in, "Dad, you're too young to retire. What are you talking about retiring?"

Jacob responded, "You both are more than capable to handle my part of the business. That new employee, which we hired a few years ago Victor Serhan can be in charge of customer service and the new clients. He's just out of college and has some brilliant ideas. You know we never really talked about this, but do either of you regret not going off to college?"

"Dad, you have got to be kidding! We were too busy to go to college."

"Besides, we could teach a class on international business just from life's experiences. The school of hard knocks and experience are the best teachers anyone could have. I think for our boys it will be different though." Omri said.

"I thought about it for about a minute but knew the business needed me more than the fraternity parties did," David laughing out loud. Omri agreed, laughing too!

"I'm glad to hear that, actually. I thought maybe I was hard on you both for your demanding schedules. The customers always wanting you both to work on their products they needed. Neither one of you ever turned down a delightful challenge, and some excellent opportunities to show what you both are made of. Several of your inventions became life changing for businesses and schools like the copier machines and electric typewriters. Just look at the bank vault mechanisms we have developed. They are being used all over the world. All thanks to your brilliant minds, integrity, and tenacity to finish a job to completion. Again, I'm so proud of you both. It's time for you both to reap the lion's share of the business while your mom and I go have some fun. Your mom would like to take Andrew and Ethan to that new Disneyland in California we have been hearing so much about." Jacob laughed.

"Now, enjoy the weekend with your wives. You won't get many chances like this very often. You both will have a lot of work to do on Monday without me," Jacob stated.

Jack then spoke up. "It will take a week to iron out all the details. Kent and I will work diligently and will have the papers for all of you to sign as soon as possible. We wish the best for you and your wife in your new life together. You will step into her domain and that might take some getting used to," as Jack laughs.

Kent looks at the twins. "You both know that Jack and I are always at your disposal. It has been a great pleasure working so closely with your dad and lately with the both of you." A bottle of Champagne was ready to be poured as Kent picked up the bottle and pour 5 glasses.

"Here is to the beginning of a new era. We are cherishing the old and embracing the new. May any new creation be developed with swiftly and integrity always is in the forefront of this company," Kent announced.

Everyone said, "Here Here!!"

Years went by quickly for Omri and David. They brought the boys to work as often as they could, just like their dad did with them. It was always such a delight to most of the employees to watch them grow up in the business and to get along so well. Now they understood the joy their father experienced watching as they grew up in the business. Someday they both knew they would also take over the business as they did, but college first. It was a different world than what it was when they were growing up. Even as young teenagers, Andrew and Ethan were learning Spanish and French to help with their Mexican and Canadian clients when their dads found it difficult to understand what the clients needed to have made. The boys were also learning German, Japanese, Mandarin, and Italian as well. Ethan had a natural talent for learning foreign languages. Andrew studied harder, but did not do too badly when he needed to. On holidays and summer breaks from college, both Andrew and Ethan were in the office or shop learning what was new and what the new clients were interested in having built. More often than not, the input the boys provided proved invaluable. Omri and David marveled at their incredible creativity and charismatic personalities. Just as Omri and David were inseparable, so were Andrew and Ethan. They even double dated until the end of Andrew's senior year of college.

Ethan and Andrew's new fiancée, Isabel, did not get along. She captivated Andrew. Ethan tried to talk to Andrew about his concerns about her, especially their differences in religion, but Andrew would not listen to his cautions. Her beauty, intelligence, and eloquence spellbound him.

Ethan himself was in a serious relationship, and everyone who met Linda loved her. They both needed to finish college first. Ethan had got his master's degree while Linda still had 2 more years for her degree in BS/ Psychology/World Religion.

Andrew and Isabel had a glorious wedding. Her family was from Lebanon. They loved their daughter and sister. They too were concerned about the difference in religion, but Isabel assured them everything was under control.

Andrew and she had worked out all the details, so it wouldn't be a problem. Her father agreed to bless the marriage, and the celebration began. It lasted for a solid week. Now that is a way to celebrate a wedding, everyone said!

Andrew started working for the company right after graduation and returned to work again a month after the wedding. He rose quickly through the company. Omri and David had decided he was to start at the bottom of the engineering department. They wanted him to learn more about the company on a full-time basis. It did not take long before he was in charge of the Marketing Department and working in accounting. After Ethan's graduation with his Masters' degree in International Business, he took over the Marketing Department with the blessing of Andrew, Omri, and David. He worked hard throughout college and working for the company. They had groomed both Andrew and Ethan all their lives to work for the company, just as they had groomed their fathers. Andrew and Ethan would now start off bringing the company to a new level.

David started off the meeting with Omri, Andrew and Ethan with "today is the beginning of a new era for Bachman's Tool and Dye Company. Andrew, Ethan, your dad and I want to tell you again just how proud we are of you. You both long ago exceeded the wildest imagination of your grandfather, God rest his soul! He knew the time would come when you both would take over the company, just as Jacob and I did. No, that time is not yet but will be soon enough." He laughs. It will involve them.

Omri explains, "Now that you 2 have become managers of your departments, Dave and I have incorporated the business. Your Grandfather suggested when we took over the business that we would start a Board of Directors. We have started the process. We would like your input on setting up this board. It will involve them in deciding decisions. Kent Noble Esq., Pastor James Deal, Michael Steele, and Veronica Murphy are who we are suggesting starting our board. We would like your suggestions as well."

Andrew was the first to speak up. "I would like to add George Chamoun. Yes, he is Isabel's brother, but he is well diverse in International business and is highly intelligent."

Ethan speaks up, "Andrew, do you think he would be an excellent fit with our company values. I've read the Quran, and we are all infidels to him. The first half of the book is very similar to our standards, but it's the second half which becomes violent against anyone who doesn't follow Allah. He himself lives in a culture which does not respect the values of women. I talked with him at your wedding and he believes Shari Law should be in America. Women don't have any rights with this law."

"Don't get me wrong Andrew; I like him as a person. I have worked with him on some business ventures dealing with the Arabic Countries, but on our board I'm not so sure. Different isn't always an offensive thing, and sometimes it's not a bad thing either. The more I think about it, I'm sure he isn't a good fit for us." *I don't trust your wife and I can't take the chance on her brother either, Ethan admits to himself.*

Chapter 7

Something's Not Right

Remembering the past with his dad and uncle, Ethan thought. *Time has changed not only for the business, but for the relationship I now have with Andrew. I would never have thought we would have become so estranged. How do we get back to some resemblance of what could be? How do I get him to see Isabel as the rest of us do? Jesus, help me to understand how I can make this better.*

Ethan rarely has down time other than his workout at the company gym or hotel where ever he is at. Making time for church, usually online, is important to him. Now he will be at home to enjoy his home church. It's a joy to him to stay in touch with his church family and can worship with them almost anywhere in the world. Ethan also teaches an Adult Bible Study and posts it online for others to take part in. He appreciates plugging in where ever his new ventures take him.

Other than "church time" his mind is usually on business of what new deal he is working on, but not now. He is consumed with the death of his close friend Robert. Something is wrong. He knows it deep down and he knows he has to find the answers. *How did Isabel do it? Was Andrew just one of her pawns?* Ethan watched her manipulate Andrew as if she has cast a spell over him.

Ethan is thinking again, *we aren't just first cousins, but more like brothers. We were as close as we were growing up.* He missed the old Andrew. Ethan and Andrew grew apart after Andrew went off to college, as time has a way of maturing a young adult. It was a few months after he introduced Isabel to the family that everyone saw a change in Andrew, and it wasn't for the better, as Ethan saw it. Business wise, he had become more cutthroat and ruthless. At first, many see this trait as excellent business sense. He could accomplish contests and promotions to push his employees beyond their normal work capabilities. Most of the employees enjoyed their jobs and the atmosphere at their job site. Those that didn't usually moved on to another job.

The turnover is very low in the company, but he also knows Isabel has a lot to do with some of their best employees, which left. Ethan talked to Andrew about it again just a few months ago.

Ethan walks into the building through the front door. As he is passing the reception area, he overhears a conversation about Jerry McFarley, which caught his attention. Mrs. McFarley is inquiring about the last time her husband was at work and that he had not come home the day before. The security officer told her that Jerry had quit after an altercation with Mrs. Bachman and that he had personally walked him out with his things, as was protocol yesterday morning.

She starts crying and says, "I don't understand where he is. I've called the police and all the hospitals. He's never, not come home," trying to catch her breath, "He's not picking up on his phone and now it just goes to voice mail."

Just then the elevator doors opens, and Ethan steps inside. Ethan is already on the phone to Esther to find out about Jerry and what she knows about the situation. By the time the elevator doors reopen, he's getting quite the ear full quietly from Esther. Though he is fuming mad, he keeps his temper in check, and heads straight to Isabel's office.

"Hiram, don't bother announcing me. I'll do it myself."

"I'm sorry, Mr. Ethan, but Mrs. Bachman isn't in yet and isn't due for another 2 hours. She has a meeting with one of her charities this morning, I believe."

"When she does finally arrive, please inform her I would appreciate her presence in my office ASAP. Thank you!!"

He turns back and asks Hiram, "We're you here last evening?"

"No, sir, I had another appointment. I left earlier than I usually do. Why do you ask?' Hiram answers.

Ethan didn't answer but immediately heads for Andrew's office. Upon arriving into the outer office, he waves at Mrs. Siegel and continues into Andrews's office.

Seeing Andrew sitting at his desk, Ethan asks, "Can't you rein your wife in any better? We lost another superior employee two days ago because of Isabel, because she is out of control again!"

"Now just wait a minute. Jerry was being sloppy in his latest project from what I understand, and Isabel had to address the issue."

"The next time you want to find out what is really going on around here, try talking to anyone else besides your wife. Oh, or her henchmen, Hiram. Isabel is his boss only, and is she not a part of Human Resources! You might have her in charge of some of your pet projects, but you know she is not permitted anywhere near any of mine. I hired Jerry to be part of my team, and he proved himself to be a precious employee years ago. Now he is missing. His wife is downstairs crying. She said he didn't come home last night or the night before."

"I don't know what to tell you, Ethan. I know for sure that Jerry and Isabel had words two days ago and he quit. George, our security guard, was called to Jerry and left the office with him and his personal belongings."

"Jerry caught her in another one of her lies and called her on it! She went ballistic on him in front of his co-workers. This is not acceptable under any conditions! Not only is her lying getting out of hand, but she knows better than to humiliate a senior executive in front of his staff!"

"I want you to know that I've decided to go to the board once again to have her removed from this business. She is a rogue executive and doesn't belong on staff. Our Grandfather had the right idea about none of our wives being on staff, and I should have never allowed you to talk me into letting her be a part of your business dealing."

"Ethan, do not be so hasty. I know it upsets you, but wait. I'll talk to her again and get her to apologize to Jerry. Just give me a day or so before you go to the board, please Ethan."

"Andrew, only because you have asked me will I wait for the next scheduled meeting. I don't know why she feels she has the gull to speak to the employees like she does, but it has to stop, and I mean completely today! I will spend more time in the office and in NY. Andrew, I've been away from the primary office for too long. I'm sorry if I've put too much of the everyday responsibilities on your lap to take care of in my absence."

Ethan turns and leaves the office as Andrew reaches for his cell phone. Ethan hears Andrew say, "Honey, you better not come in the office today..."

Chapter 8

Isabel Bachman

Isabel resents the Board of Directors, especially Ethan, for not permitting her to be part of the board of the company. When her father-in-law set up the board of directors with his brother, they followed the advice of their father Mark to not allow their wives to be on the board. She rose as far as Ethan and the board would allow. Ethan even fought to not allow her to get as far as she has. Ethan was gone so much overseas since Linda died that little by little she gained more power in the company. She could convince others to let her have an office and added responsibilities as time went on. Ethan would come back after months of being away and find out she was doing more and would redirect some of her additional responsibilities to other employees, and there was nothing she could do about it. She would complain to Andrew, but she found out he would not defend her against Ethan. The lack of support infuriates her not toward Andrew but against Ethan. Her hatred for Ethan grew to an obsession as time passed.

"Oh, what I could do with this company if only Ethan wouldn't be a part of it!" she would often say to herself and to Andrew. *How she wishes he would die too!!*

She dreams of becoming the Chairperson of the Board someday. This would be her corporation one day, and there would be nothing that Ethan could do about it. She would find a way and her gods would help her, she vows!

Growing up as a princess in a country where women and girls are the only object of which men used was difficult for a young Isabel. Though she had privileges other girls did not have, she longed for the freedom of escaping this country and moving to the free country where she had power. Even at a young age, she knew she differed from her other siblings. Her parents and grandparents knew it too.

Her father, Ethbaal[(3)], the King of Lebanon, and her grandfather tried to repress her by trying to hide her away at varied all-girl schools, but it only exposed her more to the western world. She saw the world news and saw other women who had voices and weren't afraid to speak out. She longed to wear western clothing instead of being covered up all the time.

When she started living her own life in the dorm, well as much as she could, it thrilled her to experience another world. As the daughter of the King, Isabel was always in the limelight. There was never any privacy for her until now. She knew instinctively that she would have to be careful how much freedom she would allow herself to experience. Her family is an old world tradition and believed in Shari's law. Even being a daughter of a king, it would be easy for the men in her family to say there was an accident and have her put to death for "being a disgrace" to the family by her actions.

Isabel had to set the example for all the Lebanese girls who were repressed by their fathers, grandfathers, uncles and brothers. She would have to be careful, learning to poise as a princess, yet as vicious as a king cobra. She proved girls could be highly educated and proficient in the business world. Isabel knew if she would really make her mark in this world that she would have to leave her country and marry someone from the free world.

Much to the chagrin of her family, she refused to agree to an arranged marriage, as her mother and sisters had done. She wouldn't date men from her own country, which she kept to herself. She didn't want to take the chance of falling in love and being "stuck" in such a traditionally repressed country.

The bit of control over her own body and whom she allowed herself to date gave her a sense of power, which she wanted more of. *This is only the very tip of the iceberg,* she told herself, and one very close friend. She did not get along with other girls very well. They thought she was rude and a bully. She only had her best interests at heart and couldn't care less about anybody else. Hiram, however, was different. He wasn't like other men in her family or the bodyguards she grew up with. He had a sensitive side to him and hung onto every word that Isabel would say. Hiram was gay, which made him an outcast. Isabel appreciated that in him because she felt like an outcast because of her desire to be a powerful, driven woman. Soon she learned she could confide in him and not worry that what she said to him didn't immediately go back to her father. Without fear of her father's wrath, she was telling him about her dreams and wishes. She thought, this is my best friend. She heard other girls talking about having best friends but never felt she could trust anyone to "talk" secrets too. Sure, there were a couple of girls now and then that she would try to be close to, but eventually they would report secrets back to her father.

Hiram was different. He wouldn't take a bribe from her father, and he wouldn't tell them her secrets either. In fact, he would tell her when they tried. She loved his loyalty to her. They soon were inseparable.

Hiram was not just intelligent, he was shrewd! If she didn't think of an idea, he would. They made a brilliant team working together. Isabel decided that where she went in life with Hiram would be her right-hand man. She knew secrets about him, and he knew them about her that would keep their friendship forever intact. Murderous secrets!

Her family religion was from ancient times. To the outside world, they were Muslims. They followed the laws of prayer and the rituals of the Muslim faith only for others to see. It was what went on behind closed doors, which really intrigued her, but something was still missing. They worshipped RA, but in ancient times it was Baal or the Princess Diane. She determined it was all the same gods, but over time, the names changed. The more involved she became in the rituals, the more power she could feel surrounding herself. Her family could sense there was something special about her. The gods were pleased with her and her determination. She took pleasure in torturing the people who decided not to worship her gods anymore and knew too much. They were never seen again after the "rituals" of their covens were finished. She thrived on the fear she saw in people's eyes and knew she had power over them. She secretly hoped to not just be a witch, but to be a goddess/High Priestess. Isabel dreamed of being one of Lucifer's specially chosen women for himself alone. She would do anything to reach that status and she also knew the price she would have to pay would be high! The price was, but it didn't matter. The power she gained in society was well worth it.

She had no time for people who would not further her career or spiritual goals. She used those she could then throw them away as if they no longer existed.

As her spiritual journey grew, she would do the same thing to the Demi-gods, which didn't possess enough power to quench her thirst for a higher level of knowledge of the spiritual world.

Each level brought extra strength and insights. What she didn't realize was she was becoming desensitized to demented and cruel treatment of those which entered her world. There were, of course, a few exceptions. Paul and Andrew knew her softer side.

Her children often felt her wrath. She knew the best thing she could do for Jo and Athea was to send them to boarding school abroad. She secretly, or so she thought, hated having them around. They were loud, demanding, and always interrupting her. She was expected to take care of their needs when they were home. She only had them, so they would have an heir to the Bachman Empire. Andrew insisted they be on his own. Andrew wanted them to stay home, but she would have no part of it. If he wasn't to see them, he could fly to England to see them.

After the son was born, she vowed, there would be no more, but she got pregnant twice more. She hated being pregnant. It not only distorted her perfectly shaped body, her "temple" as she called it, the thought she would also have more snotty nosed brats around her beautiful house made her sick. How could her gods let this happen to her exquisite body? She knew what she would do, but it would take some time before she could lay out her plan. She could be very patient when she needed to be like a spider waiting for her prey.

Isabel's Right-Hand Man

Hiram was from a traditional family with old traditional values. His arranged marriage would take place a year after he graduated from college. Hiram planned on attending college for as long as he could. The thought of marriage was foreign to him. He did not know her very well, but their families had been friends for generations. Not caring one way or the other about her. He secretly preferred men and was not attracted to any woman. Isabel was different. She was eloquent and sophisticated. He noticed her on the first day of orientation for his undergraduate degree in business. From a distance, he witnessed her manipulate men into doing almost anything she wanted from them. She would then toss them aside with the men and women, apologizing for letting her down in whatever situation which Isabel created. Isabel was the most cunning woman he ever met and knew if he stuck by her they would go far into the corporate world. Today, as he was sitting at his desk, even though it was Saturday morning and he really did not want to be there, he felt the satisfaction of accomplishing his own personal goal of reaching the top of his profession. He knew secrets about almost everyone in the executive corporate world. The secrets, which would easily get him killed if certain people knew what he knew. Hiram prided himself on being able to keep secrets, even from Isabel.

Of course, being a 30th grade Mason and all that happened within the Mason Society, is expected to be kept behind closed doors. He is honored for his moving up through the ranks so quickly. He is the youngest to have ever reached that level as far as the society is concerned.

The less well-known association he belongs to is his religion. Only after knowing Isabel for several years, and much grooming, did he invite Isabel to join him one night? She loved it. She told him afterwards that this was the religion she had been looking for all her life. It thrilled her with the power behind it, and it proved to be the spark she needed to build her own self-serving power on. She didn't miss a meeting after that first experience. Hiram watched her grow within the cult. The higher she grew within it, the darker and more conniving she became. He did too. They were a team and partners in the darkness of their religion. Doing unspeakable things, the potions, and curses proved to escalate their power.

He watched as she learned to manipulate those around her with such skill and finesse that they didn't even know what happened till she walked away from them. She seemed to put blinders on those around her and tell such lies to them, and they accepted it as truth. He watched this happen repeatedly. Nobody questioned her either, except for a few along the way. If a person publicly ridiculed her or questioned her about these lies, there would be very serious consequences to be paid. Her fiery would be experienced. At first those that questioned her would soon get sick with some unknown aliment which Doctors a hard time curing, if at all. Accidents would happen with serious injuries or fatalities. Some people even disappeared, never to be seen again. Hiram always knew what happened and kept quiet.

It took Isabel quite a few years after her marriage to talk Andrew into joining their coven for the first time. He didn't take to it like Isabel did at first, but soon saw the benefits of this new religion for him.

Hiram himself watched as their personalities transformed. As intelligent as Andrew and Isabel were, they were losing their compassion for other people. Not that Isabel had much to begin with, but her narcissistic tendencies took over. Andrew lost his Christian morals in exchange for the power, which the cult god promised him.

Together, Andrew and Isabel went deeper into the cult. Much is asked of them in exchange for power and wealth. The highest price was the life of their youngest son. Hiram talked to Isabel about it at one point, as they could do that to their own children. She said it meant nothing to Andrew as he didn't believe they were his anyway and she couldn't stand the germ-infected brats. She only had them because the master told her to. (Hiram understood this because he himself had 2 children die from a family curse). She also clarified that she never wanted to talk about it again!! They never did.

Hiram worked hard at keeping on top of the gossip pool around the office and keeping Isabel abreast of who was doing what. Hiram thinks he is very personable when he needs to be. Playing on his more feminine side had its advantages, he discovered. The women he works with confided in him as he was like one of the girls and men felt comfortable with him as he was not in competition for dating the women in the office. Little did they know he loathed most of them, but found them useful for his own goals!

One of the new girls would always ask why he wasn't married anymore. He would retell the story of how he was in an arranged marriage. It was just 5 years after he graduated with his master's degree; his wife was in a terrible car accident along with their 2 sons. They were killed instantly. On the outside, he played it for all its worth. On the inside, he had to force himself from smiling. He did so by knowing the fact that Isabel knew it too and used it to keep his silence.

Chapter 10

Back at the Station

Detectives Rocco and Gibbons walk towards the office of Captain Holden. He motions them into his office. On the way they hear whistles from the others in the Homicide Detectives Unit. The Detectives are welcomed back into the office with ooh's and awes and shouts about going to the Bachman Building and hobnobbing with influential society. They look at them and tell them jealousy will get them nowhere as they head into the office.

The Captain's office is wall to wall plaques of awards and graduation certificates. A picture of his wife and children is placed where he can see them every chance he gets. They are the love of his life and the reason he does his job. The Captain keeps them safe and other families in his district. He is proud of the fact that his division has the lowest murder rate in the city. He also feels he has the best police force in the city. They walk the beat and get to know the people in the community. They are honest cops and keep him abreast of any unlawful activity developing. Those who know him respect him and consider him as fair and tell his staff what they need to hear, not always what they want to hear. The Captain was also known for not pulling any punches. He is encouraging and even though most of the time they see the worst in people; he remains on the positive side in most situations.

"Please, shut the door behind you. I have word from Commissioner Newman that he wants to see you both about this case. He will want to be kept informed of the progress of your investigation. I don't have to tell you how important and sensitive this is. The Commissioner has already received phone calls from the office of Isabel Bachman about how disrespectful you were to her this morning with the questions you were asking her. Before you go upstairs, you keep me abreast first on 'the who's and where's' of your investigation and where it is leading. I want to know all the details, no matter large or small."

Gibbons is the first to answer. "Captain, there is a lot more to this investigation than what we know right now. There is at least one other person who's present death might also be associated with this case. There are several more possible as well."

Rocco interjects, "Several counties over is a winery called The Brotherhood Winery." The owner died in a car accident/heart attack over a month or so ago. We talked with one owner of Bachman's International Corporation, the new name of the company, as of last night, a Mr. Ethan Bachman which believes it might not have been an accident. He also is unsure of the death of his friend and colleague Robert Hampton, which is the one who died last night of an alleged "heart attack".

The Captain speaks up, "I know the winery very well. My wife and I go to it several times a year to this one and other New York Wineries. Veronica loves exploring the wines. New winery's come up with each year. We each have our own select favorites as she is more of a Merlot and I'm more of a Chablis lover."

All at once they both said, "Why Captain, we didn't know you were a wine connoisseur!"

"There is a lot about Veronica and me you don't know, and I plan on keeping it that way. Don't go blabbing it to the other guys either," commands the Captain.

"We didn't know Charley very well, just enough for small talk and how has this season been for you. I hadn't heard that he died. You say it was what a car accident or a heart attack. Which one was it?"

"We're not sure yet, Captain. We need to do some research on it and talks to the other officers were at the accident. I am sure the medical examiner will give us more details once we can get to our desks."

"Captain, can't you keep the Commissioner off our back for the time being. At least until we can get more information about what is going on with this case or cases as it might end up being. Isabel Bachmann is a real dragon lady with the fire breathing to go with it."

"Just be careful how and where you tread with those people. Keep your noses clean and sort this out situation ASAP. You are both two of my finest detectives. I have total confidence in you! Now go up and see the Commissioner. He's waiting for you. I can run interference for you later," the Captain states.

As Rocco and Gibbons enter the elevator, they decide it would be best to do more listening than talking at this point. They both had a feeling that the Commissioner and the Bachman's probably know each other. Isabel has already been on the phone with him, and they just left the Bachman Building.

Commissioner John Newman is waiting for them as they enter the outer office. His executive assistant is not there per usual on a Saturday afternoon.

"Detectives come in. Even though there is no one on this floor right now, please shut the door behind you. I don't need to tell you that this investigation is your top priority. You need to be kept abreast of every detail. Working with Isabel Bachmann can and will be very difficult. Tread lightly around her as much as possible. I will not tell you how to do your investigation. I'm just giving you some valuable advice. You just started your questioning and I've already received a disturbing phone call from her on your 'rudeness' with the conversation you had with her."

Gibbons is the first to speak up. His face is red with anger as he said, "Now wait a minute. We only asked her if she knew we were investigating the death and alleged murder of Robert Hampton. She blew up at us and threw us out of the office. She also had us escorted out of the building like we had done something wrong. We were not unprofessional in our momentary dealing with her or anyone else in our questioning so far."

Rocco interjected, "Commissioner, she was not only rude to us, but everyone in that building seems to walk on high alert when she is around. Before we go any further, how close are you to the Bachman's sir?"

"I know the Bachman's of course but not very well. They are involved in some of my social circles, but few. I know Ethan is a spiritual man and his wife died about 10 years ago from a heart attack. He was in Europe."

"He spends most of his time overseas, so I don't know him well, but he's down to earth, unlike Isabel. My wife has had to deal with her from time to time with unique events and finds her difficult to work with. I do, however, know Andrew well enough. He's changed considerably as the years gone by. We were friends as kids, until he went away to college. He's a brilliant entrepreneur and charismatic. He and Ethan worked together in the business growing up. The two of them were like two halves of one brain. Both are geniuses. Andrew and Ethan are the ones who grew the Bachman Empire to what it is today. Each possesses the vision and documented all they did. They're the best at what they do and would stand for no less from their employees. Only the best are hired and pay them quite well. They don't seem to have a large turnover of employees from what Andrew has told me."

"I didn't know this Robert Hampton personally, but I know that Andrew and Ethan both valued him as employee and as a friend. What I don't understand is why are you investigating this as a murder? From my understanding, he died last night of a heart attack at Isabel and Andrew's Estate. I called the Medical Examiner, and he just confirmed it as a heart attack."

Rocco answers, "We got a call from Mrs. Hampton at the precinct early this morning asking us to come over, but not in our uniforms. It is about a potential murder. She believes they murdered her husband last night. We have just started our investigation, so we don't have any evidence yet if it was or not. We'll keep you up to date on what we discover."

"Yes, keep me informed and be careful. You are on dangerous grounds if it is only a heart attack. We don't want a problem with these people when there aren't any. Got it?"

"Yes, Sir!" they both chime at once as they are turning for the elevator.

"Gibbons, I know this is a high-profile case because of the people involved. Don't you think this is getting too much attention for just being a heart attack? My instincts are telling me we haven't even scratched the surface on this investigation and we've already pissed people off. We, my friend, are in for a roller-coaster ride like we have never had one before."

"Rocco, since the name of Charley Barrow's keeps coming up; I think we need to make a few phone calls to the Washingtonville, NY police station. We need to find out what really happened at that accident. For two crucial players in this scenario to both die of a heart attack in such a short time frame from each other, it's raising the hair on the back of my neck. There's another thing which is bothering me too. We hardly even spoke to Mrs. Bachman, and she's on the horn to the commissioner about our attitudes toward her. I think she's the one who is trying to hide something, but what exactly it is will be soon found out. There is something seriously wrong with that lady and I'm not afraid to find out exactly what it is!!"

"I would like to find out what the argument was all about with the Bachman's and Barrow. Ethan might shine more light on that topic than he might realize. I think we are going to find him to be an asset, but just how much I'm not sure yet. How about when we get back to our desks you call about Charley's accident since you know a couple of guys on that force and I'll call the Brotherhood Winery? I'll find out about the Board of Directors and the deal they made for this sale." Rocco concludes.

"Hello, this is Detective Williams. How may I help you?"

"Hey Christopher, this is Gibbons from the NYPD. I know it's been awhile and we can catch up later. Right now, I need your help."

"Now isn't that a kick in the pants! You need my help instead of the other way around. What can I do for you, my old friend?"

"I understand you were the Detective in charge of the investigation concerning the accident in which it killed Charley Barrows in."

"It was pretty straightforward. He had a heart attack while he was driving to a meeting and slammed into a stone wall. You know they don't move very well when you hit them. Personally, I think he was dead before he hit the wall. It happened very quickly. I don't think he knew what happened. One moment he's driving down the road and the next moment he's waking up with Jesus."

"He was quite the local celebrity. He owned The Brotherhood Winery."

"Wait, a minute; you're not here to find out about a simple car accident, are you? What's up, Gibbons?"

"You're very perceptive, as usual! It might be something, it might be just what it is, a simple heart attack."

"I'm sure you have heard of Bachman's Tool and Dye, which as of last night has become Bachman's International Corporation. Well, one of their key employees died from a heart attack at the estate of Andrew and Isabel Bachman. They hosted the annual company gala last night."

"Robert Hampton, one of the top executives, was just about to explain the details of a new company they just acquired. As he stood up at the dinner table, he fell over with a heart attack," Gibbons continues.

"Can you guess what company they just acquired? "The Brotherhood Winery!",

I didn't know it was up for sale! Now wait a minute," Detective Williams adds. "Remember, I said Charley was on his way to a meeting when he had his heart attack. He was on his way into the city for a meeting with Andrew Bachman. He was angry, and that is what they attributed to his heart attack."

"There had been one of the Bachman company representatives in his office earlier in the day. I don't remember his name off - hand, but I'll find out what it was. All I remember was this guy really upset Charley, and he was going to straighten it out with Mr. Andrew Bachman." Gibbons said.

"Apparently you are thinking it relates somehow to these two deaths. They aren't just heart attacks, are they? What do you think is really going on," Williams' questions?

"The investigation is at the beginning stages. Homicide got a call from Mrs. Diana Hampton this morning. We went out and talked with Diana and found out that Robert had been working with Charley on a top secret buy out of The Brotherhood Winery to the Bachman Corporation. Robert told his wife if anything should happen to him like dying suddenly or become incapacitated, that she must report it to the police and to only talk to Detectives Gibbons and Detective Rocco."

"As I said before, we've only just started to talk to people and called up to the Commissioner's office already. Rocco and I are thinking there is a lot more to this entire situation than meets the eye." Gibbons responds.

"We have met Andrew and his very unpleasant wife, Isabel. Now she's the most stunning woman I have personally ever met and the most viperous at the same time. If you ever get a chance to meet her, you will understand what I'm talking about. There is something just not right about her, and I don't just mean her wanting to climb higher on the corporate ladder," Gibbons comments.

"If you hear from either Andrew or Isabel, please let us know. Oh, I'm sure you will talk to Ethan Bachman. Now he's a gentleman's gentleman. He flipped out when he found out that Andrew and Isabel bought the winery."

"We haven't learned the whole story yet. We are working on that aspect as we speak. Just to let you know a bit of history. Andrew and Ethan are first cousins. Their fathers were brothers. Andrew is the Chairman of the Board, and Ethan is the CEO. I'm not sure what Isabel is, but if it were up to Ethan, she would be out the door. Ethan has our full cooperation. You will meet him soon. I believe he will be more of a help than a hindrance. He knows all the right people in all the right places. Let's stay on the same page and keep each other informed on what is happening. I have a feeling we will talk again soon," Gibbons concludes.

"Is Rocco still your partner? I think you both need to take a road trip out to see for yourselves what and where the accident happened," Williams states.

"We'll see what I can do to make that happen." Gibbons promises.

The Brotherhood Winery

Rocco and Gibbons decide it is best to go on a road trip and visit with the local detectives at the Brotherhood Winery. They arrive about an hour earlier than they expected and went on a private tour led by the long-time production manager Mark Muser.

The winery is rich in history, especially during prohibition and the fire several years ago. Between the stone-cobbled streets and the old well-kept buildings, *it felt like stepping back in time when life was so much simpler,* Gibbons thought to himself. The walls were covered with pictures of days when the winery was young and just started out. Pictures of before the fire and current pictures show the changes that were made. There are also pictures of how the wine is processed and stored. The frames were made from old oak and blended in with the rest of the décor. Wine racks were all full of the different flavors wine and ready for customers to empty them out.

Both detectives tasted some wines just, so they knew what to bring home for later. They of course have a list from the captain's wife to fill. Brochures helped to explain what the wines represented on the scale from sweet to dry. Both detectives agreed with each other as to bring their wives with them on a long weekend trip.

"Mark, what was Charley like to work for?" Rocco asks.

Mark replies, "He was a man of perfection. For the business, he expected the best out of each of the employees. Well, we are more like family. We knew what he expected from each one of us, and we didn't want to let him down. He was an exemplary man. He worked as hard as he played. We have so many regulars which come in to see us often. I think it was mostly to see Charley. He was exciting, and people were automatically drawn to him with his infectious laughter. We really miss him. He worked hard, but I still find it hard to believe he had a heart attack. That Isabel Bachman drove him to it, I know it."

"Mark, why do you think Isabel was involved?"

"Isabel wouldn't take no for an answer. She repeatedly sent him gifts or called him. Once she even sent some goon to scare him, but I think Charley scared him off instead. He didn't want to have anything to do with her or her husband."

"Andrew was obsessed with wanting to own this company and now he does. It's only been a few days since the takeover, excuse me, the purchase. So far nothing has changed, but time will tell how things will go. Nobody here has jumped ship yet, but we expect something to happen. The shareholders have been given big promises."

"I've gotten to know Ethan Bachman over the years. He and Linda used to come here often, but since she died, he only comes once or twice a year. We are hoping to deal more with him than with Andrew."

Gibbons asks, "Please tell me what you know about Charley's accident. What was he doing before it happened?"

"Charley was finishing up with some invoices on some rather large purchases. There will be a larger than normal wedding reception here on the grounds in June, along with the normal events." Another gift from Isabel was received that morning. He usually gives them to one of us, but he kept this one for himself. It was his favorite coffee and pastries. A courier even brought them, I think. The question was why she sent them, since he would meet with Andrew and Robert Hampton shortly for lunch. He said he was going to put an end to this finally. Charley had enough!"

"Did he seem sick or not feeling well when he was leaving?"

"I'm not sure. I was in the showroom when he left. I had some customers at the time." Mark concludes.

Washingtonville detectives' approach, "Hi Mark, how's business going since Charley's passing. Sorry we haven't been back since the medical examiner said it was a heart attack."

"Detectives Dan Gibbons and John Rocco, this is Detectives Christopher Williams and Jack Martin." Mark introduces. "Come to think of it, why are you all here, anyway? I thought it was a heart attack and not a crime."

"Mark, you mentioned Robert Hampton. Did you know him at all?" Gibbons inquires, ignoring Mark's question.

"He's been coming here for about 6 months on business. He and his wife Diana have been customers here for years. Ethan, Linda, Robert, and Diana would come several times a year. They would stay locally for the weekend. I think it was a place where the four of them could really relax and enjoy themselves. They would laugh and tell stories. It's amazing how life changes. I haven't seen Ethan laugh since Linda died. Robert was the 'go between' Isabel and Charley. Charley never wanted to see Isabel in person. Robert is a good, honest man. Charley had a high regard for him and so do I. Come to think of it, the Bachman Gala was last weekend. We supplied the wine for it this year to announce they are the new owners of this company. How did it go? I'm surprised I haven't heard from anyone about how they liked the wine!"

This time it was Rocco which spoke up. "Robert Hampton died just as dinner was finishing up. He had a heart attack after the wine toast. They rushed him to the hospital but died before they got there. I'm sorry."

Mark grabbed the arm of the chair and sat down before he collapsed. "Wait, what is happening here? First Charley died and now Robert's dead. What kind of detectives are you two?"

Detective Williams put his hand on Mark's shoulder. "They are homicide detectives and they want to reopen Charley's accident. They believe it might have been more than just a heart attack. We don't know for sure if there was any foul play. We are just going to do some more investigating. I know this is a stretch, but you wouldn't happen to have any of that coffee or pastry left, by any chance?"

"Here is Charley's mug he drank from. I'm sure it's been cleaned already, but test it, anyway. He will not be using it anymore. I just couldn't throw it away." Mark pauses, "If that witch Isabel had anything to do with Charley's death, I'm going to shoot her myself!" Mark is now sobbing but trying to get his composure.

"Be careful of what you say in front of all these detectives, Mark. It might just come to be, and we don't want you to be a suspect." Detective Martin states, half smiling.

"Mark, I am so sorry. We will get to the bottom of all of this. It might be a homicide and it might not. We are just reopening the case for now. I'll keep you up to date when we can. You have my word."

"Thank you. I will appreciate it. For now, I must let the staff know so they don't hear it on the news."

"Here is my card in case you can think of anything which might help our investigation," Detective Williams' hands to him.

The four detectives leave Mark in the office, trying to regain his composure. Outside, they decide they could cover more ground if they split up. Detectives Williams and Rocco went to the medical examiner's office for more details. Detectives Martin and Gibbons went back to the station.

Dr. Kolb was examining an accident victim when the detectives enter the morgue. "Hi Detective Williams, and who do I have the honor of meeting?"

"This, my good Dr. is Detective John Rocco from the New York Police Department. He's a homicide division investigating the death of Charley Barrows."

"That was a few months ago. If I remember correctly, he died of a heart attack before slamming into a stone wall."

"It is nice to meet you, Dr. Kolb. We have reason to believe that Charley might have been given a poison which resembles a heart attack. We are working on a similar case in New York City with another victim. This is a very high-profile case and so far, we have been able to keep it away from the media. We would appreciate it to keep it that way for as long as we can."

"Well, detective, you are in luck. I still have a blood sample from Charley we can use to retest the blood. It looked like an open and shut case, but I had a feeling I shouldn't get rid of the sample. Now I know why. Do you know exactly what poison we are looking for?"

"I don't right now, but I'll have our Medical Examiner call you when he finds out if that's all right with you. The fewer people that knows about this, the better the investigation is." Detective Williams and Rocco thanks the Dr. for his time and leave for the station.

We have little to go on with Charley Barrows," said Martin as he hands Gibbons the accident report. "I don't know who this Isabel is, but she must be a piece of work if Mark wants to kill her. He's one of the most even-tempered guys I know. I've known Mark since we went to school together and I can count on one hand how many times I've ever seen him really mad, including today."

"Mrs. Isabel Bachman is the most stunningly beautiful middle-aged women you will ever meet. She is also the most viperous woman we have ever met. Mrs. Bachman threw us out of her office within minutes after meeting her. As soon as we left, she called the Commissioner and told him how rude we were to her. She's dangerous, and I believe she will stop at nothing to get her own way. Isabel might not have directly killed Charley Barrows or Robert Hampton, but she knows who did. I am certain of it." states Rocco.

"This accident report is pretty standard. I can see why it didn't send up any red flags. Call it police instincts, but this isn't what it appears. We might not have the proof yet, but we will. Just watch your back until we get her arrested. I don't trust Andrew or Isabel. She especially will try to stop us when she finds out we are investigating her. I also think these are not the only two bodies in her path."

Chapter 12

Strange Messages

Several months later,

"Mrs. Hampton just called and would like one of you to call her back," the desk clerk tells the detectives as they walk through the door. As they get to their desks, which they hadn't seen for a while, the captain calls out their names and beckons them into his office.

"I haven't seen either of you two in a few days. How's the investigation going? I appreciate the updates, but I have the commissioner breathing down my neck on this one. He wants me to keep a tighter rein on the investigation." Captain Holden states.

Gibbons speaks up. "Captain, this investigation has us going in so many directions. It's like we find one spider web and get all that information which leads us into another spider's web. I'm not sure how many webs there are, but there is more going on in that company than making tools and equipment."

Rocco adds next, "Captain, the commissioner told us several months ago that he and Andrew are friends.

I'm not comfortable letting him know about what we are turning up. I just placed a call to Ethan Bachman. We are also waiting for some blood work to come back from Charley Barrows."

"We got lucky on Charley Barrows. The Medical Examiner where he was first taken for some reason still has a vile of his blood from the accident. The Medical Examiner is running a complete chemical breakdown of his blood. They said it's going to take a while before it's completely finished. We have enough leads to follow up on. Captain, this is getting more and more complicated. We are thinking it involved some exotic drugs in these two deaths. Maybe more than just two murders, if that is the case."

Gibbons states, "The rumor mill at the Bachman's Office Building is working overtime, yet those talking to us are scared to death. We're getting crazy messages without their name or phone number to call back."

Captain Holden asks, "Give me an example."

Gibbons continues, "Here is one I got yesterday morning, 'Detective Gibbons adds, check out the missing persons report on Patty Butler. Ms. Butler was working in the engineering lab department. She had some heated words with Isabel Bachman 5 years ago and was fired. George, the security guard, escorted her out of the building with her belongings and never was seen again.' The phone hung up before I had time to respond. It was a man on the line, and there was no background noise that I could hear. I bet I've gotten at least 10 calls like this. I've been recording my phone calls lately because these calls happen so quickly that I don't always get the name when they speak. We know this one so far that was escorted out of the building, after the confrontation with Isabel

Bachman and was fired. We know she is far from the only one who has disappeared."

"Captain, one thing we need to discuss with Ethan Bachman is a list of missing employees or ex-employees."

Rocco states, "I've gotten a few calls like that myself, just a name of the missing person and little else. I will say not all of them are just from the Bachman employees. I even got one call about a missing lady that Isabel got mad at the store downtown, and another one about a server from a restaurant down the street from the office. The one common denominator is Isabel Bachman, not liking something that was said to her. Apparently she doesn't like people telling her the truth about herself."

"I did a quick name search on this Patricia Butler and the only information I could find was where she once lived and that she worked at Bachman's Tool and Dye Company. There is also a copy of a missing person's poster on the site. The poster was just updated last month by her parents. She was an only child and her parents are frantic to find her."

"I'm waiting for a call from Ethan Bachman to schedule a time to meet with him, hopefully today. I know he is meeting with his executive assistant over lunch today. Hopefully, they both will be able to assist us with a few more answers. So far we have more questions than answers."

Captain questions the detectives, "What does Mrs. Bachman actually do at the Company? I know she's involved with several large charities in the city and throughout the international world. Her name is all over the place in the influential society world. I want to know the groundwork she is doing here at the main headquarters."

Ethan Bachman should know some of these answers if you can't get a straight one from Isabel or Andrew, Rocco and Gibbons thought to themselves. He should know what her role in the company is, even though Ethan believes she doesn't even belong there to begin with. As Rocco was writing down some additional questions to ask Ethan, he thinks of one for the Captain.

"Captain, can we get a warrant to search the files of current or past employees from Human Services at Bachman's? We need to find out who else is missing since she became part of the company."

"Get me more evidence that Bachman's are involved with their disappearances and it won't be a problem. As things stand right now, we only have hearsay and that will never fly with the DA. This investigation has to be as airtight as possible. I want nothing thrown out of court because of technicalities. Isabel and Andrew Bachman already have top attorneys' on retainment."

Chapter 13

Missing Persons Division

Captain directs Rocco to go down to the Missing Persons Division on first floor to see what he can find on the names which he and Gibbons have already collected. Meanwhile, Gibbons heads over to his desk and the mountain of paperwork sitting on his desk.

"Geeze, what a pile of reports," he states to himself out loud. "I really wish I had an executive assistant!" Everyone in hear shot laughs. They also had at least one stack of papers on their desks, too!

He sits down and ignores the pile for the moment, and calls Mrs. Hampton back.

"Hello, this is Diana."

"Hi Mrs. Hampton, this is Detective Gibbons. I'm returning your call. How may I help you?"

"Thank you for calling me back. Now things are settling down a bit, I'm able to think a little clearer. I know you were here after my husband died, but I don't remember clearly what I did or didn't say. Could you and the other detective stop by sometime today, or at your convenience? I have something of Robert's I want to show you."

"Detective Rocco and I will be there about 3:00 if that is ok with you."

"Yes, 3:00 will be fine. I'll see you then. I will see if Ethan will be present as well."

"Great, we have a call into his executive assistant for him to call us back with a time he can meet with us as well. See you at 3:00."

"I better attack some of this paperwork until Rocco comes back." Gibbons again, talking to himself out loud.

Several hours later, Rocco still has not returned from the Missing Persons Division, so Gibbons finds out exactly what was taking him so long. Besides, he had enough of paperwork for the day.

"Rocco, what is taking you so long? We have an appointment with Mrs. Hampton at 3:00. We're hoping that Ethan will be also present."

"Hold your horses, Gibbons. Detective Jennifer Bubb has been kind enough to show me how the ropes work here in her department. She has quite an extensive file for the Bachman Tool and Dye Company. It dates back at least 15 years. My guess is not too long after Mrs. Isabel Bachman started working there."

Dan stretches his hand out to her. "Hi Detective Bubb, I'm Dan Gibbons. I am the other half to this working duo."

"Nice to meet you, Dan, and please call me Jennifer," shaking his hand. I inherited this mess from the Detective who started this file. I've been working on it for about the past 7 years. The stress and the frustration level I think got to him. He had a massive heart attack one night. I've been here ever since, and I understand how that could have happened. Just as I think I'm making headway towards an answer or a location of one of these missing people, something happens, and it turns into a dead end. That is what I've been explaining to Rocco.

"Here's an example. You just brought me the name of one Samantha Benson, Sammi for short. She worked at Bachman's as a lab technician on one of Isabel's projects. By the way, all the Isabel Bachman projects are top secret. Getting any information from anyone concerning the project or the people working with those projects is like talking to a brick wall. From what I gather, this Sammi Benson had some ethical issues with her project and voiced them directly to Isabel. Sammi got fired and escorted out of the building, with her belongings, by the security guard. Her husband called me the next day, saying she never made it home. I watched the video recording of her being escorted out to her car. She drove off by herself. We haven't been able to locate any other video's showing where she went from the parking lot."

"Jennifer, how many names do you have in that file?" Gibbons asks.

"I have 17, but it's not just missing people I'm concerned about. There have been some pretty bizarre accidents which have happened to some employees, but that is not my division." Jennifer states. "I've given the Traffic Division and a heads up on any employee working for the Bachman Tool and Dye Company that is involved in an accident that I want to know about it. So far they have been pretty good at notifying me, especially if it's an unusual accident. All of them have been in a fatality situation. It identifies them as accidents and not homicides, but my gut feelings are that something is not right about them. I just haven't been able to prove it's not an accident. Whoever is executing these people is very good at their job. I suspect it's a serial killer for hire and has been doing it for a very long time. We will catch the person in due time."

Rocco asks, "Jennifer, I see you are so thorough, do you also have a list of these accident victims along with the 17 missing personal?"

"Of course, I'll make a copy of the names for you" Jennifer goes over to her computer and prints out the names and gives them to Rocco.

"Please keep me informed on anything which will help clear up this menagerie of files I've accumulated over the years. I still have plenty of other missing person's files I need to attend to which; I have not presumed are dead."

Rocco takes the list and says, "I don't know how long it will take to track down family members or the person themselves. We will do the best we can to resolve as many of these cases as we can with your help, of course. I believe these cases are just the tip of the iceberg and are a lot more involved than any of us want to imagine being right now."

"Dan Rocco, it is a pleasure meeting you both. We all have a lot of work to do." Jennifer shakes their hands and as they are about to go through the door Jennifer calls out to them, "Guys be careful, only drink what you make, or open like water bottles, and watch each other's backs!"

"I'm going to call a couple of the newest names on the list. I need to give them a heads up on two Homicide Detectives that might call on them soon. They are still very skittish, and I don't want them to freak out on you if possible."

"Thank You. We have each other's backs, and we have already learned to be especially careful on this assignment. Thanks again for your help and we will be in touch soon."

Gibbons and Rocco head back to their desks. They look at the many sheets of papers they received and scanned through the names, phone numbers and addresses.

"Gibbons, aren't these new computers supposed to eliminate some of this paperwork? Look at my desk. Where did all those piles of paperwork come from?"

"Don't worry, Be Happy! Most of them I finished earlier and they only need your signature to sign off of. You can thank me anytime now," Gibbons smiles.

"Thank you very much. I was about to do some flipping out of my own. It's almost 1:30, why don't we get some lunch and head over to the Hampton's house. It will give us a chance to regroup with those names and get a game plan going on for whom to see next after Mrs. Hampton. I hope Ethan will be there too. We'll be able to get some more needed information from him." They grab their coats and are out the door before the Captain stops them.

Chapter 14

Diana's Gift to the Investigation

The Detectives pull up to Mrs. Hampton's house; they notice Ethan's car is in the front of the house. They are just looking at each other and are thankful he is going to be there as well.

They knock at the door, and Ethan answers it.

"Welcome to the Hampton's home. We are glad you are here. Man, I bet you don't hear that often," Ethan smiles.

"People are usually trying to get rid of us as fast as they can and we think we are pretty personable guys.... most of the time that is." This time Rocco smiles back.

Mrs. Hampton calls out from the kitchen, "coffee anyone? I just made a fresh batch." Everyone agrees to a cup.

"Coming from your kitchen to our lips, you make the best coffee in town. Thank you very much." Gibbons replies.

They all sit down to what they all know will be a very unpleasant conversation, but we need information and they are an end to a means. They need to know what they know and find out where they could find the other's information.

"Gentlemen, I'm glad you came to find out who killed my Robert."

This time Mrs. Hampton is dry-eyed. It has been a few months since they have talked to her and she seems to live with the situation and getting back to living again.

Ethan pats Diana on the back of the hand, reassuring her he will always be there for her. The bond between them is close, and as she is going through the worst days of her life. Ethan and her brother are pillars, which she leans on. She is now leaning on Ethan once again. She didn't think he minded, and she is thankful for him to take so much of his time to be helping her.

"Mrs. Hampton, we have some questions for you and Ethan if you don't mind but first, how are you holding up?" Gibbons asks politely.

"Well, I'm trying to get back to my regular schedule, which I've created for myself after I stopped working, but well, I'll get back to it soon, it's been a rough few months. Let's move on. Oh, and please call me Diana. Have you learned what definitively caused Roberts's heart attack yet?"

"Diana, you get right to the point," Rocco smiles and responds further, "We don't have the full toxicology report back yet from the Medical Examiner's office. The Doctor is suspecting a drug was used, but he hasn't narrowed it down completely yet. We'll let you know when we find out."

"Thank you. I will appreciate it. I'm not sure what I'll be able to do with that information, but maybe I'll have some peace of mind because I was not too hard on him for all the things I had on his 'honey do' list. There is a lot to do with an old home like this. He never seemed to mind working around the house, but I think I gave him too much to do here instead of the other hobbies he liked to do too."

Ethan puts his arm around her shoulders and holds her till she gains her composure again. He softly tells her that Robert enjoyed the 'honey do list' because he enjoyed being home as much as he did fishing and woodworking. They were all a way of relieving stress from the office for him. You were the best stress reliever for him, though. He adored you so much. You were not just the love of his life, but his lifetime soul mate.

"Ethan, you always know what to say at the right time. Thank you."

Ethan gives her a gentle hug and then turns his attention to the two detectives.

"Rocco and Gibbons, what have you found out so far as to the how and who did this? We all know the obvious person, Isabel, but she's too smart to do something like this at her own home."

Gibbons replies, "You are right, of course, Ethan. The next person on the list of ours is Hiram Haddad. I understand they do not invite the Executive Assistances to this annual Gala, am I correct?"

Ethan replies, "Yes, you are correct. There is an office party for the executive staff at Christmas time for them and the regular employees. We appreciate our staff at all levels and treat them very well. Exemplary employees are scarce and we don't want to lose any of them after we train them. As far as I know we have little of a turnover, but then again I have been out of the country for most of the past 10 years."

"Ethan, we would like to talk to you more about that, but for right now, we have some other questions. We were talking with Mark at the Brotherhood Winery. He said that Hiram Haddad had paid Charley a visit. What do you know about him besides being Isabel's assistant? We have set several appointments to speak with him, but he seems to be as slippery as Isabel is to talk to," Gibbons states.

"I know that Isabel and Hiram meet at college. They meet their freshman year and have been friends ever since. He is quite dedicated to her. It's almost as if she put a spell on him. He is at her beck and calls for whatever she wants him to do. Personally, I find him to be quite..... Creepy. He stays out of my path, and I try to do the same for him. I know he was married, but I think it was an arranged marriage. I heard something about a car accident that his wife was in, but I know nothing else about it. I am not sure he doesn't enjoy men's company as well. He has never brought his wife to our Christmas parties as other employees do. Hiram just spends time with the other men at the bar. He's Isabel's lapdog, and I really know little else about him."

"Gentlemen, if you wouldn't mind. I need to excuse myself for a few minutes. I love my coffee too, but it has a tendency to run right through me. I also have a few things I need to do as well. Please continue and I'll be back soon." Diana says upon standing and exiting the kitchen.

The guys all stand as she leaves the room. Rocco is the next to speak as they sit down again.

"Ethan now is the perfect opportunity to talk to you about something we uncovered, and it wasn't appropriate to talk to you with Diana being here. We talked with our Missing Persons Detective Jennifer Bubb and found out they have been running a list of missing persons from your company for over 15 years. That is not all. We were also told about several mysterious fatalities which have also been employees from Bachman's. These people all had major disputes with Isabel. There are other people outside of Bachman's as well, but let's just focus on these just yet."

"Wait a minute. Are you telling me there are 17 people missing that worked at Bachman's? How is that even possible? Over what kind of time period are we talking about? Over 15 years? Oh no, there might be another one. I was waiting for the elevator a couple of weeks ago when a woman was crying and asking them where her husband was. The security guard was telling her that Mrs. Bachman had fired him the day before and that he himself had escorted him out of the building with his personal belongings. Oh, what was his name... Oh yes, Jerry McFarley? Is his name on your list? She said she called the police and the hospital since he didn't come home."

"Whoa, slow down, sir," Rocco remarks! Give us a chance to answer some of these questions before Diana comes back. I see Jerry McFarley on the list. He's the newest addition to the list. There isn't any information except his wife called to report him missing and that he worked at Bachman's Tool and Dye Company. They searched the local cameras. They saw him being escorted out by the security guard. Another camera saw him drive out of the parking garage. There isn't anything else listed here after that.

"Did you know this Jerry McFarley?"

"I knew him well enough, I suppose. I hired him to be one of our many engineers. He soon moved up the ranks and became the lead executive engineer. I'm not sure at the moment why or what he was working on for Isabel, but I assure you I will know before the end of today."

Ethan was trying hard to keep his voice down as to not alarm Diana. He is furious at this point. He knows deep in his soul that Isabel has something to do with his disappearance.

"Can I have a list of names of the missing people from my company? I know you are doing an investigation on them, but I think I might find out some information which might not be freely given to you. Because of the new inventions we create, the employees are all signing a no disclosure contract when they are hired and are bound by law not to discuss the inner workings of Bachman's International Corporation. I promise to keep you posted as soon as I get any information."

Gibbons responds, "We know you are an honorable man. Rarely do we bring in outsiders to our investigations, but we will make an exception in this case. Rocco and I can use your help, as well as the Missing Persons Division. I made a copy of the list for you already. For the time being, I would like to deal with hard copies instead of emails for obvious reasons. Details, no matter how small, are important. We find these little details are usually what reveal a chain of events which gets to the truth of the situations. Nobody is perfect. Even professional hit men or serial killers slip up at some point. We will find the answers to what is going on here as well!"

Just as Rocco gave the list to Ethan, Diana comes back into the room.

"Thank you, gentlemen, for excusing me while I abandoned you for some things I needed to do. While I was gone, I remembered about something which might help you. Robert had a safe installed not long after he started working for you, Ethan. I forgot about it because I've never used it. Robert showed me where he kept the combination in case anything would ever happen to him."

"Apparently he kept journals of projects he worked on. I'm not sure what else he wrote about. I'm going to give this to you, Ethan, so he can decipher it. She hands the books to Ethan. "I do not want them back. They are for you to do whatever you feel will be appropriate for them."

"I'll take excellent care of these." Turning to Gibbons and Rocco, he said, "I'll go through these and let you know what I find out from them. I'm hoping he wrote about some projects Isabel has initiated, which she claimed were all top secret."

"Oh, one more thing, I almost forgot. When Robert came home and someone got fired, he would make a mention about another Scientist or Engineer got fired by Isabel today. He wouldn't say anything else about it. At first I would ask him about the person, but he would just say I know little about it, really. I always felt that he was trying to protect me from just how evil Isabel is." Diana says.

Diana refills their cups of coffee as they chat about Robert and his work at Bachman's. Ethan glanced through the journals. He stops and reads a page. A serious look comes across his face for a moment before covering up his emotions again.

Ethan reaches over and cradles her hand after finishing his coffee." Diana, it's always a pleasure to spend time with you, but I need to go for now. If you need anything, please don't hesitate to call me anytime, day or night."

Gibbons and Rocco stand up and thank Diana for the visit. "We should have news soon about Robert. When we do, we will get a hold of you as soon as we can. For now, we also must be on our way. Ethan, it's always a pleasure. We know how busy you are and appreciate you meeting with us today."

They all walk to the front door where Diana says goodbye. She feels much better after this meeting. The look on Ethan's face, she could tell, that the books she gave him were important and he would find answers to questions he didn't even know yet. Diana knows Isabel is a mean person, but she didn't know the extent of how far that meanness extended until Robert's death. Instinctively she knows she has something to do with it but how and why were answers she wanted to know. Now she feels much better knowing that Ethan, Rocco, and Gibbons are all working together to find the answers she so desperately needs to know. She relaxes knowing they will find the answers and justice will be served if she really had something to do with his heart attack. Diana shuts the door as she watches the men standing on the edge of the sidewalk shaking hands before heading to their cars.

Chapter 15

Ethan's Dinner Party

A bright red front door is open and those coming to it are welcome to enter. As his guests enter, they step upon the foyer floor, comprising of light beige Italian marble tiles. Straight ahead is the open staircase of solid oak with a burgundy/gold runner running up it to the landing, before splitting off to each side following up to the hallway above. The chandelier is magnificent. It is hanging down above the round oak table with a marble top in the vast foyer. With the lights on, the crystals hanging down cause prisms cascading and dancing all around the great room. A mixed flower arrangement is centered on the table, sending a scent of lilies and lavender throughout the house.

"Hello Ethan, Pastor Francis and my beautiful bride is with me.," he hollers from the foyer.

"I am so glad you all could make it to my humble abode. We are in the living room. Grab a drink of your liking from the kitchen, and come join us," Ethan responds.

Ethan stands and greets both of them will an enormous hug. "Kristy, I love your new haircut. Have you lost weight because you look fabulous?"

She laughs. "I think it's the haircut. My new shoulder length cut is so much easier to take care of. It's still long enough if I want to put it up, yet it looks great with just a quick brushing."

Everyone takes a seat. The fireplace is roaring and sending warmth throughout the room. The portrait of Linda and Ethan together above the fireplace brings back wonderful memories of each person present. As small talks begin each one shares a fond memory of either Linda or with Ethan and Linda together. Laughter fills the atmosphere.

Soon the head caterer whispers in Ethan's ear and walks away. Ethan stands up and announces. "Dinner is waiting for us in the dining room." Everyone sits where they want. Ethan, of course, is at the head of the table and sits down last. Wine is served to those who want it; others have water already at everyone's place setting.

Ethan, "I've invited you all here because I have missed being home. I have especially missed all of your company as well. I am going to be home more often so you might as well get used to being invited here more often." They all laugh and encourage him on his plans.

Esther comments, "Is that a promise or a threat?"

Ethan responds, "Both in your case." They continue laughing.

Kristy says, "I love this new light mint color you had painted in here. It brings out the color in the picture. I'm glad you have kept the picture over at the buffet table. Linda and I agreed with the Lily of the Valley being the most perfect flowers. They are so delicate yet; possess the fragrance that stops most people in their steps just to smell the flowers."

"I would get her a bouquet of those every week in May and June every year. I always stop in my tracks when I smell them myself. Let me tell you the story of that picture. We were on a walk in the city and stumbled onto at a starving artist event in Manhattan. She saw this picture and had to have it. You should have seen us trying to get that picture into the cab; I thought we were going to have to tie it to the roof of the cab." They all tried to image it and laugh. "I could never get rid of it. It's one of the funniest memories I have of us together with the taxi cab trying to help us."

"This picture is not only a masterpiece from a young artist, but it makes me laugh. By the way I have since purchased other pictures from him. Look around and see how many you can find from him. I don't think he's starving anymore!" Ethan laughs.

Smells of dinner are permeating the air, making everyone starving. "Just to let you know there are no onions in the dishes tonight. For those of you who are either allergic or just don't like onions, you have no fear of your food. If you would like some for your salad or some caramelized for the main dish, ask your server and they will accommodate you."

"Thank you!" Several said in unions. Pastor Francis said, especially loud.

"Enjoy your Stuffed Mushrooms and the Caesar Salad. Pastor Francis, will you say grace, please?"

"Dear Father, thank you for this group of believers and this food you have so generously supplied for us. Bless this home and our conversations. May you be glorified with our words and our love for you and for each other! Bless the caterers and keep us safe when we drive home tonight. Keep Ethan safe as he brings to light what has been in darkness for many years. In Jesus' glorious name we give thanks. Amen."

The crystal and china are the same which they used when Linda was alive. She had exquisite taste and Ethan would change none of these things, which they both enjoyed so much. A simple silver rose pattern on the china lines one side of the dishes with a silver rim around the edges. From the water goblets to the wine glasses and all the other pieces in between, the crystal compliments the dinnerware with an etched rose on the side of glass and a silver rim on each delicate piece.

Dinner is winding down. Some are drinking coffee or tea, while others are still sipping wine from the Brotherhood Winery. Ethan clears his throat, and everyone quiets down.

"Traveling all the time can be interesting and enchanting but there really is no place like home. As you can see, nothing has really changed in here since Linda passed away. I've left it that way on purpose. When I come home, especially from a long trip, it is nice to have her memories surround me. Yet, my heart breaks with such brokenness. Time doesn't change that hurt, it takes away some of the bitterness and stinging pain that occurs at the time and perhaps the first 2 years. Life comes in and our time isn't so focused on it all the time but the changes which happen come naturally." Ethan looks away as a tear escapes his eye. Diana reaches over and touches his hand. Without saying a word, they both understand each other's pain.

Ethan stands up, clearing his throat. Ethan turns and smiles to Diana. A tear runs down his face, but he ignores it. "I'm sorry. I hold my emotions in for so long that sometimes it just has to escape but only with my dearest of friends."

Still holding Diana's hand, "Robert was like a brother to me. Like David and Jonathan in the Bible. As they say today, brothers from another mother. I'm going to be really honest here. A part of me feels responsible," he puts his hand up as everyone voices their objections but they quiet down, "Please hear me out. I know Isabel changed Andrew into someone I don't know anymore. There is darkness about both of them that makes me uncomfortable. I however, never thought she would resort to murder to accomplish her goal of controlling her secret projects from being exposed. I sense we have only touched on information we will learn from now on. I am so sorry Diana, I didn't force Isabel out years ago when she first started showing up for work. Maybe Robert would be alive today. I failed you and Robert."

Diana stood up and put her arm around him and rested her head on his chest. "Ethan, you failed neither one of us. Robert knew what she is capable of yet. He still worked with her. He had a choice, and he made it by staying in the lab. We talked several times about him looking for a job somewhere else, but he couldn't bring himself to look anywhere else. He felt he belonged at Bachman's plus he didn't want to let you down. Ethan, he felt the same way about you. He would tell me that if he had a brother, he wanted him to be just like you. Robert loved you dearly. He did not regret for one moment working at Bachman's."

"Andrew and Isabel knew Robert was off limits, or at least I thought so until now. The investigations are just beginning, but I want this to be over very quickly. I also know this is not the way it works. If Robert and Charley were killed, we don't know the how or if it was a poison, what kind it was. It might take a year or so before they find out, is what I'm told by the Investigators. I'm already frustrated, and it's only the beginning. I need prayer from all of you to speak what I need to speak and to whom, and when to remain silent and let the officials do their job without me interfering. We need the truth to come out and those responsible for anything done which, God considers unethical to be exposed to His light and be brought to justice." Ethan comments.

Pastor Francis responds, "Dear Jesus, you and you alone know all the angles of this situation with Robert, Charley, and Isabel. Expose the truth and bring out all the problems which Isabel created working at Bachman's. Give Ethan peace within his heart, which passes all understanding. Give him the strength he needs to preserver to find the truth, and the discernment needed to know what to do with that truth. Give him your words to say and when he needs them. Let him not worry about the future because you will lay it out in front of him in your perfect timing. Pour your grace and mercy upon this home and everyone here tonight. Thank you, Jesus, for your presence here and the love you pour down on us. We love you with all our being. Jesus, in your name we pray Amen."

"That reminds me, how is your Bible Study going, Ethan? I haven't been able to get online lately. Stating this new church has my time all locked up with great excitement, I must add," Pastor Francis adds.

"I have a new one I'm posting tomorrow. It's on the 10 Commandments. I'm always surprised how many people don't know what all of them are. The study is going back to the basics. As usual, I'm going to post the study and anyone can post their opinions down below. It should prove quite interesting. Some will not react well to the truth and it will be up to us to show the truth in love and not condemnation. God created all of us and loves us all equally; right where we are and who we are. We are not their judge and executioner. We are to be Jesus to them and love them. Whatever they need to work on is between them and The Savior, Jesus."

"Well said," Diana commented. "Ethan, on that note, I must be going. I look forward to your study each week. The responses are always enlightening." They all laugh.

Everyone stands and leaves as well. Ethan walks them to the door. "Thank you all for coming. I was feeling pretty low before tonight. I know it's going to take more time to find all the answers we need, than what we would like. We have to keep praying through this situation and keep each other lifted up to God as well." They give hugs, and Ethan shuts the door.

The caterers cleaned up and left everything in order before his guests left. Now he is alone again. His emotions are still raw and lets himself cry for a time. The guilt is gone from letting Isabel stay on at the office, but that will change the first chance he gets. Ethan regains his strength and heads to the computer to finish his message to the Enlightening class blog.

Chapter 16

Ethan's Enlightenment Class

"Today we are starting a new series. I'm calling it Hidden in Darkness. We are going back to the basics. The Ten Commandments, From the New International Version (NIV) Exodus 20:1-17 [(4)]; I'll list them here, but I want all of you to go to the Bible, Torah, or your favorite search engine and meditate on their meaning."

'Father in Heaven, I pray for understanding for all who are reading this today. Guide them Holy Spirit for wisdom on what they are learning and how to apply it to their own lives. Bring them to a deeper love and understanding of you and your ways for us to live in safety, respect for others and to bring you honor and glory forever. Thank you, Jesus, and in your name, we pray Amen."

"John 14:15 states, 'if you love me, follow my commandments. So let's first go to what love is: 1 Corinthians 13:4-7 Love is patient, love is kind. It does not envy, it does not boast, it is not proud. It is not rude, it is not self-seeking, it is not easily angered, it keeps no record of wrongs. Love does not delight in evil but rejoices with the truth. It bears all things, believes all things, hopes all things, and endures all things. Love never ends.'

Now that we know what love is according to God, we need to implement it along with the 10 Commandments Laws which are:

The Ten Commandments, And God spoke all these words:

1. "I am the Lord your God, who brought you out of Egypt, out of the land of slavery. You shall have no other gods before me."

2. "You shall not make for yourself an image in the form of anything in heaven above or on the earth beneath or in the waters below. You shall not bow down to them or worship them; for I, the Lord your God, am a jealous God, punishing the children for the sin of the parents to the third and fourth generation of those who hate me, but showing love to a thousand generations of those who love me and keep my commandments."

3. "You shall not misuse the name of the Lord your God, for the Lord will not hold anyone guiltless who misuses his name."

4. "Remember the Sabbath day by keeping it holy. Six days you shall labor and do all your work, but the seventh day is a Sabbath to the Lord your God. On it you shall not do any work, neither you, nor your son or daughter, nor your male or female servant,

nor your animals, nor any foreigner residing in your towns. For in six days the Lord made the heavens and the earth, the sea, and all that is in them, but he rested on the seventh day. Therefore, the Lord blessed the Sabbath day and made it holy."

5. "Honor your father and your mother, so that you may live long in the land the Lord your God is giving you." Ephesians 6:2-3 [5]. "Honor your father and mother," which is the first commandment with a promise "so that it may go well with you and that you may enjoy long life on the earth."

6. "You shall not murder." Isaiah 44:2[6] "I formed you in your mother's womb- *Hence, Abortion is murder to God."*

7. "You shall not commit adultery. Matthew 5:27-28[7]. "You have heard that it was said, 'You shall not commit adultery '; but I say to you that everyone who looks at a woman with lust for her has already committed adultery with her in his heart.

8. "You shall not steal." (example: Malachi 3:6-10[8] tithe 10% of wages. *If you don't give back to God with 10% of your wages, then you are stealing from God). Giving back to God is any charity you give freely to, expecting nothing back. ASPCA, Church, the Blind Association, Synagogue, Food Pantry are all outstanding examples. Sometimes it's your precious time instead of money. God loves sacrifices from us because it comes from the heart.*

9. "You shall not give false testimony against your neighbor." (Revelations 21:8[9] All liars will burn in the lake of fire)

10. "You shall not covet your neighbor's house. You shall not covet your neighbor's wife, or his male or female servant, his ox or donkey, or anything that belongs to your neighbor."

"Truth seems to be a relevant term to many people today," Ethan continues to write to the Adult Bible study online. "Lies hide in darkness."

"Yahweh, God Almighty, is the creator of light and darkness. His guidelines are your measuring stick to judge for what darkness is. What is darkness/? Darkness or sin is an offensive to the Lord. Darkness hides 'from the light. Truth is light. If a person tells the truth in any situation, he will have nothing to hide. If the same person tells a lie, then he or she will have to remember the exact lie and it creates usually a web of lies to cover up the original lie in order to make it plausible. If someone is unsure of what the truth is in any situation, all that needs to be done is to go back to the original situation and the truth will speak for itself.

Let's talk about the first 2 Commandments since we can roll them all into one topic:

"I am the Lord your God, who brought you out of Egypt, out of the land of slavery. You shall have no other gods before me."

"You shall not make for yourself an image in the form of anything in heaven above or on the earth

> beneath or in the waters below. You shall not bow down to them or worship them; for I, the Lord your God, am a jealous God, punishing the children for the sin of the parents to the third and fourth generation of those who hate me, but showing love to a thousand generations of those who love me and keep my commandments."

The first commandment sounds simple enough, but what today do we worship besides or instead of God Almighty? Is it other gods, money, power, our jobs, sports, or maybe it's our families or spouse. Anything which we put above God is an idol. Matthew 6:24[(10)]. You can't serve two gods. Choose one or the other.

When is the last time you got really excited about worshipping Jesus? Do you get more excited about your favorite baseball or football player scoring a point for the team than you do for a worship song you are singing to the King of Kings? God created you. God Almighty loves you more than anyone else ever could. Jesus took a horrific beating and died a humiliating, painful death so it would set you free of death in hell. He did not create Hell for his children; He created it because of the Angels which disobeyed him and followed the archangel we call Satan. Nobody knows Satan's actual name because God took it out of the Book of Life. Satan means "deceiver". He uses it as one way of addressing who he is, yet it is only one of millions of names he uses. We'll learn more about this topic as we go on.

Jesus laid down his life for you so you could go to heaven with him for all eternity. You might say, 'I'm a good person; I'm nice to my neighbors and coworkers. I don't steal or rob anyone.' Well, let's go back to the game book, The Bible. Just like sports, in order to win the prize of being the best and winning by following the rules, so is life. The rule book is the Bible. In America we don't stone spouses for committing adultery, but we have laws which still make it a crime in some states as an example. The laws didn't change in the Bible, but society changed the laws. The family still suffers the effects of adultery, especially the children, but I divers.

Forgiveness, mercies, grace and repenting go a long way in the healing process. God is able and willing for you to come to him for all your problems in life as helping you with the consequences of our actions. We can get into that Bible study at a later time.

Some people dislike God's rules, especially for things which interfere with how they want to live. Homosexuality and abortion are hot topics of today's world. If you want to know how God feels about them, then do a word search on the topic and ask the Holy Spirit for wisdom concerning those topics. The point I'm trying to make is this; you can't serve 2 Gods or two masters. Please take the time to read Matthew 6:24 [(10)] and 1 Kings 18:21 [(11)]. Jesus promises eternal life through loving him. If you choose something other than Jesus, then you will not receive His prize at the end of the game of life, eternity in Heaven. God our Father has made it abundantly clear. There is no other way to heaven except through Jesus the Messiah, Yeshua. Read Isaiah and Revelations for a glimpse into Heaven.[(40, 41)]

Now I would like to address one more issue in today's world. It is mediums, fortune tellers, Ouija boards, tarot cards, and horoscopes. I have heard people say "Oh they are just for fun. There's no harm in seeing what they say my future is going to be." Here's what the Lord says about the topic. The Lord told Moses in Exodus 22:18[12] Sorcery is detestable to Yahweh/God. What exactly is sorcery and who are sorceresses? Let's go back to scripture again and see what God says it is. Deuteronomy 18:9-12[13] states, "When you enter the land the Lord your God is giving you, do not learn to imitate the detestable ways of the nations there. Let no one be found among you who sacrifices their son or daughter in the fire, who practices divination or sorcery, interprets omens, engages in witchcraft, or casts spells, or who is a medium or spirit or who consults the dead. Anyone who does these things is detestable to the Lord." 1 Chronicles 10:13[14]; "Saul died because he was unfaithful to the Lord; he did not keep the word of the Lord and even consulted a medium for guidance." Abortion is a sacrifice to Baal and Moloch, ancient gods which are still worshiped today, many times under different names but the same gods.

"You might say, that was the Old Testament and under the Law of Moses. Jesus did not come to abolish the law, but to fulfill it. Use your concordance to find this scripture or your smart phones," Ethan suggested.

"Galatians 5:14.[15] For the entire law is fulfilled in keeping this one command: "Love your neighbor as yourself." It should base everything you do in love. If you are in a situation which you're unsure about, go back to this statement. Not all "love" is healthy, unfortunately. The body or flesh is selfish and wants what it wants, and not what God knows is best for you. God sees the entire picture of your life. The flesh wants what feels good. God has put guidelines in your life to do what is in your best interests. He knows your future.

"Let's continue, Galatians 5:17-23.[16] For the flesh desires what is contrary to the Spirit and the Spirit what is contrary to the flesh. They are conflicted with each other, so you are not to do whatever you want. But if the Spirit leads you, you are not under the law. The acts of the flesh are obvious: sexual immorality, impurity and debauchery; idolatry and witchcraft; hatred, discord, jealousy, fits of rage, selfish ambition, dissensions, factions and envy, drunkenness, orgies, and the like. I warn you, as I did before, that those who live like this will not inherit the kingdom of God. But the fruit of the Spirit is love, joy, peace. Patience, kindness, goodness, faithfulness, gentleness, and self-control, against such things there is no law."

More importantly, there is a great deception which has been escalating as time has gone on for approximately 6,000 years. God is also known as the God of Abraham, Isaac, and Jacob, Yahweh or Jehovah. God is the Alpha and Omega, the beginning and the end. HE always was and will always be. The words God spoke started the universe, stars, planets, land, water, animals, plants, heavenly being, his only son Jesus or Yeshua, and humanity. He is the Word. He is the only true God.

Now there are millions of things or beings which humanity refers to as gods. Here is where the deception comes in at. There was an angel who led worship for God Almighty in the throne room known as the Third Heaven.[17] He wants to be a god and be worshipped as well.[18] He talked 1/3 of the other angels into believing he could be a god, so they worshipped him. Guess what his name is: Lucifer, Devil/Accuser, Serpent, Ruler of Demons,[19] Dragon,[20] The Wicked One[21], RA, Allah along with all 99 of his other names[22], Buddha, Princess Diane, all the

Greek gods, Baal, Moloch, Wicca gods and goddess, and the 3 million Hindu gods. [23, 24] Whatever name he goes by to entice people away from God Almighty." Satan is the god of this world[25, 26] Jesus watched Satan fell from Heaven like lightning."[27] If Satan was stronger than God, then how is it that Satan was the one thrown out of Heaven and not the other way around? Seek the truth. Don't rely on what somebody else thinks are truths. Investigate it for yourself. Go back to the original source and discover what the truth is for any given situation."

"Since God cast Satan into Hell and chained the fallen angels into its dungeons[28, 29] Satan has vowed to steal as many souls from God as he can. Satan is the master of lies, hate, and deception. The evil one has had thousands of years to master his craft, learning human nature. He knows how to manipulate and twist the truth with just enough to make his ideas plausible. The evil one trains his demon force to corrupt the minds of God's creations; animals and humans."

"Remember God is our creator.[30] He reigns above all that he has created. Satan cannot create anything, but counterfeits and manipulates whatever he can. Though he knows human nature and expects what we are going to do and say, he cannot read our minds. We were created with free will.

Psalms 33:6-10 states: By the word of the Lord the heavens were made and by the breath of His mouth all their hosts. He gathers the waters of the sea together as a heap. He lays up the deeps in storehouses. Let all the earth fear the Lord; Let all the inhabitants of the world stand in awe of Him. For He spoke and it was done. He commanded, and it stood fast."

"I have stirred up enough for now. Tomorrow and the following days will be questions and answers on these scriptures as you meditate on them. Seek God's wisdom on what they mean. Don't forget ALWAYS asking the Holy Spirit for guidance when reading God's Word, The Bible and the Torah. Next week's lesson will be on family. What it means to respect and honor others, especially parents. What to do if they don't deserve it."

God's many blessings to you all and love your neighbor as yourself. Love yourself because you are unique and created for a purpose in this life. God didn't make you by accident. You have a book in Heaven with your destiny written in it. You are very special to Jesus and he loves you just the way you are right now.

(In the back of this book will be a prayer for you to accept this love if you haven't already. Go there now if you wish to accept Jesus in your heart. You will never regret this decision to love Jesus in return. You will also receive peace within your heart which passes all understanding.)

Chapter 17

Digging Deeper

"Esther, I need to go to Dubai, and I want you to come with me for this trip. We will be gone for about a week. Please use this state-of-the-art Samsung Galaxy phone I gave you to make the arrangements, but make sure you are in a secure place. Motioning with his hands, they went into his office."

"As you already know, I have John come and sweep my office regularly. He was just here yesterday."

"We will need to leave first thing in the morning on Saturday. I'll meet you at the corporate plane at 6am. I'm sorry for such brief notice, but this is very important. Oh, one more thing. Who in HR do you know and totally trust with confidential information?"

"Her name is Kathy McKinney. She is not an Isabel fan and I've tested her out several times with information and it went nowhere else. She has been with us for 18 years."

"I know who she is. Thank you for testing the water for me. I've been away so much I don't know who I can trust anymore."

"Please call her and let her know I'll be in to see her in about an hour. Do you have her private number?" Esther nods yes. "Tell her I need her to pull the files for these 17 people. I'll make a copy of their names shortly. I will need the hard copies and any internet files that exist. I also want her to give you these files so nobody else can access them, including Isabel and Andrew. I will handle her boss if she has questions about this project I have her working on. Kathy is not to release any of the names I give you to anyone."

"I have some forms for you to sign that will only take a minute of your time. I can meet you at Kathy's office if you don't want to come back upstairs to yours," Esther informs him.

"As far as the trip to Dubai, I always have my passport and bag ready for these sorts of trips. I'll see you shortly. I'll make a copy of the names and I'll give you back your list right away," Esther tells him, and Ethan smiles.

"Great, tell Kathy I have John, my security guy, which will come to her office to do some technology cleaning, if you know what I mean. Tell her not to speak any of these names out loud. We don't know who is listening and how far her voice travels. Please write the names down on a piece of paper and hand it to her instead of calling her on her private number. If she has questions for you, have her write it down and you can answer her on the note. Pretend you're in school and passing notes without the teacher seeing you," Ethan jests.

An hour later, Ethan is in the office of Wendy Harvey, the Director of Human Resources. She's an older woman with short, gray hair. She wears long pants with a matching blouse and blazer. Today she is wearing a light spring dress with a sweater which accents it nicely. Dressy red shoes for comfort pull together the ensemble. She says no more heals for her. Safety and comfort over vanity.

"Hi Wendy, I hope I'm not disturbing you," Ethan says.

"No, not at all, it's always a pleasure to see you, Ethan. What brings you down to the world of HR?" Wendy replies.

"First, how's William doing? I heard he was really sick a few months ago?"

"He's doing much better. He gave me a good scare. We aren't as young as we used to be. He decided to finally, clean out the garage and overdid it, almost causing a stroke. Fortunately, it was just a warning. It sure scared the two of us. He's doing much better and is on a healthy diet. I'm on it too. Do you think I can lose weight? He's already lost 20 pounds, and it's only been 6 weeks. I, on the other hand, have only lost 5 pounds."

"You didn't come here to listen to me go on about my personal life. What do I have the honor of your presence for?"

"I have a special project for Kathy to help me with. It's important to me it just stays between her and I. I'll fill you in later about it. I know how busy you are, so I asked her to assist me on this project. It's very important that she gets me the information as soon as possible. It is a very sensitive matter, and I have sworn her to secrecy. I will tell you this much. I don't want word to get back to Isabel or Andrew that she is working on a project for me. I appreciate your cooperation and silence on this. If you see anyone at her computer besides her, please call me immediately. I do have someone coming in shortly to sweep her computer. Other than that person, nobody is allowed near her desk. She will have access to all the employee's files, present and past. I'm sorry for any inconvenience this might cause you. Whatever she is currently working on will either have to wait, or better yet, please assign it to someone else. Give no reason for what Kathy is doing. I don't want any suspicion to cast her away. If you have questions, please come to me directly. Oh, one more thing. Payroll has been given clearance on any overtime she might occur. It will be charged to my department and not yours, so you won't have to worry about your budget for this department."

"After this project is over, I'll get back to you about what is going on and what is about to happen. Secrecy is top priority right now. Can I count on you to keep it from Isabel and Andrew or anyone connected to them?"

"Of course, if there is anything I can do to help, please let me know," Wendy responses.

"If anyone interferes with her project or is too inquisitive, please let me know and they will be fired immediately by me. I believe there is a leak in this office. You are to trust no one except Kathy, Esther, and myself. That is all I can say about that for now." Ethan tells her.

"Again, I'm sorry for any inconvenience." Ethan turns and walks over to talk with Kathy.

Esther is waiting for Ethan in Kathy's office when Ethan comes in.

"Good afternoon, Ladies. I have someone coming in shortly to do some housecleaning on your computer. We'll wait for that person then how about I take you ladies out for supper, we have a lot to talk about. Esther, how about those papers you want me to sign before we start this adventure?"

Just as Ethan signs the last invoice, there is a knock at the door. Ethan gets up and answers it.

"Hello John. Thank you for coming. I'm so glad you could make it on such a brief notice. I believe you already know Esther, Kathy, this is John. He's the most fantastic computer guy I know, and one of the most trusted guys in my inner circle. He's going to be here for a while so how about we get moving and let John take care of those things we talked about."

"Mr. Ethan, it's always a pleasure doing business with you! I should be finished with the items we talked about in a few hours. Kathy, I will need your keys to your office and for the other rooms which you will use for this project. Just show me where they are, and what key I will need for them. Ethan will explain this to you shortly. Just to save some time, show me how you get into your computer and I'll do what I need to do to keep you safe and sound." John replies while shaking Ethan's hand. He hands Ethan an invoice of the items he needs for this job and his bill. Ethan signs it and hands it to Esther, along with her other paperwork.

Ethan turns to Esther, "Why don't we leave and you can take those papers where they need to go, and I'll meet you ladies out front. Your carriage will be waiting for you."

"John, Kathy and I will see you in about two hours."

"That will be perfect. See you then," John answers as he turns to Kathy, who was already at her computer to show him what she does to log into it. Ethan and Esther left the office.

Esther hands Ethan the briefcase with the files in it which Kathy had given to her.

"Ethan, these are only the hard copy files of the 17 employees you requested from Kathy. She didn't have time to look into their online files yet." Esther remarks as they walk to the elevator.

"Esther, have I told you lately how much I appreciate you?" Ethan asks as he looks down at the briefcase.

He knows how important the files are that are now in his hands. *I wonder how many more there are going to be once this is all said and done.* He thought to himself.

"Yes sir, every time we talk." They both laugh.

A short time later, all three of them are in the limo on the way to one of the finest Lobster Restaurant in NYC. There is small talk in the limo and in no time they were sitting at a table sipping on some wine.

"Please order anything you want on the menu. You both have quite a task ahead of you. I want you to know the extent of what I'm asking you to do. My circle of people I totally trust is only about one handful. You are two of these people. Here is a business card of the two Detectives I'm working with and I want you to call either one of them immediately if you are feeling that you or your family is in danger. Follow your instinct and don't just shrug off something that you're feeling is off. After you call either Rocco or Gibbons, I want you to call me."

"When we get back to your office, there will be some notable changes. Our offices are being cleaned of any listening devices. I have scheduled with John to come in and scan every few days to make sure your offices are secure. The office doors are closing whenever you leave the room. They are retinal secured so you and I will be the only ones allowed in your offices except John of course."

"You will have to pardon me. I'm afraid I didn't even ask either of you if you were ok with what I'm asking you to do. You both know how dangerous Isabel is, and I'm asking you to keep secrets from her. We all know this does not go well with her."

Esther is the first to ask. "Ethan, what exactly are you asking us to do beyond the obvious of doing our normal jobs?" Kathy nods in agreement.

"I'm asking you both to step out and keep me posted about any unusual events which you know of. I'm asking you both to do some research into certain situations which might disturb you. If Isabel or Andrew finds out what you are doing, they will want to fire you. You are to call me immediately. They do not have the authority to fire you, and I want to assure you of that. Don't argue with them, just call me."

"I am going to keep Isabel out of the building as much as I can. I am not foolish enough not to know that as soon as I leave the building, she magically seems to appear."

"Kathy, I want to ask you, how often does Isabel come into the HR Department?"

Kathy replies, "When we see her, we know she has fired someone else. She normally makes a beeline into Wendy's office. I'm not sure if you have had time to look into any of the files I gave Esther yet. You will find a form which she fills out, or has Wendy filled out for her, and she signs it why she fired that person."

"Wendy always has her personally sign these forms and likes to get her to write in her own words why she fired that person. Wendy explained to all of us that when we see Mrs. Bachman coming we are to find her immediately if she isn't in the office. We are not to get involved with her.

Wendy's assistant has taken the blunt of Mrs. Bachman's rage more than once. Fortunately, we don't see her that often, maybe once or twice a year, more often over the past few years though."

"She was just in the office the other day, as a matter of fact. I pulled his file. It's one you just received. Comments around the water cooler are that we hopefully won't see her for another year."

"Mr. Ethan, I noticed that all of these files I pulled for you all had one of these forms in them, with Mrs. Bachman's signature on them. I also know that the police have inquired about most if not all of these people and why they were fired."

"I work almost exclusively with workmen's compensation, and retirement forms and the employees associated with them. I've often wondered why some of those people never filed for workmen's compensation. I asked Wendy once about it and she told me I had enough work to do and not to worry about it. She said it jokingly, but I sort of felt it was none of my business and the topic was off limit."

Ethan quietly responds, "Kathy, what I'm going to tell you and whatever happens with this 'project' are strictly between the three of us and, of course, the Detectives. All the people on this list have all come up missing after they were fired and left the building."

We have the videos of them being escorted out of the building and driving out of the parking deck/lot. They didn't seem to make it home. We suspect there are more names which belong on this list. That is where you come in at, Kathy. Do you know of other people who were fired by Isabel and never made it home?

"Here's where I can find out. I know Wendy has kept a list of all the forms which Mrs. Bachman has signed. The list is on her computer, but I'm sure there is a hard copy somewhere. If John can get me that list, I'll pull their files. I know of some names which aren't on the list. I'll pull them on tonight and get them to you tomorrow."

Ethan speaks up, "Esther and I will leave for Dubai on Saturday at 6am. Can you meet us at the airport with the files?"

"Of course, but how am I going to get these files out of the building? The security guard has orders to check all our briefcases when we leave the building."

"I'm glad you mentioned it. I forgot about this policy. Call me as soon as you have them together and bring them up to Esther tomorrow. I'm really sorry for such brief notice and your lack of sleep for tonight. Do you have a current passport?"

"I actually just renewed it. Why do you ask?"

Depending on what you find out, you might come thought to himself, *she will be better off with us. Once certain people find out she's working for me, she will be in danger for her life. I really hope I'm wrong, but it's better to keep her safe.*

While they were finishing their supper, they notice Denzel, the driver, sitting at the other end of the restaurant. Esther comments to Ethan, "You know he's one of us. He keeps his ears open, and his mouth shut. Isabel just ignores him. She has tried to get information out of him several times but he just says, 'I'm just the driver, ma'am. I know nothing but how to give you a smooth ride and get you where you need to be.' In reality, he's a very intelligent man and knows pretty much everything that goes on around here. He talks to me, but not too many other people. He has very high regards for you, Ethan."

Thank you for reassuring me about him. I suspected for many years he was loyal to the company and not to Mrs. Isabel Bachman." Ethan laughs.

"I gave him a few good stock tips over the years. Maybe he took me up on them without hesitation. He didn't tell anyone. I knew because it never came back to me I was telling secrets."

"I think he did because he told me once a year he, his wife, and two nieces take a three-week vacation to Europe. He's a very private man, but he always comes back with an enormous smile on his face, like the cat that swallowed the canary." They all laugh.

Ethan pays the bill as well as Denzel's as usual. They chat about the lightness of other employees' attitudes now that Ethan is back at the helm again. Ethan didn't know what a difference he makes when he was actually in the building. He didn't know his beloved company is being run by a tyrant in his absence.

This all is about to change permanently, he thought to himself, and she will not like it one bit. This thought brought a smile to his face, though he said nothing out loud.

Denzel drops Esther off at her car, and Ethan walks Kathy back to her office. He wants to see if John has any news for him about the changes he is making to the office.

John meets them at the new security door. I reinforce it with a state-of-the-art retina identification security pad. He explains how he needs to set it with Kathy, looking directly into the scanner. Next he has Ethan do the same. John has already had completed his scan. The three of them would be the only ones allowed in Kathy's office.

"Moving on," John says to the next accomplishment for the evening.

"The security on these computers is very good, but nothing I couldn't hack into within a few minutes. But I went a different route. I didn't want to alert your security that I was hacking into the computer. So here is what I did. You told me Kathy that Wendy wrote a hard copy of all the people who left her with Mrs. Bachman's signed form, so I broke into her office instead. Surprising enough, her office wasn't bugged like yours was. It's all clear now, by the way. Anyway, I have a copy of the list of names for you from Wendy's office and no one other than us is any of the wiser. I made a copy for you too, Ethan," as John hands him the new list.

"John, there must be 20 names on this list."

"There are actually 17. I only made a copy of one form, which Isabel signed since they were the same. The reason for firing was sometimes different, but it was redundant since it was on the original dismissal form."

"I'm not sure what is going on here and at this point I'm not sure I really want to." John expressed. "I would like to make a suggestion, though. Instead of removing the files, just take pictures of them on your phone and leave the rest behind."

"John, I knew I liked you for a reason. Great idea! Just use the phone I gave you earlier and give it to Esther tomorrow after you are finished with taking the pictures. She'll get it to me without the security guard getting involved. Please come up to the office tomorrow and take pictures of the files you gave her earlier and return them hopefully with no one noticing they are gone," Ethan comments.

"Kathy, you now have access to one of the highest clearances in the company. Get as much done quickly and quietly as you can right now. We'll see you tomorrow and try to get some sleep tonight." Ethan adds.

Kathy, thinking to herself, *I think it will be best if I just finish up tonight and take all those pictures. Wow, all those people. How did nobody notice all those people go missing and files weren't charged on anyone? What is going on here? I love this job and this company. How did all this go undetected for years until now?*

"I'm glad John suggested about the pictures. It's going to be a lot easier to get pictures out of here. I wish I had those other files that I could put those files back through right now. It makes me nerve taking them out of here to begin with, and how am I going to put them back with no one getting suspicious?"

The first name on this recent list is Daniel James. Let me see what I can find with the physical files first on all these names, then I'll dig into the computer to see what I can find there next.

Daniel James worked in the lab with medical equipment back in early 1992. I see he had a high rating from his supervisors for performances and attitude. Oh, he worked here for 20 years before Isabel fired him for insubordination in 2012. Here's her signed form.

Click, click, click went the camera.

Next on the list is Elizabeth Brittney. I see she worked here at the same time Daniel did and was fired at the same time. She was fired for insubordination, too. I wonder if they were working on the same project.

Click, click, and click.

If I'm going to get any sleep tonight, I had better not take the time to look at these files. I'll just take the picture and get onto the computer later.

Finally, I'm done with the pictures. Now I need to get back to my office and get started with phase two of this new project.

Suddenly, there stood the security guard. He must have seen her coming out of the employee file storage office. Good thing she stashed her phone/camera deep into her bra.

"I see you're working late tonight." George suspiciously looks at her.

"I know. These workmen comp forms need to get in so these employees can get paid in a timely manner. With all the new offices starting and old offices relocating, it sure has caused me a tremendous amount of work lately. I think I need an assistant for the assistant. We both know that won't happen for sure. So here I am, but I'm almost done." Kathy responds, trying to be brave and not showing any signs she concerns about what she is actually doing there.

"Would you like me to wait around and escort you out?"

"No, that is ok. I have to get back to my office and finish up on some coordinating paperwork."

"I have to finish my rounds. How much longer do you think you will be?"

"I'm not sure at the moment. I'll have to let you know." For some reason, she was starting to feel really cheeped out. She never really paid much attention to him before and now he is making her feel really uncomfortable.

"I have to finish this, I have to go." She walks confidentially back to her room and doesn't look back until she feels safe again.

She dials Ethan, "Hi Ethan, I know you just left a few hours ago, but I just ran into the security guard, George, and he made me really feel uncomfortable. I don't mean to sound like I can't do this job for you, but there is something really strange about him. I finished the hard copy files with the camera. I took little time to look at the files, but I noticed one thing about most of them. Most of these employees worked in the medical equipment lab. Mrs. Bachman fired most, if not all of them, for insubordination after working on a project which was TOP SECRET. These projects were supervised by Mrs. Bachman only. I still need to do some research on the computer."

"Kathy, here is what I want you to do. I have to stop back at the office to pick up some papers. How about if we accidentally meet in the lobby, say in an hour and I'll walk you out and make sure you get home safely?"

"Make sure you leave a note under Wendy's door so she knows what time you left tonight, or send her an email. Take your computer home with you. You have access to everything you need from it, so you can work at home tomorrow. I really appreciate all you are doing. If it's ok with you, I've decided to take you along with us to Dubai. I'll inform Wendy that you won't be in until a week from Monday."

"Listen, Kathy, I'm very proud of you for taking on this task. I want you to be safe, so never worry about disappointing me when you ask for my help. I'll see you in an hour. Keep alert and call me again if you need to. Don't hesitate!!" They both hang up and Kathy concentrates on her work.

She felt so much better. Now to finish what she needed to do to get out of here. It was amazing how fast that time went by. Now I have to get out of here.

Just as she got out of the elevator with her laptop in hand, (her camera still in her bra), the creepy security George is standing right there. He is looking her up and down as if she is going to be smuggling out confidential files. Just as he is about to speak to her about checking her for security purposes Ethan shows up from the other elevator.

"What a pleasant surprise! Kathy, I'm glad to see you. How's your daughter doing? I bet she's all grown up by now."

"She sure is, and in her 3rd year of college already. She's a smart one and wants to be a scientist, and her goal is to work here. How about that, Mr. Ethan? She wants to be the next generation for the Company."

Ethan looks over at George and waves him off. "It's ok George; I'll walk Ms. McKinney out to her car." They continue to talk about her daughter and the lobby doors close behind them.

The Trip to Dubai

It surprises Kathy to see John at the airplane port when she got there. He is talking to Ethan when she walks up to Esther.

"I'm surprised to see John here. What's up?"

"The corporate jet is a SCIF, or at least most of it is. That means it's completely clean of any listening or visual devices. John comes through every time Ethan is ready to take off somewhere to make sure it stays that way." Esther replies.

"John has his own business and actually isn't an employee. He's the only one Ethan trusts to do his security in every aspect. We have a tremendous security IT staff and they are very competent, but as long as Mrs. Bachman comes into the building he will keep John on speed dial."

Esther continues, "I made our reservations at the Hotel Burj Al Arab. I have a feeling we are going to have many late nights trying to tie ends together. Our suite has two bedrooms, and Ethan's suite is just across the hall from ours. I've only been there once before and I must say it's the most impressive Hotel I've ever seen, let alone stay there."

"If you need anything, even a bathing suit, just go to the store or just call for room services and they will get you anything you need. Put it on the company account. This will be a trip of a lifetime, so enjoy it without guilt. Ethan will tell you the same thing, I'm sure."

"You will have some downtime while Ethan and I are in meetings. There will also be several meals you will be on your own for as well. Enjoy yourself. If you go out of the Hotel, you will have a security guard with you at all times. Dubai is an exciting place, and you need to explore it while you are here. I'll give you a copy of our itinerary so you will know what time to be back."

Ethan comes over and puts his arm around both women. He's hosting a big smile and looks ready to go.

"Well, ladies, are we ready for the next adventure in life? Our jet is ready to go. It's all clean thanks to John once again."

Kathy speaks up, "I have a question for John, or maybe you know Mr. Bachman. I need to get into some information on some project these people were working on. If I get into a department, is it going to trigger a security breach and let someone know I'm where they don't want me to be?"

"Don't worry about that. Let's get settled down inside where we can talk freely and get this show on the road or more appropriately in the air." Ethan lets the ladies go first.

After the plane levels out and the seatbelts come off, Ethan walks back into the round table room. There he lays down the journey's Diana had given to him. He handles them very carefully, as if they are the most precious things he ever owned. Esther and Kathy watch him and wondered where they came from and why they seem to be so important. Ethan is lost in thought and momentarily forgets the women are there. There is a tear in his eyes when he finally looks up and sees Esther. He straightens up and physically pulls himself together, hiding his emotions again for another time.

Ethan waves and invites them to come in. As they sit down, the attendant comes in and offers coffee or tea of their delight. Breakfast would be served shortly and ask what they would like.

Ethan orders a black coffee, scrambled eggs with ketchup and bacon.

Esther orders an Earl Grey tea with honey and creamer and Danish.

Kathy orders scrambled eggs with a cinnamon French toast, tea and honey.

As soon as they are finishing eating, the attendant cleans the table and leaves the coffee and boiling water for self-serving their own drinks. The doors are shut, and work is soon to begin.

Ethan is the first to speak. He reaches over and picks up the first of the journals. They all have dates and project titles on them. Now the ladies were very curious.

"Isabel was never supposed to work for our company, as per the founder's agreement and bylaws. How I ever let this happen is on me and Andrew. Now it's overdue to clean up this mess and make our company what our Father's intended it to be."

"I have read or at least skimmed over these journals for the past month more. The information which I read is quite disturbing especially, in the last several years of entries. I did not know just how much influence Isabel has had in our company, mostly in the medical and laboratory division."

"Since we are going to be here for many hours, I thought I would bring along some easy reading material. These are secret journals which my dear friend and co-worker the late Great Robert Hampton wrote almost from the day he started working at the Company."

"I want to go back and properly answer the question you asked me earlier when we weren't in a secure area yet. Kathy, most places today are not secure to talk in. Even though listening devices were outlawed without someone's knowledge after the Watergate Investigation, they are used everywhere. Unless painstaking measures are taken, please assume your conversations are being recorded by someone. Now I know that sound like a paranoid conspiracy. It's more of a proven fact that many influential people and companies do not want the average person to know about. For example, the cameras and devices in people's homes to ask questions, there are more ears listening than you would like to know about. Kathy, I know neither of us have one in our homes and if you do, please disconnect it while you are on this project. They are very easily hacked into. Even those doorbell cameras are spy devices. The new phones I gave you both are also not 5G because of the security breaches in them. My point is to be careful what you say and where you say it. John gave me some devices which will secure our rooms so we will also be able to speak freely there.'

"Do you have questions? I think it's important that we understand each other, and no question is stupid. If you're unsure of something or of a situation, don't hesitate to ask for help."

Kathy speaks up, "I went into the computer and got the information on what departments all these employees were working in, but not all the projects. They listed most of them as TOP SECRET and I was afraid to triggering a security breach."

"Kathy, you have the security you need to get into those departments. John has put a scrambler on to confuse the security system while you are on it and will allow you to go where you need to go. Get on and get out as soon as you can. Get the general information for now and the investigating Detectives, Rocco and Gibbons will dig in deeper if they need to. We have a lot of work to do before we get back. I'm going to have the Detectives waiting for us at the airport when we get back and fill them in on the plane what we have uncovered."

"Kathy, I would like you to get started with finding all the information you can about the projects which all the missing people were working on. Also find out what they did or said for the firing. I want to know what exactly these projects are. I want to know anything about tattooing. Who is heading them today if they are still active?"

"Esther, I want you to start on these journals. Do an Excel sheet on them so they can be easily cross-referenced. I'm not as concerned about the older journals as I am about the last 10 years or more too current. Spend most of your time with those. I am looking for a certain project dealing with equipment which uses complicated algorithms. In fact, use that word as a key to find projects and make them a priority. The other words: I want you to keep a note of microchips. These are projects I have strictly forbidden our company to have anything to do with. If you find anything in this area, please get the information together and let me know about it ASAP. If you find any other project which you feel is unethical, make sure you bring it to my attention as well."

"Now, let's get to work." With that being said, Ethan opens the laptop in front of him and works on the upcoming set of meetings they are on their way to in Dubai. Soft classical music plays in the background, which Kathy has just noticed.

Esther and Kathy each have the list of names in front of them. They sit next to each other and softly converse as they coordinate projects with names on the list.

Since Kathy has an excellent start already on the names, she assists Esther with the projects.

"Esther, whatever happened to the files I gave you the other day? I was going to file them back away yesterday but didn't make it back into the office to do it."

"I have them locked in Ethan's office. We decided they wouldn't be able to disappear if they were in there. Ethan and I also have new locks (retinal) put on our doors so they will be safe. John will notify us if anyone tries to get into our offices. I took pictures of the files like you did on the other 17 names. I have them here if you need them." Esther put her new phone on the table, and so did Kathy with hers. They open up the pictures and print out the pages they need to make easier references of them.

Occasionally, someone will get up and stretch or get something to eat or drink. Lunch is just simple, with a variety of sandwiches and soups. Supper was also light, an antipasto salad for them to share. They are focusing on their work at hand and before long the captain comes on the intercom that they will land in half an hour.

"Wow that was fast!" Kathy states. She is thrilled just how much Esther and she had gotten done while in flight. They still had a mountain of work to do, but it didn't seem to be so daunting now. They clean up their work areas and go back to their traveling seats.

Kathy sits in amazement as she looks out the window to a city which never sleeps. The view from the plane is breathtaking. She almost wishes they could stay here for just a little longer.

"Ladies, it's only about 7:30 pm to us, but it's about 3:30 in the morning here. I thought we would settle into our rooms first. I'll be escorting you to dinner/breakfast at the hotel. I'm sure Esther has already made reservations for us." Ethan looks over at her.

Esther nods.

They clear customs and the Rolls Royce Limo is waiting for them. The ride is uneventful, and they carry on small talk with the driver about his favorite parts of the city.

Kathy mentions she would like to see the camels and maybe even ride one. Ethan laughs and asks Esther if she would like to be part of the adventure as well. She smiled and said she would think about it. They all laugh.

After a quick bite to eat, they decide they need to walk a bit. They explore the hotel and are given the grand tour before heading for their rooms. Kathy has never been in such a Luxurious Hotel as this before. She thinks about the pictures she saw of this one. The pictures did not do this extravagant decor justice. This is a once in a lifetime trip. She is so grateful for Ethan to bring her along. Her head is swarming from the detailed work from earlier and the overstimulation of this hotel. It is time to put it all to bed and be fresh for tomorrow.

Kathy wakes to the smell of fresh coffee about noon. She feels delightful and ready to take on the day. She realizes she had only slept about 5 hours, and it is going to be a glorious day.

"I don't know what they did with those sheets, but I slept like a baby. I don't even remember my head hitting the pillow. I think that was the most comfortable bed I have ever slept in."

Esther laughs. "The hotels do that on purpose. They want you to keep coming back. The research they do and discover the most comfortable beds and sheets, so we get used to the best of the best. It's hard to go back to less quality when you get to experience the best there is."

"Esther, I have a question for you. All these people who are missing, do you believe Mrs. Bachman really had them murdered?"

"Yes, I do and so does Ethan: We both have seen a very evil side of her and would not put it past her to have someone on retainer who does these things for her. I have my suspicions as to whom, but I will let the detectives work on that one."

"Esther, I have a powerful faith in Jesus and I believe he will protect us as we search out the truth. It is good to know my enemy, though. I fear danger is near, yet I carry no fear for us nor for this project."

Esther replies, "I thought we were all on the same page and now I know we are. Ethan and I have a healthy respect for the powers that Isabel carries. Yet we know our Lord protects us. He will also show us those things that have been hidden from us, that need to be brought to the surface. You know He is bringing lies and deceptions out of the darkness into the light and exposing it."

Esther asks, "Do you have any of those names completed yet? You were working pretty diligently on them yesterday."

"Yes, I actually have five of them completed. Some of these projects which she authorized are disturbing. This Digital Tattooing is probably the worst one as far as my understanding in correlation to the New World Order and how it's going to be used. I think Ethan is going to be furious when I give him this information. I'm not done putting it all together yet, but I'm almost there."

"What is this Digital Tattooing?"(31)

"It's a chip or disc that goes under the skin. Then you put your smart phone on top of it and it reads all your information about you medically, your banking, shopping habits, and your location. It tracks everything. Say I had one of these discs under my skin and I went to the grocery store. When I get to checking out all the clerk has to do is to take the scan gun over the tattoo and it would deduct the amount from my bank using that chip.This could be the mark of the beast which John talks about in Revelations of the Bible."(32)

Esther just looks at her and can't believe her ears. How did our company get involved in such an evil device? Yes, she thought to herself, *Ethan is going to be furious. He must know something about it though, since it was the word he had us looking for. Umm.*

Esther changed the subject. "Ethan and I have a meeting in a few hours. Go have your meals here or downstairs. Just remember if you leave the Burj Al Arab you will have a driver and an escort. Call the front desk and they will arrange it for you. Don't be afraid to explore some. Take some time to clear your mind as to not get burnt out."

"To tell you the truth, I really want to get all this information put together as soon as I can. I'm intrigued by the mystery where all of this is going to lead to. I will probably go swimming to get my exercise in for the day, but I'll be back to work."

Esther and Kathy order room service for breakfast and talk about this trip and its importance to the company. Dubai is a hot spot for new inventions and creative minds. Ethan is an expert in his field. He seems to have a second sense about what the customer wants and just how he is going to make the equipment they need. The 3D imaging copies have made his job easier, yet it takes a personal contact to comprehend what the customer wants to have made. They are talking about the new office, which is going to start here shortly.

Ethan knocks at the door. Esther lets him in. He is dressed in an expensive suit and fits to impress.

"I hope you both got some sleep last night. I had a good workout in the weight room. I even put on several miles on the bike." Ethan grabs an apple from the complimentary fruit basket that they supplied each room with and took a big bite out of it.

"We did. I was just saying I've never slept in a bed such as that one. Wow." They are laughing again.

"Well, Ms. Esther, we must be going. I'm pretty sure it will be late when we return, so take some time for you and get some work done in the process." Ethan says with an enormous smile. They were walking through the door just a moment later.

"I think I'm going to start with that pool. She put her suit and covering on and headed downstairs. What a magnificent building this is! I'm glad I'm here.

An hour later, that pool is just what I needed and now it's time to get back to work.

Kathy stretches out the papers, files and pictures out on the table. She needs to make a chart, so she calls down to the front desk.

"Hello, what can I do for you Suite 613?"

"I need some office supplies. I need one, no two large writing pads for on an easel, plus 1 easel and white board. I need some different colored erasable and regular markers. I need a ball of string and several rolls of scotch tape and 2 double-sided tape. Please throw in a few packs of blue or black pens too, please."

"We have an office store right here at the mall. I'll order them for you and I'll have them sent up to your room right away. I'll let you know when they arrive at the Burj Al Arab. Will there be anything else, Ms. McKinney?"

"No, I don't think so at the moment, but I'll call you back if I think of something else. Thank you very much, I really appreciate it." Kathy concludes.

As soon as the supplies arrive, she writes names and taping pictures on each paper. She then put Isabel's name on a paper and places in the center of blank space on the wall. She then put the oldest missing persons around her. Working her way outward, she soon had all 17 missing persons on the wall with Isabel in the center of it all. "I know there are more names to go up here, so I'll leave room for them to be added later." She said out loud to herself. Looking at the wall, she also said, "Isabel really is the only common denominator."

Next she makes a code map of all the different projects, a color dot for each one. She forgot to order different colored string, so white is what she had. Kathy used the enormous pack of different colored makers. The package says there are 48 different colors. I hope there aren't that many projects, but just in case there are I guess I'll be using them all.

Fortunately, there were only 13, and she saved the black dot for the Digital Tattoo. Then she took the five packets she finished with and wrote the projects each person had worked on and color coded a piece of string with the color of the project. She taped one end of the string to the original person's paper and then continued it to all the other people from the board who were also involved with that project. Also, she tried to keep the same hue of colors for the same type of projects such as individual/small business tools, Industrial large machinery, medical equipment, laboratory projects and so on.

By the time she was almost done, she stepped back and looked at her creativity. It covered the walls with paper and different colored strings. Now she understood how conspiracy theorists felt. That is exactly what the walls looked like.

"What a spider's web you have woven!" Ethan's voice surprised her from behind.

"You just scared the daylights out of me. How long have you been standing there?" Kathy breathes again.

"Just long enough to be really impressed," Ethan laughs.

"I'm not done yet, but most of it is and does it show a disturbing picture. My mind still cannot comprehend just how evil Mrs. Bachman is."

"I'm just working with the missing persons, but there must be hundreds of employees which have worked on a lot of these projects. Her turnover is very high, but I'm not concerning myself over that. It's these missing people and the unethical projects which they seemed to be forced to work on."

"I think some of these situations started off with normal orders, but it meant the end products for something very corrupt." Kathy is on a roll.

"Ethan, I have additional terrible news. There are not just 17 people missing, I think there are 30 of them. I have to do more research, but I'm positive there is more. I remember a lot of these people and I know they have never filed a Workmen's Comp or Retirement Plan with me."

Ethan asks, "This is worse than any of us imagined. For right this moment, Can you give me an example of one of these projects?"

"I've just run across this one. I have little information on it yet, but something about it is giving me the creeps. It's called CHRISPR-CAS9 Gene Knockout Kits.(33) Our company is making the kit boxes for it, but I'm not sure what else is coming out of our labs for it. I think maybe the machines that make the chips. It has something to do with taking the human protein-coding gene and manipulating it or taking it out. I'm not sure why or how, but it sounds like a Frankenstein sort of thing to me. I color coded that one in brown, but the creepiest one is the Digital Tattoo chip or disc is more like it."

Esther speaks up. "Ethan, do you know what she's talking about? She tried explaining some of it to me this morning, but I'm having a hard time wrapping my mind around it."

"Kathy, first I want to say you are amazing! Did you even stop to get something to eat today?"

"I went for a swim after lunch, and then got caught up with this. I don't even know what time it is." Kathy sits down at the table, grabbing a banana.

"Yes, I know what both these things are, and they are incredibly evil. As a matter of fact, Kathy, you are right about them, making you feel uncomfortable. I had someone approach me several years ago about these projects, and I turned them down. I told certain very rich and famous elite individuals that my company would have nothing to do with them, ever. Neither one of these helps promote our society but instead has one person as a dictator ruling over the entire world with information about every living person living on it. That is too much information for one person to have access to."

"Kathy, you don't have to look into these projects any further, but if you want to learn more, feel free to explore further. It's always an education to know what the enemy is up too." Ethan adds.

"As disturbing as it is, yes, I do want to understand what these things are and how they will affect life as we know it," Kathy decides.

"It looks like we are designing the machinery to make these things and not so much as the end effect product. Am I making sense to either of you? Like with the Digital Tattoo, we are not creating the electronic device which creates the blood patterns or tattoos for the DNA. We are making machinery which makes the massive quantity of these chips or discs which go under the skin." Kathy explains.

Esther has a horrifying look on her face. "Do I understand you correctly? There is a device that goes under the skin which can track everything I do and has a complete medical and financial record of my entire life. Not only that, it also registers any new purchases I make or if I get on an airline without a passport and just use my Driver's License ID. They can just scan my hand and it will verify who I am and take the cost out of my bank account with no cards? They are also tracking my every location."

Ethan responds, "Some people are calling it the Mark of the Beast: Yes, to your question, Esther. It does all of that and more. When I was gazing through the Journals, I found some writings which alluded to these machines, but there wasn't enough information which Robert had on it. I am sure Isabel kept him as far away from that division as she could."

"This is really happening today in our time! It is a bit intimidating yet exuberating at the same time." Kathy comments.

"So Kathy, you know about the predictions of the end times, don't you?"

"Yes, I do. I know we are getting closer to fulfilling what the prophets have written about, but this is confirmation we are heading for hot and wild times ahead. 2 Timothy 3NIV describes how people are going to act in the last day and we are seeing it in today's society. Put on our seat-belts, we are in for the ride of our lives and our children's lives too." Kathy responds.

"Ethan, what are you going to do about this? I know you well enough that this isn't setting right with you. Isabel has once again deliberately gone against your ethic barometer and did what she wanted to do without the permission of the board, I'm sure. If this would have come up for approval, Mr. Noble would have notified you." Esther asks.

"Esther, I'm not sure at this very moment, but I have a few more days to decide and pray. We all need to pray for clarity, discernment, and protection I do know this for sure; I am going to make it impossible for Isabel to work at Bachman's ever again. Nobody working at Bachman's should ever be in fear of their management and especially for their life if they do something wrong. I am appalled at what has happened to my beloved company." Ethan answers.

"Kathy, you have worked so hard on this today. You can finish it later. I think we all need to get away from this for tonight. It's still early enough we can do some exploring of Dubai. Let's go have some fun. I really am impressed with all of this."

With that being said, they change into casual clothes. The three of them go out on the town for local cuisine, sightseeing, and camel rides for all of them. A trip they will ever forget.

The next morning Esther suggests they meet for breakfast at the downstairs restaurant. They have time before Ethan has to leave for a round of meetings for the day. Esther has a few of her own meetings to attend to, but she would only be gone for a couple of hours in the afternoon.

After they eat Ethan asks Kathy, "How many more people do you have to finish up with?"

"Ethan again, I hate to say this, but I think there are more people than we originally thought there were. I'll be following a project and who is working on it, and then all of a sudden that person isn't there anymore. I can't find them after that. I mean they aren't in the company anywhere yet they aren't off the employee roister either. I've made a list of who I have run across so far. I thought the Detectives should have a list of these people too."

"Let me guess, they were all hired by Isabel personally and they all worked on one of her 'pet' projects. Since they were Isabel's employees and projects, nobody knows anything about them, right?"

"I can only go by the paperwork I can find, but you summed it up correctly as far as I can see. I'm not talking with anyone about any of this except you two. I'm just following paperwork, reports, and project information as I find it. I have to say John is incredible and the information I've been able to get into with no detection."

"This has been an actual eye opener. Thank you for this opportunity. I really appreciate it, especially for last night's distraction. This is a once in a lifetime experience for me." Kathy remarks.

"Oh, back to your original question. I only have 10 on the missing persons list to finish. They are the newest ones. I worked my way from the first ones missing to the most current. So far, most of what I have is just surface information and project titles. I will finish the graph of the last 13 this afternoon. Would you like me to dig into exactly what each project comprises manufacturing?"

While we are here to find out as much information as you can:

Starting dates on each project
What the project is to manufacture
Who headed each project?
The employees who worked on the project
Their start and finish employment dates
If they are still employed, where are they working now and on what project?

"If you think of any other question which would be pertinent, please feel free to make your list longer." They all took a deep breath.

"Kathy, one thing I have learned about Ethan is he does like his lists, clean and precise." Esther adds.

"Well, ladies, I have thoroughly enjoyed our breakfast this morning. I'm going to get a run in at the gym before heading off for the day."

Esther, I will see you at least one of these meetings. We'll meet up for supper tonight. Kathy, are you going for another swim today?"

"I thought I would do so shortly before adding to the wall."

"Great, this is a stressful task and physical exercise is great for reliving it."

"I'll see you all soon." Ethan left for the gym.

Esther and Kathy just smile. Ethan is so full of energy and is like a whirlwind. They head up to their room. Kathy changes and goes downstairs. Esther walks over to the wall Kathy created. She studies these people and the jobs they did.

She thinks to herself, how could this happen right under her nose. There are so many people, so many projects which were hidden from Ethan and the board. I knew Isabel was a troublesome person, but she really is evil in the genuine sense of the word.

Esther is still in the room when Kathy comes back in. She is actually surprised to see her.

"Hi Esther, I wish I had a pool like that at my house. But then again, I would have a hard time making it to work on time every day."

Esther nods her head in understanding. "I was waiting for you. Ethan asked me if I would like to take you shopping. I told him I would hate to but would suffer through it." They both start laughing. We are going to have some fun. We are going to a special place for supper tonight, and I'm sure you won't have the proper attire for it. Don't feel guilty about it either. I will never forget the first time Ethan took me shopping. I've always lived a pretty simple life, but being around Ethan, he has changed me in that area. He works hard and loves to be generous to those who also work hard. This is his small token of what you are doing.

"Wow, really. I was worried about some of my clothes. Are we talking shoes and maybe a purse too?"

"Oh, am I going to have fun with you. We are going to buy a new suitcase or many be more."

"Give me about 15 minutes. I have to shower and dry my hair first. Oh my, I am so excited." With that, Kathy is like a whirlwind and runs to the shower.

They were gone for the most exhilarating hours of Kathy's life. She has never been so pampered. She didn't even know some of these stores even existed. Esther warned her not to look at any of the price tags until they got back to the hotel, so she didn't. They had a manicure, pedicure, spa, and all those new clothes and shoes with all the accessories to match each outfit. She even has her hair done as well as a facial makeover. "Esther, it's no wonder that the people at the top of the food chain want to stay at the top. Wow, what an incredible afternoon. I never thought I would be so exhausted and exhilarated at the same time from shopping!" Esther agrees as she slid into the limo. "What was more fun than that was watching you enjoy yourself!"

Esther has the same done with several new outfits as well. They are both exhausted yet exuberated at the same time.

"Kathy, I need to go to a couple of meetings. I'll be back about 8. I'm sure you have plenty to do too." Esther says.

"I do, and I can't wait to finish this part of it. I need to get started on the detailed projects. I'm going to do the opposite and start with the newest projects, just in case I don't get them down while I'm here."

"Sounds like a plan. I'll see you later." Briefcase in hand, Esther leaves.

The bellboy knocks at the door; he has all the new purchases. He politely asks, "Ms. McKinney, where would you like this?" She directs him to the closets in her room and has him hang them up and takes Esther's to her closet where they belong. She tips him well and thanks him. "Now it's time to get to work."

She gets lost in what she is doing. Since she has current information on the last 10 missing people, they aren't taking as long as she thought it would. She steps back and looks at her finished work. There is sadness about it. All this information is going to end up in the hands of the Detectives when they get back home.

I'm really curious about these Digital Tattoos and Biometrics. Now what does the search engine Brave say about this. Here is what the Merriam-Webster Dictionary describes:

Biometrics

Definition of biometrics. 1: biometry. 2: the measurement and analysis of unique physical or behavioral characteristics (such as fingerprint or voice patterns) especially as a means of verifying personal identity.[34]

I need more information. Here's one from Sid Roth that I can use. Tom Horn and Sharon Gilbert are talking about this very subject. [35] I know we are making the containers for the Digital Tattoos but here is what Tom Horn and Sharon Gilbert says; it's a disc that goes on your skin like your hand. "Once the disc is on, then you tap your smart phone on it and it creates a blood vessel pattern. This pattern authenticates by causing a blood pattern in your hand, which then becomes your Biometric Marker." The real ID wants Biometric markers now for Federal Building or going on a plane.

Scientists want to be able to change DNA by clipping out parts of it and then adding other DNA to the strain. That is where the Chrispr Case 9 Gene Knockout Kit comes into play. We are making the box for this.

Just then Ethan and Esther walk in. Both of them just stare at the finished wall.

"Wow, you are amazing, Kathy! I'm guessing that the wall is now finished."

"Yes, it is, but I've discovered some things very disturbing. It starts with the Digital Tattooing but gets into Germ Line Genetics. That is where they manipulate the original gene, so when it duplicates it will be the genetically modified gene instead of the original one."

"We are now moving onto Trans-humanism, Transgenic Humanism and Transgenic Animal. [36] Do you know what they are? " She didn't wait for them to answer. She excitedly continues. "Well, let me tell you. Say you wanted to do some testing on a human, but the FDA said no. You would then go to a lab which added human DNA to an animal like a mouse. You can buy these mice and do your human testing on the human DNA in that mouse."

"Now you think that is bad, just wait. Let me explain what Transgenic Humanism is. In foreign countries, say, China, they are taking humans and adding, for example, eagles DNA into their human DNA. Eagles have infrared sight and can see far beyond what humans can see. Bat use ultrasound. Dolphins can hear far beyond what humans can hear. They are using the DNA from animals with their super capabilities and mixing their DNA with Human DNA to make super warriors. Even the United States is performing these experiments in order to keep up with Russia and China because of the super humans they are creating. Now tell me this isn't disturbing. I'm glad I found out about it but I'm done looking at it for now. I do, however, want you to find out for yourselves. Here is a good starting point. Check out this website," https://sidroth.org/television/tv-archives/tom-horn-sharon-gilbert/?src=banner_disc. (35)

She wrote it on the wall for them to check out.

Ethan is the first to speak. "I've heard the terms before, but I didn't look into any of them. It makes me sick that my company, our company, is involved with any part of it."

"Have you found out what projects it has involved with any of these topics?"

"Yes, it involved all the missing people with unique aspects of these topics. We are supposed to be a tool and dye company Isabel used the medical lab to be involved with experiments in the Digital Tattooing, Transhumanism, and Transgenic Animals. I found little about it, but I found the terms in the project descriptions. I had to go deep into the computer lab records to find any information. I have a feeling there is paperwork on it and she kept it off the company computer. My guess is there is another computer, maybe her personal one, which has the information on it."

"I've underlined in red all the projects which have some attachment to these topics. I think the Detectives should know about them and all the missing people involved in them." Kathy adds.

Ethan speaks up with a twinkle in his eyes. "Kathy, how attached are you to your home? Would you be interested in moving into a more secure home, one with a built in pool? The company will pay for it so you will have no mortgage."

Kathy is speechless. She regains her composure after just staring at him for a minute or more. Her mind is going a million miles a minute at the moment. She finally says, "You're concerned for my safety, aren't you?"

"Yes, I am, very much so! When she finds out what we now know, she will not take it well. Esther and I talked today. She's been asking for an assistant for several months to work with her in the office. I have other executive assistances in other countries, but Esther needs help in the Corporate Office. We would like you to fill this position. Your salary will explode, and you will also have executive benefits. The house rarely comes with the package, but in your case I've made an exception," Ethan smiles.

"OMG, I don't know what to say except Of Course I'll take the position." She wants to cry because she was so happy, but she kept her composure even though a few tears of joy escape as she gives Ethan the biggest hug she could give him.

"Esther, it will be an honor to work with you regularly. There have been so many times when I felt so alone and didn't know who I could confide in. There is one other person, Ben Helt in HR, which is trustworthy. He deserves the office you just had John fix for me."

"Great, I know who Ben is. I will still need someone in that office I can trust and do research for me and the Detectives. I'll make it happen." Ethan exclaims

"Kathy, we work well together, and I will love to have you working with me. We will put in long hours, especially at first. I see your work ethics and I'm the one who is proud to have you assist me." Esther explains.

"Kathy, I covered for you with Wendy. I told her you had an emergency, when I was walking you out to your car, which you had to attend to. I told her you were to take off and wouldn't be back at work for a couple of weeks. I authorized you to get paid while you were off. Actually, your pay raise already started when you boarded the plane. Well, I didn't lie, this is an emergency." They all agree.

"For the rest of the time here, I want you to set this aside and look on a real estate site and look for a house. Don't have a poor man's mentality either. Look for a friendly neighborhood, one with a pool, and in a gated community. I'll have John put in a security system for you. For now, when we get back, I want you to stay in a safe place. Esther has volunteered to have you stay with her or I have a company apartment we use for out-of-town visitors. This is where I would like you to stay. You will see

Esther all day long. I don't want you to getting sick of each other yet." Ethan laughs.

"After we are finished with the Detectives, I want you to go back to your home and get the personal things you need for several weeks. I'll have a security guard go with you and to help you pack. Summer is almost here. Is your daughter coming home for the summer? She will need to be protected as well." Ethan explains.

"As far as I know, she is planning on coming home. Her finals are coming up next week and should be home the following week. I'll call her on this secure phone you gave me when I get to the apartment." Kathy comments with some excitement.

"I know I should be afraid, but I'm not at all. I feel protected, and my spirit is peaceful beyond comprehension. Thank you, Ethan, for making me feel safe too." She also points up.

Esther helps her to find an appropriate house by the end of the week. It is in a small gated community and has two pools. There is an outside and one indoor pool in the clubhouse. They show the pictures of it to Ethan and agree it would be perfect for her. He makes some phone calls and has the ball rolling on getting a tour set up on Saturday for her. Esther said she would go with her if she likes, and Kathy agrees.

The Commissioner's Office

Kathy carefully takes down her spider web of information she has collected. Once she gets back to the plane, she reconstructs it for the Detectives, for when they land. The trip is a real eye opener for her. She learned so much about so many things all at the same time.

On one hand, she feels like she needs to share the information about what the science community is doing on her social media, yet she knows she needs to maintain a very low profile until this thing with Isabel is over. She has no clue how long that will take. She will know when the time is right, and it isn't now for sure.

It's a long flight home, so she decides it would be an excellent time for an evening nap. She is glad they are leaving at night. Once she wakes, several hours later, she notices Esther is still asleep. Ethan is working on paperwork as usual.

"Ethan, thank you again, for this extraordinary experience. The trip, the clothes, the house, and the new job, but mostly for the opportunity to do research of all the information I could uncover. This has been quite the learning experience." Kathy expresses.

"Kathy, it is all you. You are trustworthy, diligent, and you have a lot of tenacity. Most of all, you have a powerful faith. These are all assets I value. I wish more people were like you. I've needed to look into all these things which you uncovered. I just never found the time to do it. This will actually be part of your job. I need you to keep me abreast of what is going on around us. You know that when we get back, the Detectives will take over all the work, you have done and they will want to interview you about it. I'm not sure they will allow you to do more on that end of it, but I want to know what pots Isabel has her hands into. I'll also be working with John to see if there is another computer with missing information on it. There is where you might find more information for me. I'm going to make sure she may never step foot onto the property again. I don't know what kind of spell she cast over Andrew, but she doesn't have one on me. Andrew wasn't always like he is now. We were like brothers, and he had a powerful faith, too. That is, until he met Isabel. In just a short time after they met, I could see the changes in him. I talked to him about his need for power attitude and he just shrugged it off as just trying to beat out our competitors. Now I see it as something else. Maybe if I can keep her out of the office, I can have a stronger influence over him. That will yet to be seen."

Soon Esther wakes up too. They are almost home.

"Good morning, sleeping beauty." Ethan remarks with an enormous smile on his face. That smile sure lit up a room, Kathy thought.

Esther laughs. "These trips are glorious and they sure do wear me out."

"The captain is about ready to announce that we are almost home. How would you ladies like some coffee, tea, and some breakfast before we land? The Detectives will be waiting for us as we land?" Ethan suggests, and they all agree.

Breakfast is served and cleaned up except for the coffee, tea and Danish. The Captain announces they will land in 30 minutes and to get their seat belts on. They leave the table and take their seats. The landing is smooth. Kathy could see two men waiting at the hanger. She assumes they are the Detectives. She is right.

The door opens and Ethan steps out to greet the Detectives. They both soon enter the plane.

"Detective John Rocco and Detective Dan Gibbons, I would like you to meet Kathy McKinney and you have already met my extension of my right arm Esther Yagel."

"Nice to meet you," they both say almost in unisons.

"We will need to step into the other room where we can freely talk without a problem." Ethan says as he heads into the other room.

Almost immediately the Detectives see the wall. They step closer to examine it. They are stunned, and that in its self is incredible.

Detective Rocco is the first to speak. After a long pause, "Wow, who put this all together? Do you know how much time you have saved for this investigation?"

Ethan smiles, "This is the work of our new Executive Assistant Kathy McKinney."

Detective Gibbons speaks up this time. "Seriously, this would have taken us months, if not a year or more, to put this all together, if ever. You have more names on here than 17. Who are these other 13?"

Kathy is beaming at the approval of her creation. "Apparently I'm not working in HR anymore," winking at Ethan, "but when I did I found these other people who were working one day and never came back to work. Some of them haven't collected their paychecks from years ago, before direct deposit was mandatory. None of them applied for workman's compensation. The other thing about these 13 is they had no family to contact from their original employment applications. They have just disappeared from our company. Maybe you can find them working somewhere else, but as far as our company is concerned they have vanished."

Gibbons speaks again. "I see your key codes, but in a nutshell can you explain it to us. Wait, a minute; I need to record this, if you don't mind. Ok go ahead as he pushes the record app on his phone."

Gibbon's phone recording mode is placed by Kathy as she speaks again.

"I started off with the 17 names you gave Ethan. I pulled their employment file and made copies of them for you. Here you will find a picture of them and a very brief description of their personal information along with the projects they worked on while we employed them with us. I then color coded the work projects they worked on and linked them with other personal working on the same project and the finish date for those projects. Many of the missing people disappeared, either at the end of a project or near the end."

"As I was working on the people working on the projects is when I found the other 13 people who no longer working for us but I couldn't find their resignations or their exit interviews. I couldn't find where they were reassigned to another position within the company, either. I looked to see if they filed for Workmen's Compensation or if they collected their paychecks for the older employees. The answer was no for all the above questions. I made a list of them for you with their employee files Ethan has given his permission for you to have them so there won't be a legal issue from the company." Kathy explains.

"I want you to know something else. All of these projects had to do with either the medical lab or the construction of materials for the medical devices. There is also one common denominator for these projects. Wait for it..."

"No, let me guess. Mrs. Isabel Bachman." Rocco guesses.

"Yes, you are correct! I haven't looked into it yet, but my guess is the Board of Directors was not informed of most of these projects. I'm sure that Mr. Andrew Bachman knew of most of them, though. I did not know of them." Ethan agrees.

"I have a question." Gibbons asks, "What is this website you have listed here? I know who Sid Roth is, but what does he have to do with this investigation?"

Ethan speaks up this time, "Gentlemen, you are in for an actual eye opener. This video is about 30 minutes long and you will have to watch it about 10 times to get the full effect of what they are talking about."

"You think you have troubles now with ex-military which have gone rogue or terrorists. You have seen nothing yet? I don't even know how you will stay ahead of what is in your future."

The Detectives, just look at each other and wonder what he is talking about. They know it is serious for Ethan to make such a comment about it. The video will have to wait for now.

"I see some of these projects are self-explanatory, but what is this Digital Tattooing, and Transgenic Humanism? I've heard a little something about Biometric Marking because of the Real ID but what does that have to do with a Tool and Dye company?"

Ethan, Esther, and Kathy in unisons say, "Watch the video." The three of them look at each other and smile.

"I am livid about all of this. I am very glad I've had time to digest this before going back to the Corporate Office. I will sit on most of this information out of respect for the investigation. I want you to find out what has happened to these missing people and who is responsible for their disappearance."

"Through Kathy's investigation on all of this, we believe Isabel has a separate computer which has more information about these projects. We can't find the information we need about them on any of the company computers." Ethan states.

Rocco and Gibbons thought without speaking it out, 'If she is responsible for any of these missing people, it might also be on this computer they don't have custody of.'

Kathy, you have done an extraordinary job for us. Without your help, we would never accomplish all that you have done for us in such a short time."

"Ethan, we want one of her for Christmas this year," Rocco requests! They all laugh.

"Sorry Rocco, we are keeping her!" Ethan states with an enormous grin on his face.

Kathy blushes as she carefully gathers up her creation on the wall and hands it off to Gibbons. "Unfold it from the top very carefully, and it should go back up easily on your own wall. If you have questions, please call me and I'll walk you through it."

"Kathy, we can't thank you enough for all of this. I'm sure we will have plenty of questions for you as we dive deeper into the investigation from this angle. I'll take great care of this for you," Gibbons comments.

Rocco states as they are leaving, "Everyone please take extra precautions and stay safe. If you see something, say something. Ethan, that goes for you too! As this unfolds, all of you will be in danger. I'm sure you already know this. I put nothing past Isabel. Get extra security, especially body guards, Ethan! Be careful. Be aware of your environment. Don't hesitate to call either of us immediately. Don't be a hero. Let us do our jobs. That is what we are here for." He hands Kathy and Esther both of their business cards.

"Rocco, I don't know about you but I've never experienced such leg work already done for us and we didn't even ask for it. Can you imagine the leg work we would have had to do just to get court orders and warrants? We would need to get just some of this information? We might not have been able to get all of it. What about these other 13 names that Kathy found? I sure hope they aren't missing too, but when we get back to the office, we can hand them over to the Missing Persons Division and let them investigate their whereabouts."

"I agree with you Gibbons, I want a Kathy for Christmas. For only being gone for a week, she saved us a years' worth of investigations. I'm really impressed with what she accomplished. You know the Commissioner isn't going to be happy when he finds out how much Mrs. Bachman is involved with a possible 30 missing persons, which are probably all deceased by now. She seems to be the only common denominator at this point, anyway."

Gibbons continues, "Have you seen Isabel's body guards, Paul Blumenthal and Sid Jehu? They are enormous men. There is a look about them that makes me suspicious of what they are capable of doing for Mrs. Isabel Bachman."

Rocco comments, "I noticed that too about those men. Let's get this stuff back at the office and figure out our next move. We will also have to get the Captain more involved at this point. I know the Commissioner will want to hear from us too. I think we have to do some more interviews before we take this information to him. What do you think?"

"I agree. We need to have more information and solid proof before we take this keg of dynamite to him. You start by going to Missing Persons and filling her in with the new 13 names we got. I'll start by reconstructing this elaborate spider web which Kathy created for us. Then I'll get the Captain involved." Gibbons explains.

"Listen, I'm really concerned about the safety of all three of them. They need our protection. Maybe not right now, but soon. Once Isabel finds out about some information we have dealt with, the projects which she is in charge of, she is going to be a furious witch on the warpath!," Rocco states.

"We will have to talk to the Captain about getting them police protection. I seriously doubt that Ethan will accept our protection. He will be more inclined to hire his own security guard. I hope he will get at least one guy. Pride has a way in getting in the way of doing the intelligent thing to do," Gibbons comments.

"Well, we're back at the precinct. Time to get the ball rolling again and now we have a lot more evidence to proceed with this investigation. I'll see you shortly," Gibbon's remarks.

Gibbons works diligently on all the sheets of paper and trying not to separate the strings which are attached to them. The longer he works on trying to recreate the "wall" the more he appreciates all the work which Kathy put into her creation. He has to keep refocusing on the task instead of looking at the names and the projects they had worked on. It is fascinating to him all the unique kinds of things Bachman Tool and Dye Company make. They would take an idea and make it from scratch until it was perfected for that company. He didn't consider himself to be very creative. He's a facts and figures kind of guy. However, he appreciates the talents of others to do the things he had no ability to do.

Gibbons notices other people listed on the different projects. I bet they still work at Bachman's. We will work out a strategy to talk with them about the missing people from their department without causing Mrs. Bachman too many suspicions for as long as we can. I want to start with the projects which Robert Hampton had worked on. I wonder if they are all listed on these sheets. If they aren't all here, I am sure they are in the books Ethan has. He told us earlier he was almost finished with them and would give them to us shortly. He promised he would warn us when he exposes Isabel with the misuse of the lab for her own devious projects.

Ethan said he would keep her out of the office as much as he can. That will help. We know the influences she had in the elite community, and they didn't want any unnecessary problems along the way.

They want to have all the solid proof of her involvement with the missing people before confronting her. He needs to know exactly how Robert Hampton died. They know it was a drug-induced heart attack. The drug which was used is still being investigated on its orients. As he is deep in his thoughts, Rocco comes walking into the room.

"Gibbons, Wow, you put that up just the way Kathy had it. I'm impressed you didn't get any of those strings unattached while you were doing it! Buddy, it looks great."

"I have Detective Jennifer working on those other 13 names. She had two of the names on her list. She didn't know they were associated with Bachman's though."

"Let's get the Captain in here and I thought we could start at the projects which Robert Hampton worked on." Gibbons suggests.

"I stopped by his office. He'll be here shortly." Rocco says.

"What do you think, Captain?" They notice him standing there while they were discussing their strategy plans.

"This is quite impressive. Gibbons, you didn't need a warrant for any of this?"

"No Captain, Kathy McKinney works or did work in the HR Department of Bachman's Tool and Dye Company. She's the one who put all of this together. She was looking for information concerning the 17 missing people who left the Company after being fired from Mrs. Isabel Bachman. We have the videos of each one of them being escorted out of the building and driving out of the parking deck, but they never showed up at home."

"While she was trying to figure out what project they each worked on, she found an additional 13 people who have also disappeared. Rocco just gave the new 13 names to Detective Bubb a few minutes ago."

"Did Ms. McKinney have authorization to release all this information to you?"

"She sure did. Mr. Ethan Bachman is the one who actually pulled her out of HR and took her to Dubai with him and his secretary. She's been working on this for 2 weeks with Ethan Bachman's blessings. Mr. Ethan is the one who wants this investigation to be complete, expedited quickly and thoroughly," Rocco states.

"Captain, this is a lot bigger than we thought at first. We are working closely with Missing Persons and with the staff at The Brotherhood Winery. The Medical Examiner believes that Charley Barrows was also given the same drug which Robert Hampton was given. I know it's been several months since they died but they still haven't found the origin of the poison they were given."

"We know Isabel is involved, but we haven't been able to get close enough to get any information on what, where, and when. These people have to be somewhere. Most, if not all of them we presume, are deceased. I have a gut feeling that Isabel's two body guards have something to do with their disappearance and probably her Executive Assistant, Hiram Haddad. We also know that George, the company's security guard, is the one who escorted all of them out of the building. We also know that each of the missing people worked in the lab department under the direct management of Isabel Bachman." Gibbons adds.

"You know your next stop is going to be with the Commissioner. He will not like what you have to say, but he's an honest man and won't interfere with your investigation."

"Maybe it would be better if the Commissioner came down here to see this than us going up to see him." Rocco suggests.

"Take a picture of it and show him what you have going on with the investigation. He has been inquiring how it's been going for some time now. He'll have a few questions for you and some advice as well." Captain Holden states.

The Captain calls up to the Commissioner's Assistant to make preparations for the Detectives to give him their report. He is told to send them right over to the Administration Building at City Hall.

The Detectives go up the elevator a bit on nerves but confident of what they are doing. They only have to wait a short time before they are summoned into his office.

"Come in, Detectives. I'm looking forward to hear what has been happening with your investigation. From what I understand so far, there is a connection between your investigation and the Missing Persons' Division. They have 17 people missing from Bachman's from over the past several years with no leads as to what has happened to them." Commission Newman states.

Rocco adds, "There are actually an additional 13 people we have just added to those 17 missing people. I would like to show you a picture of what we have at our Prescient in the department. Ethan Bachman had one of his employees put together a 'spider's web of information for us. In this picture you will see all the missing people and the projects they were working on when they disappeared. Ms. Kathy McKinney worked in HR and was given authorization to have special access into the lab and the projects worked on in there. Please understand, Mrs. Isabel Bachman does not have any idea of this investigation. Commissioner, she is the only common denominator in all of our findings besides all working in the laboratory or in engineering under her supervision."

"There is another situation which is also connected to this investigation. We have some news about Charley Barrows from The Brotherhood Winery? He died several months ago, before Robert Hampton died. The same poison which killed Robert Hampton murdered him."

"The poison creates paralysis of the muscles of the heart, thus causing a heart attack. The Medical Examiner's office is still trying to locate the origin of the poison. We suspect Isabel's Executive Assistant, Hiram Haddad, has something to do with it, but we don't have the proof we need to prove it yet."

Commissioner Newman speaking, "I have met him before. It wouldn't surprise me if he didn't have contacts which could get him some exotic drugs capable of an assortment of different ailments, including death. Get some more information on him. Check out his snail mail, email; both personal and business. Ask Ethan if he will authorize getting a list of expenses that Isabel and Hiram have had over the past 15 years. We can eventually get a warrant, but if Ethan Bachman will authorize it, you will save valuable time. Maybe this Ms. Kathy McKinney will get it for you with Ethan's permission."

"I wonder if this poison was made in the lab. Does the Medical Examiner have the ingredients used to make the poison?" The Commissioner adds.

"I'm not sure, but I'll find out." Gibbons says.

"This 'spider-web' as you call it, is quite extensive. You said she only worked on it for a week or 2. Maybe we should hire her." They all laugh. "We tried that but Ethan stated we can't have her."

"I don't think we could afford her with the new job she was just promoted to."

Gibbons asks, "Commissioner, we know you have close ties with Isabel and Andrew Bachman. Isabel is involved with these disappearances as well as possibly involved with the deaths of Charley Barrows and Robert Hampton."

" What can you tell us about the Bachman's?' Gibbons continues.

"Isabel is originally from Lebanon. Her family is royalty. If they still had kings and queens, she would be a princess. In her world, I am sure she still is. Her assistant has been her right-hand man since their college days. He is extremely loyal to her and her alone. He would throw Andrew under the bus if he were cornered, but as far as Isabel is concerned; you won't even get her date of birth from him, even if you serve him with a warrant."

"She's a very prominent part of the city's elite society. She is also as intelligent as she is beautiful. If she has any inkling that you are intimidated by her, she will chew you up and spit you out without you even knowing it until it's over."

"Rocco and I have been working around her so far. I don't think she knows how much we know about her involvement with the missing people. We will work closely with Detective Jennifer Bubb and Ms. McKinney from Bachman's." Gibbon explains.

"Thank you for keeping me posted on your progress. We'll talk again soon, I'm sure," Commissioner States.

Gibbons and Rocco take that as a cue they are being dismissed. They exit immediately. On the way out of the elevator, they decide to stop in to see Detective Bubb.

"Rocco, I'm glad we have Detective Bubb working this end of the investigation. This is so much more complicated than we first thought it was going to be, and we even said it was complicated."

"We also need to stop in to see the Medical Examiner to see if he found the source of the drug they used yet. I wonder how many other people they used that drug on," Gibbons comments.

He looks over at Rocco, but he seems to be lost in his own thoughts. He is right.

Rocco is certain that Isabel and Hiram are involved in all of this. How they were going to find the evidence they need to arrest them both is something only the future holds.

Andrew is a brilliant man in his own right, but how much of this is involving him? When it comes to his wife, he seems to let her do whatever she wants to do with his blessings. He keeps himself busy with the Bachman Empire. Andrew needs to know what she is doing, but that would tip our hand on investigating her. Ethan promises to keep a lid on exploding on Isabel until we are ready to expose her corruption.

Ethan has his own issues with her. He promised to keep her out of the business without interfering with our investigation. She is sly and; I bet when she is in that lab when Ethan isn't around, like last week when he was in Dubai.

"Rocco, earth to Rocco!" Gibbons announces as he is driving back to the office.

"Wow, was I lost in thought. Gibbons, we have to find a way to get the evidence to stop Isabel and Hiram from destroying any more lives. I know we are good but are we going to be able to pull this one off without either of them finding out what we are doing. When Ethan gets some protection as well as Esther and Kathy, it might be a signal to them we are investigating them." Rocco shares some of his thoughts.

Rocco continues, "I was also thinking this is the opposite of how we usually work. We usually have the body and the where, but not in this case. We have 'the who done it' and the possible motive but we don't have the bodies and the method they were killed, presuming they have died of course."

"Rocco, we are two of the best of the best when it comes to the Homicide Division. We will not let them get away with what they have done. They might be brilliant and have gotten away with this for years. That is going to stop, and we are going to be the ones who stop them. It might take us awhile, but we will get what we need to put them in prison for the rest of their lives."

"I don't remember ever working a case such as this one. It is backward, but we will get the evidence we need to convict all of them and see them in Reichert." Gibbons assures Rocco.

Chapter 20

Ethan Goes Ballistic

Ethan has his driver take him home to drop off his suitcases. He changes his clothes after a quick shower. Before he heads to the office, he makes a phone call. The phone rings only once, and Ethan hears a very familiar voice.

"Hi Ethan, I'm surprised to hear from you so soon. What can I do for you?" John asks.

"John, I have an enormous job for you, and it's going to take most of your employees. I need your help this weekend. It's going to cost me a small fortune, but it will be worth it to me. You are really busy, but I need you to drop everything and come over to the office with as many of your guys that you totally trust. I'm having you change all the locks on the doors for the entire building. This includes the elevators, especially the executive elevator. I'll have my people in IT help, but I want you and your people to oversee the project."

"Does this have anything to do with Ms. Kathy McKinney, and her investigations? Wait a minute, where are you?" John questions.

Ethan smiles to himself. *A much needed reprieve from his current thoughts.* "John, I'm at home right now, but I'll be heading into the office shortly. We just got back and do I have news for you. This is so much worse than I ever thought possible. I can't go into the details right now, but someday soon I will."

"This is really short notice. I really appreciate all you can do for me this weekend. I'll pay the staff double time if they can have this all done by the time the staff comes back in on Monday morning."

"Wow Ethan. Whatever is happening there is some major business. I'll make some phone calls and meet you at the office in an hour." John hangs up from Ethan and starts dialing again.

Ethan is furious with Isabel. *How could Andrew allow her to do some things she has done is beyond his comprehension? The Andrew he grew up with is not the Andrew he is today,* he thinks to himself.

His company will not assist The One World Order to advance in their agenda. Doesn't Andrew know how devastating Socialism would be in this company and our own country? No free enterprises, no competition to create better companies. Who would be the dictator? Satan himself! No, thank you. I will not be a slave to the Cabal, The Bilderberg Group, Trilateral Commission, Area 51, nor to the Illuminati's. I'm sure there are other groups as well. We will fight these groups as every human being should. Who are they to say they are better than everyone else? God Almighty created all of us. He is the only one better than everyone else, and He gave us freedom of choice.

This trip has been an extraordinary experience. What an education on so many levels! How did 30 people come up missing and nobody alerted me? Am I so untouchable that my executives are afraid to come to me with their problems? Why didn't Robert come to me when he suspected Isabel was doing experiments which I wouldn't have approved of? Now he's dead, and she's the cause of it. I can't go backwards, but I can go forward. I want people to talk to each other. I certainly do not want our employees walking with the fear of being the next missing person. That is no way to live, especially in the workplace. How did I let this go on for so long?

My first line of business when I get to the office is to take the steps possible to getting rid of Isabel once and for all! Hiram is going with her for good, too! My next stop will be at Andrew's office. He and I need to have a serious conversation about what he knows about what is going on around here without letting the cat out of the bag about the missing people. He is so blinded by his wife that he isn't the same person I used to know. I have to make him see the reason to keep her out of the building permanently, even when I'm not in town. There are enough charities that she is involved in, I would think that would be enough to keep her busy and out of Bachman's business. She is sneaky, though. Isabel is stunningly beautiful, intelligent, poised, and extremely evil, and I don't use that word lightly. Ethan acknowledges to himself.

Ethan pulls into the parking deck and drives into his parking space. He looks over and sees Isabel's car in her spot.

"Umm, that will change hopefully today." He tells himself out loud and with a smile.

"I wonder where I'm going to find her. Maybe I'll just go to see Andrew and see if she shows up there."

"This is going to be very interesting because she knows she is not supposed to be here and she must not know that I'm here either."

Ethan takes the elevator up to the executive floor. As he gets off the elevator, he motions to the receptionist. Not to mention he is here. He walks directly into his own office, calling Wendy from HR to come up to his office telling no one he was in the building. She is to bring a stack of exit interview forms with her.

Ethan asked Wendy, who filled in for Kathy while she has been away. She found Ben Helt to be quite competent as a replacement. Ethan informed her she might consider hiring him for that position permanently, and he explained to her he has hired Kathy for another position in the company. He would give her details later that day.

After he gets off the phone with Wendy, Ethan leaves his office and heads straight to Andrew's office. He also motions to Andrew's Executive Assistants, not to mention to anyone that he is there. He is pretty sure the grapevines are already at work, but at least he tries to keep his presence under wraps the best he can.

"Andrew" Ethan shouts.

Andrew bolts straight up. Ethan laughs and feels young again.

"Ethan, I didn't know you were back already. You just scared the life out of me." Andrew stands up and shakes Ethan's hand.

"How did Dubai go? Did you seal the deal?"

"Of course, it was a trip that I will never forget in so many ways." Ethan adds.

"Andrew, I'm going to be in the office for quite a while now. I have no plans for going out of town for at least 6 months, probably longer."

"I'm going to insist on Isabel staying out of the company business as our bylaws state. I have reasons for this which I will not get into right now."

"Whatever her responsibilities have been, I am sure you and I are more than capable of taking care of them. I know she has been working in the lab and I am more than willing to take on that responsibility. I've already hired another assistant to work with Esther with the addition work load." Ethan catches him off guard.

"Wait a minute Ethan, what is this really all about?" Andrew questions.

"It's about Isabel working on projects which neither the Board nor I have authorized. I'm sure you don't even know half of the things she has her hands on in our business. What is worse of all is our employees are all walking on eggshells? She has our employees terrified when she is in the building, to which she is here now; even though I made it extremely clear, she is not welcome here. After today, she will no longer have a parking place reserved for her."

Ethan softens his tone, "Listen, I know you love her and she can't do anything wrong in your eyes, but trust me there are major problems with her working here."

Before Andrew could respond, Isabel comes into the office. Isabel is speechless to see Ethan standing there. Thinking to herself, *why didn't anyone tell me he was back from his trip and in the building. Why she wasn't told by Mrs. Siegel? Heads are once again going to roll for it. Visibly angry over her surprise, she hated surprises, and this one was at the top of the list.* Quickly, she regains her self-control.

"Ethan, it's so nice to see you again! I didn't realize you were back from Dubai already. How was your trip?"

Ethan turns his attention to Andrew, ignoring Isabel, which he knows will infuriate her even more. "Andrew, are you going to inform her of our current conversation, or would you like me to clue her in?"

Andrew looks disheveled. Ethan waits a pregnant moment. "Since you're not speaking up, I will! Isabel the bylaws of our company state very clearly that the wife of Andrew or if I had a wife, they are prohibited from working here. I personally never authorized you working here. I have tolerated your presence here for a time, and now it's over. As of right now, your labor contributions to this company are over. I told you that the last time I was here. I believe that was only a few short weeks ago, and to stay out of the building, yet here you are."

"ANDREW!" shouts Isabel. She is now a banshee woman. She is so angry she can't get herself under control. "DO YOU HEAR HOW HE IS TALKING TO ME? YOU CAN'T AGREE WITH HIM. I HAVE RESPONSIBILITIES HERE THAT WOULD BE UNETHICAL FOR ME JUST TO ABANDON." The employees on the next floor down could hear her screaming.

"There is nothing you are doing here that Andrew and I can't take over. For example, I am now taking over all the projects in the Laboratory Department. Your keys will no longer work in that area specifically after today. They are being changed immediately." Ethan responds calmly to her, screaming at Andrew.

Isabel, still ignoring what Ethan is telling her, continues yelling at Andrew. **"I am not leaving this building.**

I have authorization to work here by the Board. You can't let Ethan get away with this. He isn't here to assist you with running the home office. You need me here and you know it. ANDREW SAY SOMETHING! Just don't sit there without addressing this outrageous insult to me!"

Isabel is red faced with fury. She can't believe that Andrew still isn't saying anything to defend her. Of course, she isn't giving him time to respond before screaming at Ethan herself.

"ETHAN, YOU ARE OUT OF YOUR MIND TALKING TO ME LIKE THIS. WE STILL OWN THE MAJORITY OF THE STOCK AND I'M NOT LEAVING! I WORK HERE, WHETHER OR NOT YOU LIKE IT. DO YOU HEAR ME! I'M NOT LEAVING TODAY OR TOMORROW OR ANYTIME SOON. WHEN I LEAVE, IT WILL BE ON MY OWN ACCORD." Isabel retaliates.

"Isabel, I'm sure the entire building hears you and it is very unprofessional. This is exactly why you are being fired as of today. You will not intimidate me, as you have all the employees in this building. The terror reign you have initiated on our employees as of today, ends. You've been warned time and time again not to talk to the staff as you are talking. Excuse me, screaming at me right now. You have fired staff which you had no business firing. Leave on your own accord, or I will have you escorted out as you have done to so many of our other employees who have not agreed with you. The choice is yours. By the way, take Hiram with you. He's not welcome here either." Ethan is furious, but kept his composure and voice under control.

Lowering her voice but still seeping madly and teeth clinched, "Andrew, you idiot, say something! You can't let him get away with this. You can't let him talk to me like this. I'm valuable around here. I work hard, and so does Hiram. You just can't fire him just for working for me. He has his responsibilities and he will need time to train someone to replace him. It's not fair to him. I understand about the bylaws, but Hiram is not a part of them. He's always been a part of this company almost since the day he graduated from college."

"Andrew, say something!" They both look over at him, and he just sits there with a stunned look on his face. *The employees aren't the only ones walking on eggshells,* Ethan thought to himself.

Finally, he speaks up as he stands to address his cousin. "Ethan, be a reasonable man. You can't just walk in here and fire my wife and her secretary. They have done nothing wrong. They all have their jobs to do and have responsibilities to the company. At least give Isabel a month to reassign her projects to other people and train them how to do them. We all understand the bylaws, but to fire Hiram. Come on, Ethan. He is a hardworking employee. Hiram has broken no company rules. He doesn't deserve to be fired. Ethan, you're not being reasonable. You have jet lag or something."

"Andrew, yes I have some jet lag but that isn't even close to the problem here." Looking at Isabel, "He does not know what you have been up to. It's going to stop today. You have overstepped your authority in the company and who knows where else. Our employees tremble in fear every time to walk down the corridor, any corridor. Our employees deserve much better than that. You have fired employees you had no right to fire. I could go on, but I won't. I've called a Board Meeting with all the members this afternoon. The first thing on the agenda is you and redistributing your responsibilities."

"By the way, as I've already told you, all the locks will be changed. Anyone caught allowing you into the building will automatically be fired. Your company phone and laptop will be left here today as well." Ethan tells her as he opens Andrew's door and motions for her to leave.

Isabel continues screaming at Ethan on her way out of the door, "YOU WILL HEAR FROM MY LAWYER ETHAN. THIS ISN'T THE END OF IT! ANDREW, I WILL SEE YOU AT HOME AND IT ISN'T GOING TO GO WELL FOR YOU." She slams the door behind her.

There are two security guards waiting for her as she exits Andrew's office. Hiram is already packing up his personal belongings when she entered her office. There is one Security Guard with Wendy from HR. She has finished his exit interview and has his signed papers in her hands. They give him a four months' severance package of benefits and four months' salary. Ethan added a condition with his severance package. He is not to be in contact with any of the employees at Bachman's. If he does, the severance benefits package would stop immediately and however much of his monthly salary is left will also stop. He would be paid his four-month salary one month at a time instead of a bulk amount.

Wendy explains to him he will leave his keys, company phone, and laptop at the office with the passwords for said electronics. Someone from IT would be here shortly to have these items handed over to that person.

"Isabel, what in the hell is going on? Wendy walks in to the office with a security guard and tells me I'm fired and

I have to leave immediately. What did I do wrong? I don't understand what is happening."

"I know Ethan is behind this because he puts a condition on my severance package and salary. He said if I talk with anyone from Bachman's after I leave here today, my package and salary will cease immediately. It's for only four months. I have no notice. Is this legal?" Hiram babbles, which were unbecoming of him.

"Hiram, Ethan just fired me, too! He will hear from my lawyer from both of us. This is outrageous! He will not get away with this. I refuse to clean out my office. It's my office and I will be back. Don't anyone touch the things in my office. Do you hear me! Not even one pen!" Isabel shouts for everyone in hear shot to hear, mainly the entire executive floor.

One of the security guards speaks up. "Mrs. Bachman: I must ask for your company phone. You must leave it here with your laptop."

"These are mine. I'm not leaving them with you and anyone else." She retorts.

"I'm sorry but I must insist." He tells her.

Ethan appears at the doorway. "Don't give George a hard time, Isabel. After all, he's just doing his job."

Picking up a book, she throws it at Ethan. "Get the hell out of here. You have caused enough damage for the day. You will hear from my lawyer shortly."

"Not with the company cell phone. Now be a good girl and give it to George like he asked you to do." Ethan has fire in his eyes.

"FINE, here George" She slams her phone down on the desk and storms out of the office. Hiram follows shortly behind her with his box of personal items with him. The security guard patted down Hiram to make sure there were no stick drives on his person, nor in his box of personal items. George found 2 stick drives and gives them to Ethan as he passes by him. Ethan nods and smiles.

The two security guards that are waiting for Isabel outside of Andrews's office walk slightly behind her and the other security guard is behind Hiram. They are being escorted out like a common criminal. They are furious and go out with their heads held high.

Everyone in the corridor or at their desks just look at each other. They all knew that when Ethan came back from Dubai that Isabel wouldn't be welcome here. Ethan must be back because Isabel is getting the ax. Everyone is afraid to say anything. They either have their mouths covered in shock or just have their mouths dropping to the floor. You can hear a pin drop. Nobody says a word. Is this really happening?

She is being escorted out like she had done to so many others. Now she herself is leaving. OMG are the whispers. Mrs. Isabel Bachman is being escorted out of the building. People just stare at disbelief. They are afraid to say anything in fear that as soon as Ethan leaves again for another trip, she will be back.

"What are you starring at? I'll be back in no time," she screams at onlookers.

The next line of business is to set up a meeting with all the department heads. The atmosphere in the office is going to change and for the better. I want our employees to enjoy coming to work. I want them to be efficient and creative. They can't be much of those things with how things are right now.

Ethan heads back to his office. In an hour the Board will be in the conference room. So it has begun. He meditates on the job at hand. *I promised not to bring that there are 30 people missing. This is driving me more than the entire things that Isabel has been doing around here, not only behind our backs. The abuse she caused to so many employees. I wonder how many people left here because of her. Exemplary employees that would have helped humanity by the inventions we develop here. Well, it's in the Detective's hands. I have to let that part go for now. I have a tremendous amount of damage control to do now. I have to make that my focus.*

There is a call from the receptionist that broke his thought pattern. "Mr. Ethan, there is a Mr. John here to see you. He wouldn't give me his last name."

Ethan laughs. "He doesn't have a last name. Send him in."

Moments later, John is knocking on his door. "Come in. John: I can't tell you how thrilled I am to see you. Can your crew start right now?"

"Well, that depends on what you have in mind besides what we talked about earlier," John smiles. He knows whatever Ethan asks of him, he will gladly do.

"I need all the locks in the building changed for our floors. I also need the code for the elevator to the executive floor to change immediately. I need Isabel's company cell phone programmed so I can tap into her old phone calls and text messages. I also need to find out if there is anything in her company computer we are now in possession of that we didn't have access to."

"Whoa buddy, what just happened here? It was only a week ago you flew to Dubai and you just got back today? Kathy must have found some pretty serious things for you to be this excited. You got rid of Isabel, didn't you?" John observes.

"John, what she found is so beyond what I ever could have imagined. What Isabel has done here has been evil. I can't get into right now but just know the police are involved, but that has to stay between you and me. I'm only telling you because there might come a time when you will be asked a few questions from a couple of Detectives I know and respect." Ethan explains what he could.

"I'm going to assume you fired Isabel just a short time ago, hence needing the locks and codes changed. I'll start with the elevator and get the code to you right away."

"What is going to prevent Andrew from giving her the new code and a new key card?" John questions.

Ethan responds, "I've already informed Isabel that anyone who lets her into the building will be fired immediately. As far as Andrew, I can't stop him, but I can have her arrested for trespassing. She knows I will do it so I don't think she will want to be humiliated by that situation."

"You know it's going to take me some time to get the new fobs and key cards to all the current employees. Since today is Friday, I'll have my crew work on it all weekend. You know this is going to cost you a pretty penny for all that overtime. I'll work with your IT guys and we'll have it done by Monday morning. I'm also assuming that Kathy's office is still ok with how we set it up 2 weeks ago."

"Yes, that office is fine, but it's not Kathy's anymore." Ethan laughs. "I promoted her to Esther's new Executive Assistant. What she did in a 2 week's span was so amazing that it is beyond words. I couldn't let her go to a menial position when she is capable of so much more," Ethan smiles. "Come to think about it, I wonder how many people working for us have been wasting their talents like Kathy has for so many years. I will have to work on that aspect of all this in due time."

"Wonderful. I knew she would be great. I could sense it about her and how intelligent she is. I only showed her once how to do something and she like read my mind and took off with it. Good for her with such a significant promotion. Now I need to get started. I'll start with getting a crew together and make my way to the IT Department. I'll see you on Monday morning. Have a great weekend and be at peace about your security problems." John and Ethan shake hands and John exits Ethan's office.

Ethan takes some time to meditate on what is about to take place. Finally he is ready and enters the Conference Room. Those who can't make it on such short notice are there by Zoom/Video Conferencing. Everyone quiets themselves as Ethan enters the room.

Andrew is the first to speak. "What the hell do you think you're doing firing my wife. She has a job here, and she does it better than anyone else. You have no right to fire her and you didn't even have the respect to even tell her or Hiram why you are firing them. What do you have to say for yourself, Ethan?"

"I have a question for the Board before I get back to you, Andrew. Does anyone in this room know what Digital Tattooing is and what the process is for it?" Ethan asks.

Kent Nobel is the only one to raise his hand, surprisingly. "I know it has something to do with The One World Order and they were looking for us to create something for it. I know it was up for a vote for the Laboratory Dept. but we didn't have enough information on it. We didn't want to have anything to do with it or The One World

Order. That was about 10 years ago or so. I don't think some of the current Board Members were even here at that time. Why do you ask?"

"Thank you, Kent. Does anyone else here know anything else about it?"

Everyone shook their heads no.

"Andrew, therefore Isabel was fired earlier today, along with her sidekick Hiram. I never did trust that guy. She went behind our backs and has been developing a variety of One World Order products without the Board's approval. I don't have a complete list yet of all the 'projects' she had going on yet, but I will. I am going to be taking over the supervision on the Lab until we untangle all the Top Secret Projects she was involved in. As far as what Digital Tattooing is I'll explain it in a simple term. It creates a tattoo involving an individual's blood system and a microchip which goes on the person's right hand or their forehead, whichever they prefer. The chip is installed, then the person's smart phone taps it and it forms a blood pattern. Through this blood pattern, an individual can be tracked through GPS. It can access their financial situation and their medical information throughout one system."

"Every single person living will eventually be mandated into having this chip. It is now offered voluntarily, but those who resist it won't be allowed to get medical help or won't even be able to buy groceries. There will be no money exchanging hands. All purchasing transactions will go through your chip."

"If this doesn't scare you, it should. Free enterprising as we know it will all be controlled by a few designated elite's. Does anyone here want to be a slave to the dictators who will control this system? I certainly don't and will fight it from happening as long as I can. As far as I'm concerned, this company will also not be a part of it any longer!"

"Does anyone else know of projects Isabel was working on?" Ethan inquires.

"I authorized all of her projects, Ethan. I am the Chairman of the Board and I told her she could do all of them." Andrew retorts.

"How dare you authorize projects without going through the Board first? You don't have that kind of authority alone. Why do you think we have a board to decide on serious projects such as this situation?" Ethan is now burning with anger.

"What is wrong with you, Andrew? Has she cast some sort of spell on you, don't have your own mind anymore? I'm serious. You would have never agreed to some things she is doing in that lab." Ethan responds.

"Ethan, whether or not you like her, she is still part of the executive branch of this company. I made her part of it." Andrew shouts back.

"We will see about that, Andrew. It's against our bylaws and I for one will never allow her to not only be a part of this company. I'm making sure she never steps on foot in this building again. As we speak, all the locks are being changed. I will give new name tags with fob codes on them out on Monday when the employees arrive. The code on the executive elevator will be changed shortly. I'll give you the new code before you leave. Anyone allowing Isabel into the building will be fired immediately for those who can be. For those who can't be fired will be dealt with in another way. Believe me Andrew, when

I say if she shows up here again I will have her arrested for trespassing."

"She has terrorized the employees long enough in our workplace. Our employees are terrified of her. She's insulting, abrasive, a racist, and ill-tempered. She has fired people who simply disagreed with her. Outstanding employees were let go without reason. She was wrong in so many cases, and those who bravely stood up to her were humiliated and degraded. She either fired them on the spot or they quit. Nobody should be afraid of another employee, no matter where they work. Respect for your upper management is one thing, but to work out of fear is another thing altogether. She's not welcome here, Andrew, ever. She's your wife and our bylaws are very specific about her not working here. You have proven time and time again you can't rein her in to have respect for our employees. We as a company will no longer tolerate her behavior. How many lawsuits have we had to endure because Isabel was out of line and verbally abused an employee and we settled out of court?"

"Andrew, I will not continue to argue with you about Isabel. We need to take a vote to keep her out. Remember the Bylaws. I know many of you in here are also afraid of her. You are voting what our Company laws state. Set aside your feeling. If you feel you need security against Isabel, which will be arranged for you. Talk to me after the meeting and I'll arrange it. We will take the vote on a written ballot. Fill out the paper in front of you. Just check yes to follow the Bylaws and keep Isabel out. If you want Isabel here, vote No. Even though we are voting here, I do have our lawyers reviewing it right now, so it might be a moot point. Vote now and don't look at anyone else's vote."

Ethan collected the votes. He read each one out loud.

"1 yes,"

"1 yes,"

"1 yes,"

"1 no,"

"1 yes,"

"1 no,"

"1 yes,"

"1 yes,"

"1 yes,"

"1 yes,"

"1 yes,"

"The Yes's have it. 9 to 2."

"Andrew, if any of these people have a mysterious accident, I will make sure Isabel is arrested and thrown in jail without bail."

"Andrew, I know you are going to experience the wrath of Isabel when you get home but the Board has spoken."

"Thank you for being here. I also feel I must reiterate the laws of this official Board Meeting to total silence on the content of this meeting, especially including but not limited to the discussion on Digital Tattooing. I do highly recommend you do your own research on this topic. We will discuss this topic again, in the near future. By the way, this especially applies to you and what you can discuss with Isabel. Other than the vote, you are forbidden from talking to her about the meeting." Ethan states.

"Ethan, this isn't over, and you know it. You could careless of what is going to happen when I get home because you have caused it. Isabel works hard and has very valid projects going on here. She has financially contributed to our business. Why did you fire Hiram? He has been a dedicated employee. What did he do wrong? He's done everything anyone has ever asked him to do. Yet you fired him why, just because he was Isabel's Executive Assistant?"

"You know as I as I do, she is probably on the phone right now with the top lawyers in NY. She will claw her way to get her job back, and I don't blame her. She's been working here for 19 years." Andrew's voice was raised and cracking as he spoke.

"Andrew, I objected to her being here right from the start. Every time I was away on business, you allowed her here. It wasn't right and you know it. I should have put a stop to her being allowed to work in the office in any capacity years ago. I can't go backwards but I can start today to make things right and having her in the building working was the wrong thing to do from the start. I just didn't know how bad it was until recently. She's gone from the building and she's not coming back!" Ethan is angry, yet determined to put an end to Isabel's evil reign at Bachman International Corporation.

Andrew storms out of the conference room. The two people who voted no also follow him. They are trying to console Andrew. They tell him they will stick by him no matter what. Ethan notices the security guards stop them and direct them over to Wendy.

Ethan continues to talk with the rest of the Board and answers some direct question, but he has to reply that he will have more answers for them later and that it involves the police. He told them that this information is to remain confidential, and it is important that it remain that way so the police could do their job without interference. Ethan makes them swear their allegiance and cooperation to the company before they leave the room. He assures them he knows what he is doing and has the company's best interest at heart. They trust him and his judgments' and want to be kept informed of what was going on. He assures them he will as much as he can.

Ethan goes back to his office. Next he calls all the Vice Presidents and Department Heads to the Conference room. The grapevine is working overtime. Everyone has questions, especially with the entire IT Department busy changing locks and giving new keys to the Department Heads. The Department Heads were told to hang onto the keys until Ethan or their VP talked with them first.

Within an hour it seems the Conference Room is standing room only with one chair available. Ethan's of course. Soon Ethan enters the room and immediately the room, which is loud from chatter, becomes still and quiet.

"Ladies and gentlemen, I am sure by now you have heard that Mrs. Isabel Bachman is no longer an employee here. Actually, she never really was, but that is another issue being dealt with."

A huge applauds erupts. Ethan smiles, but concerned as well.

"Was I so unapproachable that nobody could tell me that Mrs. Bachman was terrorizing the staff? I am sorry that I was so caught up in my own affairs within the company that I didn't notice what others were dealing with. For that please accept my apology."

Peter Loy, a long time established employee, Vice President of Engineering, speaks up next. "Of course we accept your apology. We all have been waiting a long time for today to happen, so we are very grateful to you." Another round of clapping and shouting starts again, but soon quiets down. "What will happen to the projects we are doing for her. Who do we get authorization for the expenses which we accrue?"

Ethan addresses the issue and more. "I want to say I know some of you in this room were some of her 'pet' employees." He notices several of the people in the room trying to be secretly using their cell phones. "Please turn off your phones and lay them on the table, please. That would be a best thing for everyone here to do; you might get them back before you leave."

"Now that is done, we can go on to other business. I must begin with this. Is there anyone here who feels they can no longer work here without Mrs. Bachman's being your supervisor?" There are three people who raise their hands.

"Wendy from HR is here with exit interview forms for you to fill out. You are excused, but first I want to know why you feel so dedicated to her?"

Sandra Sved, Vice President of Human Resources, explains first, "She has always worked with me and I don't have a problem with her. I am not comfortable with what you are doing, Ethan. Count me out." Sandra stands up and leaves with Wendy close behind, papers in hand.

"Sandra, I'm sorry to hear that. You are a fine worker, and we will miss you. I'll have a conditional severance package for you. Wendy will explain it to you. Thank you for leaving your phone here. One of the security guards will go with you to help you clean out your office." She gave Ethan "the look," as she exits the door.

Ashley Puritan is the next one to stand up. "I agree with Sandra. I'm out of here too for the same reason. You are the one who is wrong here, Ethan!"

"Ashley, Vice President of Public Relations. Please don't leave until you have received your conditional severance package. It won't take you long. Sorry to see you go as well."

She gave him a flip of her hand as she walked out the door.

"Is there anyone else? I only want people here that want to be here." There were two more people who also walked out, with Ethan repeating the same comments he gave to Sandra and Ashley.

"Well, folks, it looks like some promotions are going to be happening shortly. Think about your loyal staff, which has proven to be excellent employees over this weekend, those next in line for those who left I'll be talking to by the end of next week. Also, I need you to give me a recommendation for positions within the company, not necessarily in your department, for those hard workers which you feel the need to move up."

"Since today is Friday and the locks and new name tags with fobs are being made this weekend, I want you to release all the employees in your department to take the rest of the day off with pay. When they come in on Monday, they will get their new name tags. They will need to gather in their departments in the lobby at scattered hours. I will meet with all of you in the lobby at 4 on Sunday."

"If you see a department that didn't get the memo to be here, please send the department head up to me immediately. For example, I didn't see Jonathan Kilpatrick from the Lab Dept. here. Is there anyone else you didn't see here that should have been?" Everyone shook their heads. It was five minutes later Jonathan was in the Conference room.

"Didn't you get my memo about the executive meeting?" Ethan inquires privately.

"Yes, I got it, but I was in the middle of something I couldn't stop at a moment's notice." Jonathan stiffly responds.

"Jonathan, I'm sorry I didn't have time to talk to you earlier. I've been busy too. I know you and Isabel worked closely together over the past 13 years. As of today, she won't be employed here anymore. This leaves an opening for you to receive a promotion and a substantial raise. If you choose not to take it, I'm going to offer you the same exit package that a few others have accepted. Which would you prefer? I don't want anyone to work here that doesn't want to be here." Ethan states.

"What are my options?" Jonathan asks.

"Option 1: If you stay, I demand total loyalty. Any employee found communicating with Isabel except for Andrew will be fired immediately. You will become the Vice President of the Laboratory Department and you will answer to me directly. I already know more that you can imagine what is going on in the Labs. There is a sizeable raise involved and additional benefits along with additional responsibilities."

"Option 2: If you chose to leave you will be given a four-month severance package which also includes four months' salary. I will give the salary one month at a time with the condition of no communications with Isabel within those four months. If you do your benefits and salary with stop immediately. What is your decision?" Ethan inquires.

"Do I have time to think about it?" Jonathan asks.

"Sure, you have five minutes. I'll wait." Ethan says firmly.

"Why are you being such a hard-ass, Ethan?" Jonathan snarls.

"You tell me, Jonathan. You have worked side by side with Isabel. You know better than anyone else what she has secretly been doing in the lab. You know the projects she's been working on, which the Board would never approve of. You know the secrets nobody should know, don't you. Talk to me, Jonathan. She's not here anymore. We can get protection for you." Ethan encourages.

"I don't know what the hell you are talking about. You're out of your mind. Give me the severance package and salary. I want out of here." Jonathan demands. He talks tough, but Ethan sees the fear in his eyes.

"Jonathan, you will not be safe. You know how dangerous she is. I think you know where the bodies are buried. Let us keep you safe and get you some security, even if it's for a brief time." Ethan offers.

"You can't keep anyone safe from Isabel! If she wants someone to disappear, they are gone, and nobody is going to find them. I know nothing other than that. I still know nothing else of what you're talking about. I wasn't involved with her secret projects. What do I need to do to get out of here?" Jonathan again demands.

"First, I need your cell phone." He slams it down in Ethan's hand. Next, Wendy from HR will do your exit interview and the details you will need to sign. She's right outside the room. Here, take this card. It's for Detective Gibbons if you need some help." Ethan offers. He snatches the card from his hand and exits the room without an incitement.

Ethan picks up the phone and calls the Security office.

"George here, what can I do for you, Ethan?"

"George, are you finished with escorting Isabel and Hiram off the property?"

"Yes, sir, what else can I do for you?"

"I need you to come up to the Executive Conference room and escort Mr. Jonathan Kilpatrick to his office so he can get his personal belongings. Please make sure he stops to talk to no one and especially not to make any phone calls. He must also leave any electronics behind, including any digital sticks which might have company business on. Double check his belongings, briefcase, and pockets. When you take him out to his car, also go through it for any paperwork and electronics like you did for Hiram. The parking deck it is still on our property. Please, report to me after you're done. I'll be in my office."

Ethan picks up the phone. "John, I need you to go down and secure the laboratory in the basement. I'll call down there and talk to the remaining employees still there and give them the weekend. As soon as the last one leaves in 10 minutes. I want you to lock it down. The security guards down there will make sure they have all left immediately." Ethan hangs up and calls the security guards in the lab and the next in command after Jonathan. He then dials another familiar number.

"Hello, Detective Gibbons speaking."

Chapter 21

The Ball is Rolling

"Ethan here, I want to give you a head up. I fired Isabel today and needless to say, she was not happy. All the locks are being changed to keep her out, at least the best of my ability. There have been a few top executives which have quit. The last one which is having his exit interview completed right now is one I want to talk to you about. His name is Jonathan Kilpatrick. He worked directly with Isabel in the Lab. He is a man of interest to you. I am also concerned about his wellbeing. I gave him one of your cards."

"Hi Ethan, I'm glad you called. Do you have a phone number for Jonathan? I'll call him shortly." Gibbons asks.

"We have given the new list to Missing Persons. Her department has made this as a top priority. She is grateful for the help and wants Kathy to work for her, but I told her it is now below her pay grade." They both laugh.

"Also, Rocco and I just left the Commissioner's office. You know they have been hiding these missing people for a long time, but someone along the way either has or will make a mistake. We will find out where these people are.

There are just too many of them not to have any trace of what has happened to them all." Gibbons concludes.

"Gibbons, I know you don't know the answer to this, but I'm going to ask it, anyway. What kind of time frame are we talking about? I've kept it quiet about the Missing Person's investigations. I have only talked to Isabel and others about the projects she was doing in the Laboratory." Ethan asks.

"Ethan, I'm going to be honest with you. They have been doing this for years with little being on the radar. We have no bodies or any clue at this point what has happened to any of them. We will, though. This might take a few months or it might take years. I do guarantee that we will do our best to find out what has happened to them. Hopefully now that Isabel is out of the building it will at least stop." Gibbons assured him.

"I have a question for you. Did you read all the journals? Was there any information about any of these missing people? Did Robert even know they were missing after they left the building?" Gibbons asked.

"I only had time to skim over most of them. The only thing that I saw was starting on the end of the first book was a mention about the firing of Phillip Bryant and Joseph Harris. Their spouses were here the next day looking for them. I'm sure there are more. I just wasn't focused on it. He wrote that the rumor mill circulated the fact that making Isabel mad made people disappear permanently, but nothing was proven. He also mentioned that Hiram, Isabel's executive assistant, was pretty creepy, and the employees didn't like him being around. We all felt that way, so I fired him too when I fired Isabel. If anyone had something to do with people missing, I'm sure Hiram and/

or her two bodyguards, Sid Jehu or Paul Blumenthal, had something to do with her dirty work. I can get you the phone numbers for all three of them if you need them. I'm sure Kathy can discover them for you. Come to think of it, ask her." Ethan and Gibbons agree.

"Thanks for the heads up and for keeping the Missing Persons Investigation quiet for now. It will break open soon enough. As much as I want these people found yesterday, I know from experience it will take a while to find them. Don't get discouraged if it takes longer than you think it should. Rocco and I will see this through to the end. I want to make sure we have the evidence we need, that those involved will never see the light of day again." Gibbons again assures Ethan. They both say goodbye and hung up.

Chapter 22

The Laboratory

Ethan has been quite busy for several months. Positions are reassigned. He promoted people who deserved promotions and demotions or firing of others which were not loyal to the company. Through Kathy, and her keen skills of observation, he was kept up to par with the progress of the Laboratory. He finally cleared his schedule enough to get down to the laboratory for himself. While Ethan was busy with administrative business, he instructed Kathy to find out the distinct divisions within the Laboratory. What the divisions are working on and the staff who are working on them. Isabel had managers over each division and a supervisor over 5 divisions. Jonathan Kilpatrick was the official Vice President but Isabel was the real Vice President for all intent purposes. Everyone in the lab knew this. If fact, everyone in the building knew Ms. Bachman she was in charge except Ethan. Jonathan was really the Head Director over all the supervisors. Since Jonathan's resignation, it has left a void Ethan, temporarily is filling until he knew exactly what is going on that Isabel was so secretive about.

The laboratory is on the subfloor of the Bachman Building. The only people allowed on that floor had to have top clearance. There is a separate elevator which only goes to the sublevel and comes up to the main floor. The door to the elevator looks like an office door with a retina eye security clearance to even open the door. Each employee leaving the floor also is scanned. They search their briefcases and purses each time exit the floor. They even check their lunch sacks and drink containers. Security is tighter than Fort Knox.

Ethan enters the floor of the laboratory. The two security guards greet him as he passes through security.

"Good morning, gentlemen. It's very quiet down here." They both nod.

"I sure would appreciate a two cent tour." Ethan suggests, as he could see how nervous both men are. Ethan has his list with him what position each person has, but other than the top administration he did not have a face to go along with these names. He would get to know all of them in time.

"Gentlemen, I want you to know I am not Mrs. Bachman, nor am I Mr. Haddad. We do not require you to walk on eggshells when I am here. Call me Mr. Ethan. I plan on working down here till I know who everyone of you, what you do and how proficient you are at what you do. I want to learn the inner workings of this entire laboratory. Here is my card. I want you to relay anything that you see as suspicious and call me immediately. Call your supervisor next." Ethan continues. "How many guards have clearances to work down here?" Ethan asks.

"Mr. Ethan, I'm Edward Rudeck. There are 23 guards who have clearance for this area. Some of them work in other areas sometimes, but when someone calls off, they are available to work here."

"There are more guards at the other locations like at the warehouse by the docks and some in Albany if we run into a crisis and need more but we never have had to." Edward continues. "I don't know if Mr. Bryandt here has been at the other locations or not, but I've been to both on different locations."

"What are the primary functions of having labs at these two locations?" Ethan asks, trying hard to keep a level head and open mind. He didn't know they had two other lab locations.

Edward Rudeck comments next. "I've only been to the docks once. They were using some sort of test on a shipment they had just received from China. Later on in that day I saw the shipment from China getting loaded on a truck and they drove away."

Mr. Bryandt stayed behind and waited at the elevator post for Mr. Ed to return after the tour. He thought to himself, *I sure hope Mr. Ethan can fix this department so we can finally enjoy our jobs. My wife keeps telling me to retire before I have a nervous breakdown. Well, wait till I tell her that Mr. Ethan Bachman himself is taking charge of the Lab. I hope she will be as happy as I am. I feel I can finally breathe again without worrying about getting screamed out for just being here.*

Mr. Ed is very nervous for about the first hour walking with Mr. Ethan. The longer they talk about the very basics of what he knows about each department, the more relaxed he becomes. Even though he was working here for many years, he only knew very little about what each department was working on. If it was a gigantic machine, he had some idea of what it was going to be used for. There were many departments which use dangerous chemicals, and he had to know about them. However, he didn't know what they were used for sometimes. He talks to Mr. Ethan about these chemicals, and the dangers associated with them. He shows him the stocks of different labels, and supplies only associated with this department.

Mr. Ed introduces him to everyone they come to encounter with. Of course everyone knows Mr. Ethan. Each employee, Ethan, tells them just to call him Mr. Ethan and he would give them an encouraging smile. He of course knows all the department heads speaking cordially for a few moments. Mr. Ethan explains they will have a meeting with them shortly but wants to meet the entire staff face to face before settling into his downstairs office, as he calls it.

It surprises Ethan how large the lab is and the extreme security. Each Department is sectioned off with their own iris scans to enter their department. Of course Ethan knows about the scanners, but he didn't know just how many different sections of the lab there are. Some rooms hold large equipment, while others are only big enough for a few employees. The atmosphere is thick with anxiety. Even though Ethan tries to make light with the visit, he can still feel the presence of Isabel in the area. One of the first things I need to find out is who is going to tell me the truth about the last time she was actually in this area. I don't think it was that long ago, even though it's been months since she was fired. Everyone is still skittish.

Of course, Ethan knows some supervisors and knew the old Vice President, Artie Watkins. Artie worked closely with Jonathan and knows the inner working of the Lab.

Ethan doesn't trust him enough to talk to him about the missing people. For now, Ethan needs him, but his instinct tells him to tread carefully with him.

His new temporary office fills up with the Supervisors and managers. He scans the unfamiliar faces and wonders if there is anyone here that knows all of what is going on down here. Does anyone have all the pieces of the puzzle besides Isabel? He knew instinctively that Jonathan would know most of them, but Haddad would know them all, and maybe even more than Isabel. Haddad would know where all the bodies were buried.

"Hello ladies and gentlemen and welcome to the first meeting of I'm sure many to come. Call me Ethan or Mr. Ethan; just do not call me Mr. Bachman. We'll leave that title for Mr. Andrew Bachman."

"I'm looking forward to getting to know each one of you and your staff. I want you to talk to me without feeling you are walking on eggshells. I am not a screamer, I am an excellent listener. If you or your staff have any ideas on how to improve your jobs or the environment, my door is always open." Ethan states.

"Each and every one of you has extremely important jobs here and I want to feel you are to do them to the best of your abilities. If you or your staffs run into a situation, pass it by me. We'll talk it out and come up with a solution together. We will bring this department together as one well-oiled machine. I understand there is a level of privacy and secrecy within each segment of this department. Of course, that will remain in effect. However, there are some levels of camaraderie within our department down here which can be enjoyed by all. For example, I've noticed how sterile each area is. I do not mean cleanliness issues; I don't see any pictures of family or children at the employee's stations. Each employee should be free to make their station their own. They don't have to, but I want each person here not dreading coming to work every day. Having a reminder of why they work so hard might help them relax and be more creative."

There are no secrets between each of my Directors and supervisors and myself. I want to know how each segment of this department works. Under the previous administration there were many secret hidden agendas. I will not tolerate this practice to continue. Keep me informed of everything which happens down here, great or small. Things which have happened down here, both past and present, I want to know. I don't want to be surprised by something which happened and I didn't know about. This is where you each come in. A report from each of you in needed, explaining to the best of your ability what has happened down here from the time you started. I want to emphasize that I will hold these reports in complete confidence and do not share with anyone else unless necessary for clarification, etc. Unless you give me specific permission, I will not use your name for this process. There must be total honesty between you and me. I would like to receive these reports no later than the end of next week, if not sooner. If you need more time, please let me know. Because of the nature of this report, unless necessary I would like you to keep these issues to yourself and in your own words and in your own perspective. If you know of an employee which you work with that has additional information which you need, have them write their own report concerning this matter and attach it to your report, please.

"A job description in your perspective is also required. I also want a report of what I expect from each of your employees and what encompasses their job. Present goals and what you see as to the future of your segment 'accomplishments. Please, this report needs to be finished first and I expect it by tomorrow morning." Ethan continues.

"I am a fair and honest person. I expect the same from all of you and your employees. It will take some time to build this trust because of the past administration. I already have set this up several months ago, and I want to reiterate this. Under NO circumstance is Mrs. Isabel Bachman allowed in this department ever. If she tries, I MUST know immediately. This is so serious of a situation that anyone who knows she is here and doesn't tell me will be fired immediately. You already know this. Just because I'll be working down here most of the time doesn't mean she won't know I'm gone and will try her best to infiltrate this department again. She can be really nice when she wants something, and she wants back here more than anything. I must know everything that goes on down here."

"Time to switch gears, it's your turn to talk to me. I'm sure you have some ideas already of what we can do to build up the moral in your segments and with the Department as a whole. We have about an hour before lunch will be served, so I want some really brilliant ideas." Ethan concludes as the conversations begin.

The reports start being placed on his desk by the end of the day. Now that he has his management motivated, he could feel the atmosphere is changing in the building's basement. He is thinking in many ways this department is part of the foundation of this building as well as the business. How à propos it is for this to be on the sub-level.

As the last of the employees exit the floor for the evening, Ethan scoops up the reports on his desk and heads out for home. It has been a pleasurable day. It is great to see people smiling and chatting softly as they walk past his office. He wonders how long it has been since these employees smiled at one another. The past is past. On to the future!

Ethan scans the reports as Denzel drives towards his home.

"Sir, would you like to stop for a bite to eat before I take you home?"

"That is a wonderful idea. How about ordering a medium pizza for me and a large for you to take home? No arguments." They both agree.

As Ethan continues to review the reports, he founds no surprises. Kathy has done a very thorough job with their job descriptions of each employee in the lab. What he is really interested in seeing are the other reports he requested from them. He wants to see if any of them will mention the missing people. Do they know? Will they tell? Will the grapevine be working throughout tonight? He will find out soon enough who will be honest with him over time, he is sure.

The next morning, after a pleasant run in the neighborhood, he is eager to get back to work. He expects the rest of the reports on his desk. He is not disappointed. Again, as he looks through them, he did not find any surprises. He wonders about Jonathan and if the Detectives ever talked to him. They said nothing, and he didn't ask. There has been too much time which has passed to open that can of worms back up.

He talked to financial and asked for all the departments' records for the time which Isabel was involved with this department. How in the world did she ever get permission to control this department was beyond his imagination? Why is Andrew so blinded by her? It was hard for him to understand but it is what it is and for the moment he has a full plate with cleaning up her mess.

Ethan is reviewing the financial statements from years ago. He is thankful they computerized them and he did not have to go through stacks of paper documents. Very few of the supervisors are still here from the beginning, which is a shame. We had some exceptional employees in this department. So far nothing seems out of place. He had to call the actuation Department for some clarification on some items. He is looking for changes especially, when the first person went missing. What were they working on? What caused their disappearance? He knows instinctively something is more than wrong. He needs to track these people from the beginning.

Though he kept to himself for several days, he scours over the massive amount of invoices and financial reports, and welcomes an employee asking him a question every so often. He checks and double checks invoices and inventory items. Matching items needed for the construction of ordered products. Ethan is actually impressed as to the quality of the final products and how the managers could keep the costs down as best as they could without skimping on the quality.

He learned what the company made other than the items he personally contracted out for. Even Isabel in her early days had sales, which he knew nothing about. She had these items made, and it seemed all legitimate. This realization caused more questions than answers. Did the Board know she was making sales, ordering materials to have these items built and doing the billing for these items? She was doing the entire process from beginning to end. He bet most of the Board didn't have a clue what she was up to, as well as himself. These were good contracts, as far as he could tell. That wasn't the point. I bet Andrew knew all about of these early contracts at first. I wonder when it changed that most of what she was doing at the end nobody knew about, not even Andrew. I can't bring myself to believe he knew about the missing people.

The days flew by and before he knew it the recent reports; he requested from last week to come across his desk. He stops what he is doing and thumbs through the new folders.

Though he didn't specify, some reports are handwritten. Most however are sent email or printed out and put on his desk, taking a special interest in the handwritten reports. He immediately pulls those from the pile and separates them. Curious is Karen Allen's report going to be handwritten.

Ms. Karen, as he addresses her, has become almost a right-hand woman to him for the past several days. She worked closely with Jonathan and is a wealth of information. Kathy's report on her was very favorable. Because of Kathy's report, Ethan had met with Karen several times before officially coming down to the laboratory. He still didn't trust anyone here yet, but she has been an asset he appreciates.

So far none of the Directors has asked for an extension. As he has taken time to walk around the facility at least once a day, since his arrival, he notices the employees stay within their area. There isn't a gathering around the "water cooler" as is customary on other floors of the building. They mostly ate lunch together and leave together within their own department without associating with anyone else in the other departments. He assumes it is because Isabel was so secretive about the "projects" she had people working on that she discouraged camaraderie with other departments.

He organizes the reports, separating not only the handwritten ones but also the ones of the projects which he ordered from his sales. Reading those first to make sure everything lines up according to the client's specification. The departments are doing a supreme job of carrying out the client's projects.

There is nothing in the reports about anyone in their departments missing or having any altercations with Isabel. The reports are done on the computer mostly and sent through email.

Maybe, he remarks to himself, that Isabel was smart enough to leave his clients alone with whatever she was doing in the laboratory.

The next category he looks into is the other executives who work directly with him in sales. Most of their sales deal with the large machinery which is built outside the laboratory but sometimes use special oils or paints which needs the lab's involvement. The director's reports again are all in order and list nothing about any missing persons in their departments.

With all the departments he is sure were clear of any "complications" he went on to the projects Andrew was involved with. His involvement with the company, besides being the Chairman of the Board is the administrative end of the business. The VPs of Finances, Laboratory, Human Services, Executive Secretaries except for Ethan's, the Secretary Pool, Janitorial and of course Isabel. Since Ethan was overseas so much, he was the CEO and the VP's from Engineering and Sales/Marketing answer directly to him. He took over Production Supplies, Security, Transportation, and now the Laboratory to name a few since the day he fired Isabel.

As Ethan ponders about how the responsibilities were divided up between Andrew and himself, he realizes how unfair he has been to Andrew. He has equalized the workload by taking over some departments, yet it still seems an overload for Andrew. Everything moved so fast with Isabel leaving and Ethan being "In the House" full time that Andrew is busy putting out fires from Isabel's removal. Andrew did not give Ethan a hard time about taking over the Laboratory. Even though Andrew said he approved all the projects Isabel was involved in, Ethan is positive he did not know the "projects" Isabel was involved with or he would have fought to maintain control over the Lab. Ethan is also convinced that Andrew didn't tell her that Ethan now has control over it. He would have heard the fireworks go off if he had told her.

Ethan's private phone rings. "Hello Kathy. How's life on the top floor?" Ethan laughs.

"It's fabulous as usual, Ethan! Listen, I need to show you something which isn't making sense to me. Can we meet somewhere like where we did when we first started working together?"

"Sure, have Denzel pick us up and see if Esther can come with us for dinner tonight at 6:00."

"Great, I'll ask her now and we'll see you at 6 out front." Kathy walks over to Esther and invites her to dinner with Ethan and herself.

"Hi Esther, have I told you lately what a really superb job I have and just how much I appreciate you and Mr. Ethan?" Kathy smiles to herself.

"You only tell about every other day." They laugh out loud.

Kathy is unsure about how secure their offices are, so she handwrites her notes instead of speaking. "Esther, I keep running into these weird statements coming from China. They are being sent to Isabel's phone and emails to her company computer. I think Isabel still has a computer getting these messages and doesn't realize I have access to her old computer. I know this because it's coming up read when she reads them. I can get into them without the acknowledgement of it already being read, fortunately. She deletes these messages as soon as she reads them. The messages are some sort of code that she understands. I'm glad that Mr. Ethan gave me her electronics instead of the IT Department. They would have bleached them and given them to another employee."

"Kathy, I would love to go to dinner with you and Mr. Ethan." She acknowledges and also handwrites, "WOW, are we going to have a very interesting conversation tonight. I am excited to find out what you are thinking."

"Wonderful, I'll come over and get you just before 6," she says as she returns to her office, which just happens to have been Hiram Haddad's office.

"Now, this is what I call perfect timing, ladies!" Ethan comments, as he seems to have come out of a closet and into the lobby. Laughing because he sees them jump, he says quietly, "You didn't know that is the hidden elevator entrance to the subfloor where the Laboratory is located. Well, where one of the Labs is located at, anyway."

Esther and Kathy just look at each other with a surprise look on their faces. They are both thinking the same thing. "How could they have worked here this long and not even know it was there?"

Denzel has become the Director of Transportation with all the staff changes. He is responsible for the hiring and firing of those trustworthy to be the company drivers. He himself only did the driving for Andrew, Isabel, Ethan, and their Executive Assistants. It is always a very interesting drive for Denzel when Andrew and Ethan ride together. Ethan makes sure the privacy window is always down.

"Good evening, Denzel, we'll be going to our favorite Lobster House tonight for dinner. Enjoy yourself with dinner, like usual. Well ladies, it's been sometime since we have done some catching up over dinner. My apology, especially since I enjoy both of your company so much." They all agree.

"Yes, Mr. Ethan, we both feel quite neglected." They banter.

They continue with small talk until after they order their meals. John's devise comes in handy to use when out in public and needing to secure conversations in a small area. Tonight's meeting is a perfect example of its use. The separate dining area which was requested when Ethan made the reservations is perfect for their time together.

"Kathy, as far as I'm concerned, you are one of the smartest people I know, and if you are having trouble understanding something, it is a concern of mine. Describe to me the problems you are running across?" Ethan inquires.

"I've kept Isabel's and Hiram's electronics up and running. I mostly monitor her company computer and cell phone. I'm getting strange messages on either or on both items every once in a while. The sentences make little sense. It's some sort of code from someone in China. You said there is more than one laboratory. Could there also be one in China that you know of?" Kathy questions.

"Wow, you don't pull any punches, do you? The mystery continues and the spider web becomes much more intricate. Can you give me an example of one of these sentences?" Ethan asks.

"Certainly, this is the one which has concerned me the most and I've been monitoring to find out more but have found nothing else to relate to it. Less than a month after you fired Isabel, she received this message from China;

"We received the 2 Golden Threads you sent, and the packages were a bit banged up but still intact. Since they are not the normal packages you send please advise, as to the location you want them in.'

"What do you make of it, Mr. Ethan and Esther? I have an educated guess but I want your analyzes first." Kathy requests.

Esther questions," Could you please repeat the Golden Thread part?"

"Sure, 'we received the 2 Golden Threads you sent, and the packages were a bit banged up but still intact. Since they are not the normal packages you send please advise, as to the location you want them in." Kathy reiterates.

"I know nothing that she has access to from the company after they escorted her out. To the best of my recollection, I have not heard of her trying to get back into the building to get anything which didn't personally belong to her. Even then she didn't come here Mr. Andrew took some pictures from her office home with him." Esther mentions.

"I've heard of the Golden Thread in different literature. I've also heard the expression with dark spiritual issues. For that reason, I'm very concerned with what they might mean. As far as the Laboratories, I know of a large one on the subfloor in the Bachman Building, one at the docks and one in Albany for patents and alterations which might be needed immediately for legal reasons. I don't know of any outside of those, but I will look into it. This is the first I have heard of the possibility of one overseas. If this is the case, nothing good is coming from it." Ethan responds.

There dinner appetizers or salad are ready for them so they pause the conversation until after dinner is finished and they are onto coffee or tea. They all decline dessert. As they relax after an extraordinary meal, the conversation drifts back to The Golden Thread and what it can mean.

Kathy did not want to talk about what she is pretty positive it means. She already hinted some information to the Detectives from Homicide and to Detective Bubb. Before she talked to Ethan and Esther about her suspicions, she did more research on Jonathan Kilpatrick and Sandra Sved. They were both single and were only children. Only Sandra had a mother still alive and has few friends. Both Jonathan and Sandra were totally dedicated to their jobs and worked approximately 60-70 hours a week. They were dedicated to our company, but also to Isabel Bachman. Kathy swallows hard and begins to express her concerns.

"Mr. Ethan and Esther, is it possible that they put Jonathan Kilpatrick and Sandra Sved into Witness Protection right after they were escorted out of the building?" Kathy asks.

"Kathy, I gave Jonathan the Detective's business card before he left. I haven't heard whether he called him or if they got a hold of them. I gave the detective Jonathan's phone numbers later on that day because I was concerned for his safety. Wait a minute, Kathy, what are you insinuating? Are they missing?" Ethan now is really concerned.

"Mr. Ethan, Esther, I've been trying to find out if they are missing on their own or because of Mrs. Bachman. I didn't think about anyone else missing since you fired her until I found Golden Thread email. I called the Detectives, and they told me to call Detective Bubb from Missing Persons. Detective Bubb and I actually talked for a brief time, and I told her what I could. I've looked into their Severance Packages. They both had Direct Deposit and none of the funds have been used. I told Detective Bubb about the email, about the Golden Thread and another code word, Home Brew."

"I'm sorry I've kept this from you for the past few months, but Detective asked me not to talk to anyone about it. I just couldn't keep it from either of you any longer. Detective Bubb knows something but can't tell me but assures me she isn't the only one working on this "problem". I gave her the IP address from the computer in China. The only thing that she told me was this was a lot bigger than any of us expected it to be. She also said it's going to take several months, if not a year or so, to find out the truth of all that is happening. I know we want results yesterday, but they need to be thorough and we need to be patient."

"On the upside of this I have found no one else from Bachman's that is missing. I also have noticed the environment within the different departments has changed for the positive. Employees are talking to each other, and production is up. People are smiling and happy to be working here." Kathy shares her observations.

"Kathy, this has been a very heavy load for you to carry alone. I'm glad you shared it with us. I understand why you had to keep it to, but I want you to know that no matter what you find you can always talk to either of us." Ethan reiterates.

"Mr. Ethan, I just thought of something. Maybe Denzel knows the answer to this. Has Isabel used the company plane to go to China or anywhere else overseas?" Kathy asks.

"Kathy, you are a genius. I think it's time for him to join us for coffee." Ethan gets up from the table and invites Denzel to join them.

Esther joking says, "Denzel it's so nice to see your face instead just the back of your head and shoulders." They all laugh. Denzel seems very nervous, though.

Ethan reaches out and shakes his hand before he sits down with them. "Denzel, I want to thank you for your faithfulness and dedication to Bachman International Corporation. Are you enjoying your new position and promotion?"

"Oh, yes, sir. I really appreciate all you have done for me and my wife really thanks you too, sir," Denzel smiles.

"You have been with us for over 20 years, and I appreciate you and your services. I bet you have seen and heard many things which you had to bite your tongue so you wouldn't say anything to anyone."

"Denzel, we have a question for you. Are you also in charge of the jets and the scheduling for its use, and who uses it?" Ethan asks.

"Yes sir. I make sure it's ready to go for those authorized to use it. Is there a problem I don't know about?" Denzel asks.

"How often do Andrew and Isabel use one of the planes, and where do they go to? Does Isabel use it without him?" Ethan inquires.

"They usually go to England to see the kids or they will send for the kids and go to their summer home on St. Thomas. He gets together with the children more often than she does. She might go once a year to see them."

"She takes the plane to Europe, Lebanon, and China. I think she was just there last week for several days."

Denzel thought to himself, maybe she isn't allowed to still take the plane and a worried look must have crossed his face.

"Denzel, why do you have a worried look on your face? You're not in trouble for what she does. She's Andrews's wife and is entitled to use the plane." Ethan reassures him.

Immediately Denzel relaxes. "Thank you, sir. I thought I was in trouble for letting her use the plane. She still uses the limo service all the time, but she has someone else drive her where she needs to go besides me. Is that still ok?" Denzel asks quietly.

"Is this other driver loyal to her or to the company?" Ethan wants to know.

"I've had no problems with him, sir. He's been mostly the only one to drive her anywhere for many years. She always requests him to drive her. He pretty much keeps to himself and never gossips with me or anyone else. Is there a problem, sir?"

"No problem at all! I would like to know when she uses the plane, without her knowledge, and what her itinerary is. Usually how much notice does she give you before she leaves?" Ethan inquires, knowing what he will ask next.

"She usually reserves it a week ahead of time; sometimes it's only a couple of days' notice. She went to Lebanon for the last time to see family. She has reserved plane #3, her usual plane, to go to China next week and will stay for four days. The plane has 2 scheduled stops. First stop in London, then Athens for refueling, since this is one of the smaller planes in the fleet. She used to take Jonathan Kilpatrick with her, but since they fired her, she usually goes alone. There might have been other people on the plane before she boards, though. The only reason I say that is because they order extra food and drinks to be stocked on board." Denzel responds.

"Denzel, do you know where she flies into when she goes to China?" Ethan wants to know.

"She always flies into the same airport. It's called Guangzhou Baiyan International Airport. Now that took me awhile to learn to say that one," Denzel smiles.

"I want you to do me a favor. Since I know how difficult Isabel can be on hired help, I would like you to give her usual driver 2 weeks off with pay for his dedicated service and you do her driving for him. I would also like you to be the one to pick her up from the airport when she returns.

Please check back with me after you drop her off each time." This time it was Ethan, who was smiling.

"Not a problem, sir! Now if you will excuse me, I must visit the restroom before taking you all back to your cars or home, whichever you prefer. I can always pick you all back up in the morning to go to work." Denzel assures Mr. Ethan.

After he leaves the area, Kathy is the first to speak up. "Wow, is that a wealth of information? I didn't think to ask him before. I'll call Detective Bubb and inform her we just learned and see where it might fit into the scheme of what is going on if, she can even tell me where it fits in at all.'

"I'm sure it will. I can't help but think that it is some if not all the missing scientists and engineers from Bachman's." Esther says still in amazement.

"I think you are right, Esther. I'll call Detectives Rocco and Gibbons and let them know what is going on and that you will call Detective Bubb. That way we are all on the same page." Ethan adds.

"Esther, Kathy, would you mind if Denzel took you home and picked you up in the morning? I'll be in the office later on tomorrow. I have some things I need to do first, so I'll need my car." Ethan suggests.

They look at each other and agreed.

Chapter 23

How Dark are the Secrets

"I know it's late, but I really need to talk to Detective Bubb from the Missing Persons Division. Is she still there?"

"Hold on, and I'll connect you to that department. I believe she is still in the office." The desk clerk responds.

"Missing Persons Division, Detective Bubb. How can I help you?"

"Thank you for still being there. This is Kathy McKinney from Bachman International. We need to talk right away."

"Hi Kathy, I know you have you been researching again as our past conversations lately. You saved me months if not years of work the last time," Bubb smiles.

Kathy, laughing, says, "How did you know? I need to talk to you. I know it's late but I need you to come over, in plain clothes, this evening to my home."

"Absolutely! I was just getting ready to leave for the evening. What is your address and I'll be there as soon as I can? Does this have anything to do with what we have been talking about lately?"

"I'll call the gate and let the security guard know that you are on the way. Thank you. I'll tell you when you get here."

Before long, the guard calls and says she would be there shortly.

"I am so glad to put a voice to a name. That is one reason I invited you over." Kathy tells her as she answers the door.

"I am too! Before we get started, I would like to record our conversation. If it's anything like your spider web, there will be more information than my mind can retain in a short time." Detective Bubb says as she enters the foyer.

"Not a problem. Another reason I wanted you to come here is because I know this house is a safe place to talk. I've been doing more research about our laboratory, or I should say laboratories. We have one very large lab on the sublevel of the Bachman Building. We have one at the Docks and one in Albany for patent reasons. I talked to Mr. Ethan tonight and I think we have an additional one in China which none of us knew about. Mrs. Bachman is still involved with it and takes the private plane there on a semi-regular basis, even though she no longer may work for Bachman's."

"We talked with the Director of Transportation, Denzel, tonight and he filled us in on the plane situation. You will want to talk to him. He will give you dates of when Mrs. Bachman or her assistant Hiram Haddad went to China, and how long they were there."

"According to Denzel, they always fly into Guangzhou Baiyan International Airport and go somewhere in Guangdong, China. I have the ISN number of the computer they use the most. I'm sure your IT Department can trace it and find exactly where the location is."

"You are amazing. I need to clone you," Detective Bubb smiles to himself.

"Hang on, there's more. This information we just got tonight from Denzel. I have information from Mrs. Bachman's computer and cell phone, which Mr. Ethan gave me instead of the IT Department. Since you are recording this, I'll reiterate some of the information I've already told you. I've been monitoring both of them ever since I received it. Believing that Mrs. Bachman has a computer at home she is still using for company business. Notifications come to me when she gets an email or text message on her phone. I can read them before she does without her knowing it. Once she reads these messages, she deletes them. They are in code and I don't know what most of them mean or who they are from or for in some cases."

"Do you have a copy, of these messages by any chance?"

"I was afraid of making a copy but I made notes of them and some code words they use. The one which caught my attention was the one less than a month ago after they fired her. It stated: 'We received the package, a bit battered but intact.' I looked to see if there were any more missing people from our company that she could have been talking about as a package. I found Jonathan Kilpatrick and Sandra Sved had activated none of their Severance Packages or salary since they quit the same day Mrs. Bachman was fired. I'm hoping they were put into Witness Protection by the Detectives Rocco and Gibbons."

"Jonathan started working here right after he graduated from Grad School. He never married, and as an only child, he took care of his parents until they both died about 5 years ago. The lab was his life and worked here 60 or 70 plus hours every week. I'm not sure what friends he had outside of Bachman's. What I'm getting at is that I'm not sure anyone would miss him to file a Missing Persons report on him."

"Sandra Sved has a mother still alive but doesn't seem to have much time to visit with her. She again works 60 or 70 hours a week so outside of Bachman's I'm not sure who would report her missing either," Kathy stated.

"I don't know either of those names, so my guess is at this moment they have not been reported missing. I will double check with the others working on this case after I leave here." Bubb remarked.

"Besides the package, were there other words which you felt were codes for something else?"

"Yes, there were words like Golden Thread, Home Brew, Evergreen and Renegade. I think Evergreen and Renegade referred to people, but I don't know who. I do, however, believe these people are high on the food chain, if you know what I mean. The reason I say that is that one email asked if approval was cleared by one or both of them for something to do with Trans-humanism."

"I didn't know what Trans-humanism was, so I goggled it when I was in Dubai. Here is what the Encyclopedia Britannica defines it:[38]

Trans-humanism, social and philosophical movement devoted to promoting the research and development of robust human-enhancement technologies. Such technologies would augment or increase human sensory reception, emotive ability, or cognitive capacity as well as radically improve human health and extend human life spans. Such modifications resulting from the addition of biological or physical technologies would be more or less permanent and integrated into the human body.

"Some of this Trans-humanism is a miracle for many people who need Bionic parts such as hands, arms or legs. These machines enable people such as wounded soldiers who have missing parts because of explosions while on duty overseas. However, there is a negative side to Trans-humanism. This is my opinion, I want to make that very clear, I think this is what Mrs. Bachman is working on. It has to do with DNA of different animals such as the DNA of Eagle's eyes and the capabilities of seeing mice from 2 miles away just as an example and putting it in 'volunteer' humans to create Super Humans. Since this has been going on for years, are these scientists now working on first and second generations?"

"If I am right about this, it would explain why it would have to be done in China. It is unethical for the United States to officially do any kind of these experiments on humans. What they are doing to animals by blending DNA from other animals into humans is unbelievable to me? My guess is yes as they have done to our vegetables, hence Genetically Modified Organism (GMO). Are these vegetables healthy for people? That is for you to decide, and I suggest doing your own research into it. I personally go for certified Organic myself. It's sad to me I have to pay more for natural organic vegetables and they pay less for vegetable which have been modified. It makes little sense to me and that GMO products don't have to be labeled as GMO's. Where is the FDA labeling when we need them? Sorry, I'll get off my soapbox now." Kathy laughs.

"Kathy again I reiterate, You Are Amazing! The information you have just given me is more valuable than you can ever imagine. I can't tell you much right now, but I will tell you this much. This is much larger than you would ever dare want to comprehend. There is an international task force involved and I think the information is exactly what they have been looking for. I wish I could tell you more, but I can't. Detectives Rocco and Gibbons don't have this information, so please keep it private. Please, you can't even discuss this with Mr. Ethan as much as you feel you need to. You might not hear from me for several months, or maybe even a year or more. Rest assured we are working hard to resolve this very delicate situation with the best probable outcome." Detective Bubb assures her.

"I'm sorry, but I have already discussed it with Mr. Ethan and Esther this evening. Denzel told all three of us about the jets and all the information I just gave to you. Also Mr. Ethan was calling the Rocco and Gibbons to fill them in with what we have learned tonight." Kathy informs her.

"Oh, one more thing, Mrs. Bachman is planning on going to China next week for 4 days. Denzel is going to drive her to the plane and pick her up again when she gets back. I'm sure you and your International Investigators might do something with that information. I sure hope you do with no one getting hurt. Take care of my friend and be safe along with your team."

"Thank you so much for all of your research and priceless information. Can this Denzel keep things quiet if we question him about Mrs. Bachman and the timeline of the trips she has taken?"

"Absolutely, that is why Mr. Ethan promoted him to Director of Transportation. He is Mr. Ethan's driver and has been for years. He keeps to himself and doesn't gossip to anyone about what is said in the car's privacy, except maybe to Mr. Ethan. I'm not privy to that information." They both laugh.

"As far as I can tell, Mrs. Bachman does not know we know about China or about the Missing people. We certainly don't want to spook her. We keep it amongst ourselves and always in a safe location." Kathy adds.

"Thank you again, and we'll get together again soon. It's been nice getting together in person for a change." Detective says as she gets into her car.

Detective Bubb was overwhelmed by all the information Kathy just gave her. She is glad she recorded it because she didn't want to forget anything. Let me see, it's almost 10:30. That means it's about 3:30 am to Chief Harry Campbell in London. I owe him a few early morning phone calls, and this is going to be one of them.

"Good morning, sunshine. I hope I didn't wake you like you like to do to me." Jennifer says smiling.

"Good morning, I think, or should I say good evening to you. Have you been to bed yet?" The Chief says trying to sit up in bed.

"I have an actual eye opener for you. If you weren't awoke a few minutes ago, you will be now. The Queen is going to Chinatown next week for 4 days. This is the break we have been waiting for. I'll get you the details and meet you in London in a few hours. I'll catch the red eye. Oh, and we have two more to add to our list." Jennifer says, smiling. She is beside herself with excitement. Sleeping tonight, even on the redeye flight, is going to be hard to find for her.

"Jennifer, you are a delight to wake up to. I am looking forward to hearing from you later today, or should

I say tomorrow, for you," Harry tells her as he gets up, preparing for the day ahead. He has to get the team together, and fast.

London

Detective Bubb stops by the home of her Captain of the Missing Persons Division, William Weber. "I'm so sorry to wake you at this hour, but it's extremely important. We got a break in the investigation on those missing people from The Bachman Corporation and possibly many more. This information is so valuable that I can't take the risk of explaining over the phone to Scotland Yard and the other international organizations which are also working on this case. I have found the missing pieces in this extraordinary case which we have been in searching for so many years. Captain, I need to leave for London tonight and get this information to the right people without causing alarm to the wrong ones. This situation is international as you know and with the information I just received from Kathy McKinney from the Bachman's and with Mr. Ethan Bachman's ok, we have to move on this information immediately. I'm sorry, but I've already booked my ticket and must leave. I'll be back as soon as I can, hopefully tomorrow night." Briskly turning around and ran to her car without waiting for a response. She stopped at her apartment long enough to grab her already packed bag, which she keeps by the front door with her passport and a few hundred dollars just for emergencies like this one. She also mailed off a package to her Captain in case she doesn't come back.

Jennifer arrives at the airport with only a few minutes to spare. She alerts the clerk at the front desk who she is and where she is going, shows them her badge and tells them the importance of her making this flight. The supervisor is called and they hold the plane for her. They literally run through the airport to make the flight on time. Detective Bubb is thinking to herself, *it's a good thing I called ahead and got everything done I could do before getting to the check in line.* As she sits in her seat and tries to get comfortable, she notices her surroundings. She the air flight Marshall is sitting in the same row she is in. She takes some comfort in his presence and puts her headphones on and puts her head back. Sleep might not come, but at least she could rest for now.

Jennifer's head is still spinning for all the information Kathy had given her. Part of her felt negligent for not thinking of talking to the head of Transportation of the Bachman's. Thank God Kathy didn't. We have been looking for the location in China for years. We knew that there was a place these people were going to in China, but we don't know the where and exactly the why or when.

When the plane lands, the Airline Attendant asks everyone to remain seated and comes over to where Jennifer was sitting. She leans over and quietly whispers, "Are Detective Jennifer Bubb?" Jennifer nods. "Please come with me." Jennifer follows her and the Air Marshall follows behind her. She is escorted off the plane, which actually had a comforting effect on her. She knows the information she carries is valuable, but as a second thought, she is now wondering how many other people know what she knows.

Harry is waiting for her at the airport along with 4 other people which Jennifer didn't know personally but their reputation preceded them such as George Stork, the Secretariat of Interpol, the assistant for Mark Mitchell the head of our CIA, the assistant for Nelson Basel of Counter intelligence from Scotland Yard, and Geordan Lenz from Israel. Jennifer is really impressed, especially since she was very limited in what information she had given Harry on the phone.

"Greetings Jennifer, It's so good to see you again," as he shakes her hand. "I would like to introduce you to some very special friends of mine, but first let's go to a place where we can talk privately and safely." Immediately Harry and Jennifer along with their entourage head to another part of the airport where the private jets are located. They enter the jet where they are led to a secure room. There is Mr. Mark Mitchell and Mr. Nelson Basel waiting for them. They rise and introduce themselves to the only person in the room they didn't know personally. "Detective Jennifer Bubb, it is an honor to meet you." Mr. Mitchell states. Jennifer tries to be professional but blushes, anyway.

"It is I who am honored to be here. I hardly gave Harry any information on the phone, so I'm surprised you are all here. The information I have for you is going to be worthy of your time. I assure you!" They sit at the oval table with the assistants, get ready to take notes. Drinks are served, and the work begins.

"As I'm sure you already know, I've been working at the Missing Persons Division for several years. I have been working almost exclusively on the people missing from the Bachman International Corporation. The first person was reported missing about 16 years ago. Several months ago, that list was at 17. This is until Mr. Ethan Bachman found out about it. He was livid and had one of his loyal employees, Ms. Kathy McKinney, who has been working in HR for the past 18 years; assist him in finding out about these employees. She is one of the most amazing investigators I've ever met. Here is a copy of the "spiders' web" she created while on a trip with Mr. Bachman and his executive administrator. She put this together all in less than 2 weeks. I've been trying to find out this information for years. The best part is that Mr. Ethan, as I have been instructed to call him, gave us permission with no search warrant. Mrs. Bachman has been forbidden to step foot in the Bachman building again. So far she has complied with the orders. Just because she isn't allowed in the building doesn't mean however that she has stopped working on her 'top secret projects from the Laboratory.' Mr. Ethan has taken over the operations of the Lab in the basement of the Bachman Building, the lab at the docks, and the lab in Albany. It wasn't until last night that he found out there are additional labs or at least one in China."

"Kathy was given Mrs. Bachman's company computer and cell phone when after she was escorted out of the building the day Mr. Ethan returned from his business trip with Esther and Kathy. Instead of the IT department getting a hold of her computer and her assistant, Mr. Hiram Haddad computer and cell phone, Mr. Ethan made sure Kathy got it with the passwords for each. Apparently Mrs. Bachman doesn't know this computer has not been swept clean and still has access to the information on it.

Mr. Ethan has a special IT expert he uses to let's say get information with no one knowing someone else is seeing the same thing. I'm sure you all know what I'm talking about. I know I'm being a bit long winded, but please bear with me. These details are important. Kathy's has been monitoring the computers and lately strange messages have been coming across her emails or texts. Before you ask, they are coded words which Kathy didn't understand. She's talked to me slightly about them starting about a month ago. I had her keep quiet about them, to Mr. Ethan and Esther. She did until last night. The 3 of them went to dinner with a secure room and Kathy told them what she had found and if it meant anything to them. Words like Golden thread, special packages arriving in China and they not knowing where to put them. Other words like Home Brew, Renegade, and Evergreen. Kathy is certain the last 2 are code names for prominent officials."

"What did she tell you about Renegade and Evergreen?" Mr. Mitchell asks nonchalantly.

"She said the email asked about permission from either of them for a situation dealing with Trans-humanism. There wasn't any other information concerning the email which she could find. I have a good idea who these names are for, but more importantly I have other information which will fill in some of the missing solutions to your intricate puzzle you have been trying to piece together.

Mr. Ethan's driver, Denzel, is the head of the Transportation Division of Bachman's. While Mr. Ethan, Esther Yagel and Kathy were at dinner last night, they asked Denzel if he might know about the use of the company jets. They invited him over to their table for coffee and asked him if Ms. Bachman ever uses one jet and when and where she goes. It just happens that she will leave for China on Sunday morning and staying until Thursday. They will have 2 fueling layovers. One is in London and the other in Athens. Their eventual destination will be to the Guangzhou Baiyan International Airport and they are then picked up by limo and go somewhere in Guangdong, China." Jennifer could tell by the looks are their faces she had hit pay dirt with this information. "By the way, I do have all of my conversation with Kathy from last night recorded." Kathy had made 3 copies, one for Harry and an extra one for herself. She mailed it to a friend for safe-keeping in case something happened to her. She would have made more, but she did not know the other gentlemen would be there.

"Detective, do you believe these 17 missing people could still be alive?" Geordan Lenz inquired.

"I must fill you in on something else Ms. McKinney found. When she was putting the 'spider web' together she found an additional 13 people, which only 2 had been reported missing with my division. All of these 30 people, none of them have collected their paychecks, nor have they filed for workmen's compensation or unemployment. Now I have to add Jonathan Kilpatrick and Sandra Sved to that list..Jonathan Kilpatrick was the Vice President of the Laboratories. Sandra Sved was the Vice President of Public Relations. Both were very close to Mrs. Bachman and worked closely with her. Jonathan was also with Mrs. Bachman on several of the trips to China, as Mr. Denzel confirmed. Both people have also come up missing. They have not collected their severance packages when they quit when Mrs. Bachman was fired. Nobody has heard from either since they were escorted out to their cars.

The video in the car garage shows them getting their cars cleaned out from any Bachman paperwork and computer sticks by the security guard. They got into their cars and drove out of the garage. We have no information after that on either of them. Both were only children. Nobody has come forward to file a missing person's claim of either of them."

"To answer your question, Mr. Lenz, I wasn't positive they were until the Golden Thread email. I believe the 2 Golden Threads refer to these 2 people. Their leaving Bachman's that day was not planned by Mrs. Bachman. She had no time to prepare for their departure to China, but grabbed them after driving out of the parking deck. I believe they were kidnapped as she had done to the others. I also believe George the Security Guard had something to do it but I don't have any evidence of it yet. I know he was the security guard which escorted out all the other missing people." She handed the copy she made to Mr. Mitchell instead of Harry. He agreed with her discussion with a nod to her.

The room grew silent as the gentlemen digested the information she just gave them. She again spoke up boldly, 'I know the information I just gave you is way above my pay grade, but I want involved with the conclusion to this situation. I have dedicated a major part of my police career trying to find these people and I have earned the right to see it through to the end! I say this with all due respect, gentlemen.

George Stork is the next one to speak up. "Detective Bubb, the information you have brought to us today is invaluable to all of our investigations. If you would be as kind as to give us a few minutes to discuss what we have heard with each other, the attendant will show you where you can freshen up and get whatever you would like for breakfast. You must be famished. We will join you shortly for breakfast as well." The attendant appears as on cue and brought Jennifer into a different section of the jet where she needs to use the facilities. She gives her order to the attendant and then proceeds to the restroom.

The attendant is close by when Jennifer emerges from the restroom. "Wow, that sure isn't the same kind of restroom from the airline I just came from." Jennifer laughs. The attendant agrees and brings Jennifer back into the same room the gentlemen were still in.

She sits down, and breakfast is served to everyone. The conversation is light and quite comical. Jennifer didn't know these men are so funny and how down to earth these prominent officials are. She finally relaxes. Breakfast is finished and cleaned up. Coffee and tea are served. The attendant leaves, and the room is secure again.

Mark Mitchell looks at Jennifer and begins asking her more about Kathy McKinney. "We have some information about Ms. McKinney, but we would like to know more about her."

"I really know little about her other than professionally. I know she has a daughter which is graduating from college shortly and will work for Bachman's this summer. I know she was promoted to her current position because of her work on this project. Now, Kathy is the Executive Assistant to Esther Yagel, the Senior Executive Assistant to Mr. Ethan Bachman. Kathy received a very large pay raise, benefits for the executive staff and a new mortgage free home in a gated community where Ms. Esther also lives. Mr. Ethan is very protective of his assistants. I also know that their homes have the best security that money can buy. She is loyal to Mr. Ethan and to Esther. I must say, Kathy is an extremely intelligent person and has a powerful faith in Jesus. She can be trusted without regards to her own safety. Other than that, I know little more than that." She smiles.

"We would also like to talk with her and check out the electronics in her position. We would also like to bring you up to speed on what we can in this situation. Welcome to the team with the blessings of your Captain Weber. He only asks that you come back long enough to bring your replacement up to speed on your other cases."

"Welcome on board Jennifer!" Mike states as he stands to shake her hand. "I must add this. As far as your department knows, you are going on assignment to locate information concerning these people, for right now. Officially you're now part of the CIA, if you so choose to take the assignment."

Laughing, Jennifer says jokingly, "Am I joining Mission Impossible? Of course I accept the assignment and position! There goes another check off my bucket list!"

"Congratulations! Now let's get started on what you don't know." The gentlemen filled her in on their part of the situation, which put all of them on the same page. It was very interesting to her to see all the different countries working together for a solution to a very intricate, sensitive situation with as little carnage as possible. A game plan is created with each leader developing strategies to work together as a well-oiled group, setting aside political differences. This problem is an international, not just a NYC police problem.

Not Saying

The next day Detective Jennifer Bubb works diligently at her desk when Detective Rocco appears from nowhere, or so it seems to Jennifer, startling her. Rocco laughs as she jumps.

"What are you working on that you are so engrossed in this paperwork of yours?" Rocco asked politely.

"Hi Rocco, you scared me half to death. I'm sorry I haven't kept you or Gibbons in the loop for the last several months. We have been busier than you would believe. This case of yours, well, isn't yours. It's mine, and it's huge. We have undercover cops that have been working on this for a few years from other divisions. Scotland Yard is even involved. You do not know what you have stumbled upon. I couldn't really talk to you before about it, and I really can't now. I will say this much. Your department won't be involved with the 30 missing people who used to work at Bachman's International Corporation." Bubb tells him.

"Wait a minute. Are you telling me that you found them all and they are still alive? How can that be? Where are they? Did Isabel have something to do with their disappearance?" Rocco questions her excitedly.

"Whoa, there cowboy! Hold up on the questions. Perhaps I've said too much already. You will know soon enough. I know it must frustrate you but know it's coming to a head soon, well maybe within a year, I pray. It's been amazing working with people from all over. There are so many angles on this investigation bring worked on. Everyone involved seems to have a unique piece of the puzzle. All I can say is the puzzle is almost complete. I'll give you a head up when arrests are going to start. I'm sure there will be some people you will be interested to see in handcuffs." Bubb concludes, giving no answers to his questions for now. "What I have just told you absolutely must be held in strict confidence. I already know you will tell Gibbons, but that is it!"

"That is a lot of information without really saying anything. That actually explains a lot. Usually the Captain is on our case about not making a significant inroad. We still have more questions than answers since this investigation began almost a year ago. I would appreciate being there when Mrs. Isabel Bachman gets arrested and Hiram too!" Rocco says, leaving her back to her paperwork.

"Gibbons, I finally could see Bubb. From what she didn't say, we opened Pandora's Box when we found 30 missing people from the Bachman's International. I don't know what's going on but from what she said there are going to be arrests ASAP or within the year, and she'll let us be there when they make arrests. Hopefully, it will be Mrs. Isabel Bachman and Hiram Haddad." Rocco is excitedly wishful.

"Bubb also said Scotland Yard is involved, and it wasn't our case, meaning it isn't Homicide's Case but Missing persons, except of course Robert Hampton. Gibbons, I don't know how, but from what she implied they are all still alive." Rocco whispers.

"Rocco, how is that even possible." It surprises Gibbons.

"Gibbons, I don't know, but I know it involves Scotland Yard. I bet the CIA and FBI are involved too. She said it was huge. Could it be that Isabel had them all kidnapped, but why and where have they been," Gibbons questions?

"I don't know. I couldn't get any answers before she dismissed me politely." Rocco responds.

"All we can do is to sit on the situation for now. Bubb is going to give us a heads up when they are ready. I sure hope it's soon, for Ethan's sake. He has been extremely patient with our side of the investigation. I know he has had his hands full with the lab at his company since he fired Isabel. I think she's still involved somehow with the company plane and some foreign destinations. Ethan didn't elaborate on the specifics. He said Detective Bubb is working on it with Kathy. She just isn't one to take no for an answer." Rocco continues.

Chapter 26

Back to the Laboratory

After Ethan talked with Detective Rocco this morning, he went directly to his desk at the Lab. He is more curious than usual to see if any one of the Directors or supervisors wrote anything about Trans-humanism or missing people from their departments or divisions.

He went to the Director of the Medical Division report, Deb Williams. He was thrilled to see it is handwritten. Next, he found Karen Allen's handwritten report. He reads Ms. Deb's first.

Dear Mr. Ethan,

I first want to say Thank You sincerely and business career for removing Mrs. Isabel Bachman from the presence of Bachman International Corporation Building. I started working here right from Graduate School 14 years ago. I have been walking on a tight wire almost from day one. That is, until the day she left. We all down here felt like we could breathe for the first time. Though we were unsure of her return, we are now confident she will not.

In the time I have been here, I have witnessed many strange things in this department. We have worked on designing and testing medical equipment for an assortment of special needs clients. Notable prostheses for athletes involved with the Paralympics. It involved many of the clients in a variety of accidents. Many were in car accident or in the Military. They started off simple enough, but as time has proceeded, it has become more Bionic. Some of these replacement limbs are beyond one's imagination. These inventions have changed lives of many disabled people.

Mr. Ethan, I know I didn't totally do as you asked for this report, but please help us find our friends and make our jobs enjoyable instead of terrifying.

Sincerely,
Deb Williams

"Thank you, Deb, for your honesty." Ethan says to himself. Now let's see what Karen has to say.

Dear Mr. Ethan,

You asked for a thorough report, so here it is. I first want to thank you for the honor of being promoted to Director of the Laboratory. I never really thought it would happen with Mrs. Bachman and

Jonathan Kilpatrick in leadership. I thought I hit the glass ceiling.

I have been here for 17 years. I have my PhD in Genetic Disorders and Orthopedics. I have always worked on the research portion of the business to assist people with special physical dysfunctions. I believe we can make their lives easier with the equipment we design specifically for each client. Over the years I have seen this occur many times, and this alone has kept me loving my job.

Every employee still working here today is here because they are creative, dedicated to their job, and are paid well for it. Those I have seen leave here have either left because of Mrs. Bachman or Hiram Haddad. Now that is a man who gave all of us a case of uneasiness.

Mr. Ethan, there have been so many people who have left here and have never been heard from again. They are all from the Medical Division. Most of them have worked on Mrs. Bachman's "special projects" such as Trans-humanism. This is the Bionic prosthesis part which I specialize in. There is another part of Trans-humanism with I will have no part of.

I know there is another laboratory overseas as I overheard different bits and pieces about over the years but I couldn't talk to anyone about in fear for my life. I know Jonathan has been there wherever there is.

I can talk to you more about this outside of this building. I don't think it is a secure place to talk. I am sure she still has this entire department under surveillance, both audio and visual.

I know she still has spies working here. I can guess who they are, but it would only be a guess. Mrs. Bachman has not been back here since you fired her. There are some here who are asking questions about what we are doing on our jobs, which before we're not of any interest to them.

Ethan stops reading her report at this point. Thinking, *I'm sure she has surveillance all over here and maybe right here above this desk. I will call John and take care of that right away.* He took all the reports and stuck them in his briefcase "I've been so busy with trying to get things in order that I totally forgot to have John sanitize the lab."

It is a Surprise

"Hello, Gibbons, here. How can I help you?"

"Hi Gibbons, this is Ethan. It's been over a year and I was wondering how the investigation is going with Robert Hampton's and Charley Barrow's murders?"

"Ethan, you won't believe this, but I was just getting ready to call you. Are you sitting down? First, I want to thank you again for the formula for the drug that killed Robert Hampton and Charley Barrow. To think they made it in the lab with no one else knowing what they were doing. The Medical Examiner's both here and for Charley Barrow concluded that this was the drug that was used for both of their untimely deaths. It took a while, but we discovered how and when Hiram and Isabel used it."

"Hiram put it on Charley's steering wheel of his car just before he got in it to come to the meeting at your office with Andrew. It was a clear powder which absorbs into the skin, causing the heart to become paralyzed."

"Isabel had put it into Robert Hampton's wine glass knowing he would drink the wine that was going to be poured for him. This way nobody else would be affected by the poison. She herself took care of his glass during the commotion of Robert's heart attack. There were enough people who saw her with the glass, which is how we could connect her to the poison. She didn't know anyone was watching, and perhaps they wouldn't have thought anything about it if it wouldn't have been out of character for her to clean up after anyone."

"Second and most importantly, are you ready for marvelous news for a change? Wait for it, wait for it."

"We have all 30 missing people on the way back to the United States shortly. It's taken all this time to get all the different legal organizations such as Interpol, Scotland Yard, and many other country police actions compiling all the pieces of the puzzle to put this together. With the cooperation of the CIA, FBI, Mossads, Scotland Yard and numerous other police forces all over the world, they broke a human trafficking ring of scientists. I know I'm repeating myself, but this has been incredible. The information you and Kathy have provided saved not only years but many lives as well." Gibbons slightly pauses.

"I will go into more details later for you. Right now I have a big favor to ask of you. Will you call Isabel and Hiram into the conference room along with Andrew and Effie Siegel?"

"I have coordinated our Homicide Investigation with the Missing Persons Division to arrest all four of them at once, hopefully with little incidence. Can you make this happen ASAP?" Gibbons requests of Ethan.

"I sure will, and I want as many details as you can give me later. I'll call you right back and get this show on the road today." Ethan promises.

"Hello Isabel, Ethan here."

"What the hell do you want? Haven't you caused me enough grief? What are you calling me for? "Isabel questions.

"I would like you and Hiram to come to the Conference Room at 11 today, if that is possible. I am sure you and Hiram have kept in contact, just to make sure you both are here. I have something special for you both. I'm on my way to Andrew's office to invite him and Mrs. Siegel to be there, too. I think we can resolve these issues all at once. It would mean the world to me for all of you to be here."

"What kind of trick are you trying to pull on Hiram and me? You've done nothing in the past year but humiliate me by having me escorted out of the building the way you did. I didn't deserve that, Ethan! Are you planning on doing that again with me and Hiram? We aren't coming if you are!" Isabel retorts.

"I promise I will not have either of you escorted out. Just be here at 11 and I'll explain everything to all four of you at once. Will you be there?" Ethan asks politely.

"Yes, I want to hear what you have to say for yourself. Hiram is in town for the next few days before flying back overseas. Send a car to us. We'll be at my house." Isabel snarls.

"Thank you. I'll see you both at 11:00," Ethan smiles.

Ethan walks down the hall, and Mrs. Siegel is sitting at her desk as usual. She reaches over to press the intercom button to alert Andrew that he is on his way in, but Ethan is already through the double doors.

"Andrew, I just got off the phone with Isabel. I've invited her and Hiram to the Conference Room at 11 this morning. I have come up with a solution to this situation of ours. I am here to invite you and Mrs. Siegel to join us at 11 as well. Do you think you both can join us?"

"Ethan, I would love it if you and Isabel would bury the hatchet. I love you both so much. This feud between you both is going to give me a heart attack." Just then Mrs. Siegel announces on the intercom that Mrs. Bachman is on the phone and wants to talk with him immediately. He picks up the phone.

"Andrew, what the hell is Ethan up to? I don't trust him. In fact, I never have!" She is yelling so loud that Andrew has the phone away from his ear and Ethan is hearing everything she is screaming.

"He's standing right here. Do you want to ask him?" Andrew offers.

"No, I don't want to talk to him. I will be soon enough. I just want to know what is going on." Isabel lowers her voice.

"I'll call you back. Bye, honey." Andrew says as he is hanging up the phone.

"So tell me, Ethan, what is going on?" Andrew inquires.

"I just need all 4 of you to meet me at 11? It's a surprise." Ethan states as he is leaving the office.

"Hello, Gibbons here, how can I help you?"

"Hello it's Ethan again. I've arranged them all to be in the Conference Room at 11:00. That's not too early for you, is it?"

"No, that's perfect. We'll see you shortly and will meet you at your office in plain clothes. Detective Jennifer Bubb will also be with us." Gibbons hung up.

"Rocco, call Bubb and tell her we are all set for 11 this morning. They will all be in the Conference Room. I'll meet you in the Captain's office and I'm sure we will have to go see the Commissioner." Gibbons says.

"Missing Persons' Division, Detective Bubb speaking."

"Rocco here, we are hitting the bird's nest at 11 this morning. All 4 hawks will be present at a known location."

"We are ready to fly the coup. We are all on standby. See you there. The swat team will be in place." Bubb responds.

"Captain, we will make the arrests for the murders of Robert Hampton and Charley Barrow at 11:00 today at the Bachman's conference room. Detective Bubb and her team will be there with the swat team. They will charge kidnapping and human trafficking amongst other charges after we are through with them. They want to get our victims back to the United States first, and they will land in Dover DE by 3:00p today," Gibbon states.

"I know. Bubb explained it to me earlier. You still have some time. Go see the Commissioner. He will want to be filled in on what exactly is happening. Take Bubb with you. She can finish filling him in on her part of this investigation. Great job by the way. I'll see all 3 of you when you get back this afternoon," The Captain states.

"We are here to see the Commissioner." Detective Bubb tells his assistant.

"He is waiting for you and knows you have a time restriction." He assures them.

"First, I want to congratulate all three of you for jobs well done. This has been a lengthy investigation. I just want to make sure you all have your ducks in a row. I want these charges to stick and you know they are going to try to debunk everything you have done. The Bachman's have the money to do it to the best of their lawyer's ability." Commissioner Newman states.

"My department and entities from all over the world have been working on this case for years. When these two guys gave the additional names a year ago plus the dates when everyone disappeared, it fit into place with investigations of other departments which needed names to go along with the people they were following which they knew were kidnapped." Bubb says.

"There are people from all over the world involved with this Human Trafficking ring which was arrested this morning. Andrew and Isabel Bachman, Hiram Haddad, and Effie Siegel are only four of the big names being arrested right now. There will be more today and also within the next few days. It fit in perfectly with the timeline with Detectives Rocco and Gibbons. We are all set for the arrests to take place at the Bachman's offices at 11 this morning for the Bachman's and for their Executive Assistants." Bubb continues.

"Ethan Bachman has set it up that Isabel and Hiram will be in the office at 11. This way we can do all the arrests in one place with the least amount of resistance. We have enough evidence on Isabel and Hiram for the poisoning of Robert Hampton, and Charley Barrow. Andrew, with his secretary, Effie Siegel's for the knowledge of the death of Charley Barrow. We have proven they both had full knowledge of it before it happened. We have them for conspiracy to commit murder." Gibbons points out.

"What has been so incredibly amazing to me is how long this trafficking ring has been going on, over 50 years, with little to no detection. All these people from all over the world were kidnapped and forced to work on scientific projects for the Chinese. It was only by the grace of God and talking to the right people with a new piece of information that we found where they were. It's taken the cooperation of police departments all over the world to pull this off. We are getting all 30 of our people back from Bachman's. Others weren't so lucky. The labs from deep within China were raided several hours ago. Some didn't make it out. The Chinese government wasn't very cooperative. I am in awe of our undercover attack forces. There are over 200 scientists which have been rescued, over 100 from the United States alone. Our people should arrive about 3:00 in Dover, DE. Military planes sure fly faster than commercial airlines. Oh, and by the way, if it weren't for the President's assistance none of this would have happened. He has been incredible. Doors were opened for the use of military I didn't think would ever open. Anyway, our people are safely on their way home." Bubb concludes.

"Again, your jobs were well done. I'm very proud of all the work that went into these arrests. Thank you all!" Commissioner exclaims proudly.

Chapter 28

The Set Up

Ethan is working on some paperwork when Isabel and Hiram walk into the Conference room. She does *know how to make an entrance,* Ethan thinks to himself. *Like a bull in a China Shop*. Isabel is already yelling at him as usual. *I haven't missed this at all this past year. I bet our employees haven't either.*

"Nice to see you too, Isabel," Ethan says sarcastically. "Andrew is on his way here. Then we will get started. Hiram, how has China been? I've heard you have spent most of this past year overseas." Hiram didn't answer him. Just then Andrew and Effie Siegel walk into the room.

"Now we can get started. Please, everyone have a seat." Ethan looks down at his phone. He has just received a text stating the police are in the lobby and are on their way up.

"I'm going to make this short. Isabel, you are one of the most beautiful, intelligent women I have ever met in my life. You are elegant and poised. Just as glorious as you are on the outside, you are also the darkest and most evil woman I have ever met. With that being said, you never should have been allowed to work here. You took advantage by creating products our company would have never allowed."

"Hiram, your dedication to Isabel is admirable. Few people in this world find such dedication for as long as you two have known each other. I understand you have been by her side since the beginning of college." Hiram nodded.

`Hiram, you helped her in ways you should have never done. Does she have something hanging over you would so blindly follow her into the darkest realms of life? Maybe it's the other way around; perhaps you have something over her, maybe both!"

"Andrew, I have always loved you like a brother, and I have missed our closeness. We could talk to each other about everything and anything. That unfortunately has not been the case for a very long time."

"Effie, your dedication to Andrew has also been admirable. I understand you and Hiram are close friends. Perhaps you are the only other's friend in the entire building. You have known about what has been going on in the Laboratory from almost the start. Have you filled Andrew with all of your knowledge? I would like to think that you kept him in the dark about most of it without his knowledge. I have a hard time believing Andrew knew all of what you three were up to!"

"Andrew, you allowed your wife to have free rein over the Laboratory without really knowing what she and Hiram were doing, but now you will find out. You all are responsible for the disappearance of 30 of our most outstanding and intelligent Scientists, we have had employed here in the Engineering, Medical Division of the Laboratory." Andrew has a questionable look on his face as he looks over to Isabel."

"Isabel, what is he talking about? Explain it to me. What Scientists. Who has disappeared?" Andrew wants to know.

"Oh, my dear cousin, it gets worse. They had Charley Barrow and Robert Hampton murdered. They were two of the most precious people I had ever known. For what Andrew and Isabel were they murdered for, a winery, an obsession of Andrew's. Was that really that important to you, that they had to be murdered so you could possess something you weren't meant to own? They were wonderful people and now they are dead."

Ethan is now gaining more strength again. "The four of you are responsible for some of the most outrageous behaviors and actions, and the time to pay the piper has arrived." With a simple gesture, the police come around the corner with guns out.

Rocco, Gibbons and Bubb each state, "I have arrest warrants for Isabel Bachman, her executive assistant, Hiram Haddad, Andrew Bachman and his executive assistant, Effie Siegel.

There are more than enough police officers to make the arrests of all four individuals. The rest of the police are going to the offices of Effie and Andrew's searching and confiscates their computers and office materials, which relate to the Laboratory and China.

Rocco states, "We have arrest warrants for Andrew and Isabel Bachman on the charges of the murders of Robert Hampton and Charles Barrow. A warrant is also for the arrest of Hiram Haddad, for murder of Charley Barrow and other unrelated deaths. We also have an arrest warrant for Effie Siegel for conspiracy to commit murder. All four are also being charged with kidnapping, and International Human Trafficking. The charges include over 50 charges which will be explained to you each at the station, The warrants also includes the search and seize of Effie Siegel's and Andrew Bachman's computer, cell phones along with any objects of electronics and digital products. The warrants also include all paperwork related to these charges for the offices here and at your homes. Please stand up and put your hands behind your backs. I will now read you your Miranda Rights," Rocco states.

"You are under arrest. Before we ask you any questions, you must understand what your Miranda Rights are:"

"You have the right to remain silent. You are not required to say anything to us at any time or to answer any questions. Anything you say can be used against you in court."

"You have the right to talk to a lawyer for advice before we question you and to have him or her with you during questioning."

"If you cannot afford a lawyer and want one, a lawyer will be provided for you."

"If you want to answer questions now without a lawyer present, you will still have the right to stop answering at any time. You also have the right to stop answering at any time until you talk to a lawyer."[(37)]

"Do you understand your rights?" He asks each one of them.

Andrew" Yes", Hiram, "Yes", Effie "Yes"

Isabel responds with, "Of course I do. What do you think I am, an Idiot! No, we have our own lawyers and don't need you to get us one.

Once they finish reading the Miranda rights to all four of them and they say they understand their rights, they are led out of the conference room.

"What the hell have you done, Ethan? You haven't heard the last of me! Let go of me. I can walk by myself. You don't need to put those things on me. Stop it, they are too tight. They are hurting me. Take those cuffs off of me. I demand it. Take them off. I am not walking out of this office with those cuffs on. Take the cuffs off of me. Are you listening to me? Do you know who I am?" The police ignore her demands.

Isabel and Andrew Bachman, Hiram Haddad and Effie Seigel are being led away with their hands cuffed behind their back and Isabel yelling at Hiram to call their lawyer. Hiram is also being arrested for his involvement in several other unrelated unsolved murder cases, such as missing men from his local bar establishment he frequencies. Isabel didn't notice that he was handcuffed as well. She is only concerned about herself and Andrew.

The office staff are standing there with their mouths wide open and whispering as to what is going on. Esther and Kathy watch in amazement and whisper to each other they were so glad this part is finally happening.

The docket at the courthouse is so full the four of them are sent to jail overnight. They schedule the preliminary hearing for first thing in the morning, and the lawyers for Isabel and Andrew can't do anything about it.

The charges of double murder and kidnapping are being filed. They are standing before the Judge for the preliminary hearing. Of course, they plead not guilty and "didn't know what the Prosecutor is talking about."

" The two counts of murder in the first degree of Robert Hampton and Charley Barrow are now on record. It is also my understanding that there will be more charges to be filed against Isabel Bachman, Hiram Haddad and

Effie Siegel for kidnapping and human trafficking, but at a later date." The Honorable Judge Peter Lovecchio pronounces as he brought down his caviling hammer. Isabel and Andrew Bachman, and Hiram Haddad and Effie Siegel were being charged for 1st degree murder, 2 counts contracting for murder for Isabel Bachman and Hiram Haddad. Their smooth talking lawyers got the Bachman's out on house arrest and with a $500,000,000.00 Bond along with turning over their passports. They will also not have access to the company jets as well. They sent Hiram and Effie to Reichert until their trials. Because of Hiram's direct involvement in the two murders and Effie's trial for conspiring to commit murder is the reason for their direct incarceration. They're also considered both as flight risks."

The press with all their cameras and microphones are waiting outside of the courthouse as the Bachman's are exiting through the heavy oak doors. Isabel raises her head and put on her most dignified appearance. Without saying a word, both Isabel and Andrew got into the Company limo, waiting for them.

The Aftermath

Patty Butler, Elizabeth Brittney, and Sammi Benson hug each other when they got to the plane. They are so excited to see each other. It has been years, and both lived the past several years as slaves for Isabel and the Chinese Government. Never in their wildest imagination did they think living as a slave would even be possible as an America citizen. Yet here they are. They were forced to work as slaves, kidnapped from American and forced to work on things unethical and immoral. What they had to do to survive made them sick, literally. Nobody cared. They watched other scientists from other countries refusing to do what they were told and murdered on the spot. Someone else was forced to take their place. If they refused, they were shot in the head immediately and someone else was forced to do the job. The rest of us were just told to get back to work. They were also abused in many horrific ways. Now for the first time in years there is hope. Now they were getting on a military plane. They feel safe for the first time since they were escorted out of the Bachman Building.

"Nothing was the same after I got fired and escorted out to my car by George. I got to my car and put my belongings in the back seat and drove out of the parking deck. Within 2 blocks my car stopped and was out of gas." Everyone in earshot was all agreeing the same thing happened to them.

"I know I had a full tank of gas when I drove into the garage that morning. A tow truck shows up suddenly without me even having time to call my insurance company to help. The driver comes over to my car so I open my window and without warning he attacks me with chloroform. The next thing I knew was I was on a plane with my legs and wrists bound. Once we landed, I was blindfolded and put into the back of a car and taken to a lab somewhere in China. I wasn't alone. There were about 4 of us altogether." Patty comments.

Even though they were kidnapped at different times, the routine was the same as they determined. Now they just want to go home to America. They all are relived once the plane is in the air and over the ocean.

"Ladies and Gentlemen, we are now in International Air Space." The pilot announces. They cried with tears of joy while others passed out from exhaustion and while others felt they were safe enough to let go of their paralyzing fear.

Without incident, the plane lands in Dover, DE. The military plane had approximately 325 people on it from China and military personal. All the passengers felt some degree of trauma but thankful to be back on American soil. Some passengers like Philip Bryant and Joseph Harris it had been almost 18 years since they were kidnapped.

They gave up hope from every having freedom again, let alone finding themselves back in American again.

Philip and Joseph sit next to each other on the plane. Most of the time, they were in the same lab, working side by side together. Every once in a while they were taken somewhere else in China to work at another lab, but they were blindfolded and we not allowed to talk while on these excursions. There were always several armed guards, and they meant business. "

I'm glad we were smart enough to keep our mouths shut most of the time. Sometimes someone new would arrive and mouth off to one of guards. It did not go well for that person. They usually received the butt end of the rifle across their skull. Once I saw them shot this guy dead right in front of all of us just for saying where am I? The guard got screamed at killing one asset. We never saw that guard again. Philip thought he was saying to himself, but Joseph heard him." Joseph recalls the same situation. "I was thinking about the same thing," as the plane is landing.

"It's been so long since I've cried that I don't even know if I can anymore. I'm just so thankful to be in the USA." Philip states.

Many of the passengers are very emotional, others are wide eyed and looking around and making sure they are really in America. All the passengers need a shower and a place to clean up. They need to put on regular clothes too.

Everything happened so fast. The shouting, the sound of bullets close by then the mix of American Military, Scotland Yard, CIA, and maybe even the Navy Seals were all there. They came into the Laboratories with a full blaze of glory. People were screaming in Chinese and English.

There was so much confusion. The scientists weren't sure what was happening. The Chinese were screaming at them to drop on the floor and be quiet or they were going to shoot them all dead. Yet there were American voices gathering people out of the different Laboratories and escorting them down the halls with guns firing.

The Laboratory which Jerry McFarley worked in only had one guard left in it. " As the other guards left to find out what was going on, we were lying on the floor. We knew we were being rescued. A few of us fought back. While the guard had his back turned away from us, I got up and tackled the guard. There were 3 other guys that helped me hold him while we got the other people out and into the halls. We knocked out the guard and took his gun and escaped. We found the other people leaving and joined them. There were four of us that wanted to go back in and try to help others, but we were told to stay with the group. They would get everyone out safely." The Commander told them. Jerry was recounting the events which occurred only a short time ago to all those who were listening.

"I can't believe I'm back. Thank you, thank you, and thank you." He says as he hugs one soldier. "I don't know how to thank you for saving our lives. We never thought we would ever get out of there." Jerry continues.

"Ladies and Gentlemen, please keep moving. We need to get you indoors." The Officer commanded.

Once they land they are directed inside the hanger, the Americans from China are separated into groups. Canadians gather together. People from the west coast are put in one group. The Midwest is next to stand together. East of the Mississippi River and south of the

Mason Dixon line stood off to the side in another group. The last group standing is those from the Northeast. This is the largest group.

"I need all those that worked at Bachman's Tool and Dye Company to stand over here." The Officer said. "All 30 missing personal are all here and accounted for." One soldier announces to the Officer.

"As much as I wish we could send you all home tonight, I'm afraid you will have to stay here for a day or so. You will need to be debriefed. Doesn't a good hot shower or bath sound good along with new clothes? How about your favorite meal brought up to your room? We have arranged rooms for all of you."

"Everyone will move onto our next destination shortly. Water and restrooms for those who need them right now are available. We are waiting for a plane to arrive momentarily. The people on that plane are those responsible for putting the final informational pieces together, which were essential for your rescue. Without their investigations, it might have been several more years before we found out where you were." The Commander explains.

In the distance they hear the private jet coming in for a landing.

Immediately after the arrests of Isabel and Andrew Bachman, Hiram Haddad, and Effie Siegel leaving the Bachman Building, there was a flurry of excitement. Ethan made an announcement for all personal to enjoy a long weekend. They were free to go with pay for the rest of the day off. Meanwhile, Ethan, Esther, Kathy, Denzel, Detectives Jennifer Bubb, Dan Gibbons, and John Rocco boarded the Bachman Company jet and flew down to Dover. DE. The plane from China had landed almost an hour ago. The pilots are ordered to land next to the military plane at the same hanger.

Upon entering the hanger, a great applause broke out as the group whistled and shouted, "Thank you." The Scientists are sobbing with tears of joy again. "I see even the soldiers standing guard for their safety wiping away a tear or two." Patty whispered.

"Ladies and Gentlemen, Let me introduce you to the people responsible for breaking this case wide open and supplying the vital information which enabled your rescue. First, let me introduce Detective Jennifer Bubb. She has been working in the Missing Persons Division for over 8 years and has been working on the missing people from Bachman's Tool and Dye Company ever since she started working in that division. She has worked closely with Scotland Yard with their missing scientists amongst other law enforcement divisions throughout the world." Applause erupted again for Detective Bubb. Commander Drew Brandon pauses.

"Next up are Detectives Daniel Gibbons and Detectives John Rocco. They work in the Homicide Division in New York City. They were working on a murder investigation of one employee, Robert Hampton, from Bachman's International Corporation. The company was new named as of last year as I understand it. The Detectives 'stumbled' on the list of Missing People from Bachman's. At the time of Mr. Hampton's death, the Missing Person's Division only knew of 17 people missing." The Commander continues.

"For those of you who do not know this gentleman, this is Mr. Ethan Bachman. He is one owner of Bachman International Corporation. Working closely with the Detectives on the homicide, he accidentally found out one of his scientist had come up missing after the murder. This is when he pulled Kathy McKinney out of Human Resources to work with him and Mrs. Esther Yagel, his Executive Assistant. Mrs. Kathy McKinney is the person, ladies' and gentlemen, who found where you were and how long you have been there. We didn't know most of your names from Bachman's until Kathy found you. Mr. Denzel unknowingly had the ultimate pieces of the puzzle." The people started crying and rushed in to thank them. "Hold on, there's more. Through a series of events, these 4 people put together where you were and notified the Detectives where you were being taken. They also found out how you were being smuggled out of the country and when. These people are your genuine heroes, along with your rescued squad," The Commander smiles.

"Mr. Bachman has arranged for your flights home when you are given the clearance. The Doctors will check you out and make sure you are ok. If you have questions, please don't hesitate to ask. You all have gone through quite the ordeal and we want to make sure everything is ok with you."

"Some of you will have to be caught up on the latest technology for the average people like the new iPhones, wrist watch computers, and Tablets. Not the kind Moses had." Everyone either laughed or shrugged their shoulders.

"Ladies and Gentlemen, Welcome Home. We all worked as a team and got you home as quickly as we could. You will also go home as quickly as we can get you there. I want you to hear this from me before you hear it on the news. Concerning the employees from Bachman's the wife of the other owner of Bachman's International Corporation, Isabel Bachman was responsible for your disappearance.

They have arrested Isabel and Andrew Bachman as of a few hours ago. Their Executive Assistants, Hiram Haddad and Effie Siegel, were arrested as well for their knowledge or involvement in your disappearance as well. There is still an active investigation going on and the end is not in sight yet. We found you and got you all out of there as fast as we could. Hopefully, your testimonies will help close more doors and they will make more arrests. For now, we thank God you are here and safe." Ethan notes.

A line forms and everyone comes up to shake their hands or give hugs to all of them. Jonathan Kilpatrick and Sandra Sved were the last in line.

Jonathan approaches first. "Mr. Ethan, I am so sorry for all of this. I knew where they were and couldn't do anything about it. I was married when I first started working at Bachman's. Isabel had her murdered. It was an 'accident' but Isabel let it slip one time that it was on purpose. After that slip she never let me forget it and it would happen again if I tried to leave without her permission. Every time I tried to get away from the situation, someone else close to me would die. Both of my parents have died because of Isabel or Hiram. I didn't know what to do. I am so sorry. When you fired Isabel that day, I knew I was in serious trouble. I left to go into hiding. Hiram knocked me out as I got out of my car when I ran out of gas. I think he did the same to Sandra. All I know is we woke up some place dingy and were chained to our beds. I'm not sure how long we were there, but I think it was several weeks. They drugged us up most of the time and before I knew it I woke up on the plane going to China where the other scientists disappeared to. What is going to happen to me now?"

Sandra speaks up next. "Mr. Ethan I knew she made people disappear, but I didn't know where or how. I too was afraid of 'disappearing' myself. I kept my nose out of it, but now I wish I hadn't. What an awful place, what an awful and evil woman she is. How could I have been so deceived? I always thought of myself as an excellent judge of character. How could I have been so wrong about her? Mr. Ethan, what they did to us and all those people, and how they were forcing them to live, and the working conditions are right out of a horror movie. I wouldn't have believed it had I not seen it for myself." She begins sobbing. The flood gates have finally opened. She pulls herself together. "The world needs to know what is happening in the medical field. It's not just China but other countries are creating inhuman distortions of people's bodies. They are making super humans but those the experiments don't work correctly are like Frankenstein's monster. It must stop. I'll be glad to testify against her and Hiram."

Ethan whispers quietly to both of them, "I'm not sure what will happen to you both for your knowledge of this before they took you. I'm sure the courts will find lenience on you for your own ordeal in this. I'm very thankful you both made it back here safely." Ethan truly means it."

The Fall

Denzel was driving the limo from the courthouse. "Sir, Mrs. Bachman, where would you like me to drop you off at? Mr. Bachman, your car is still at the office."

"Take us to the office. I'll drive us both home from there." Andrew answers.

Isabel and Andrew get into his car. Isabel is humiliated and angry. Andrew gets home with no news crews following them. Andrew is driving into the garage and neither Isabel nor Andrew notice Ethan's Jaguar parked by the entranceway. Most of the way home from the Court House, Isabel is unusually quiet. She keeps looking into the mirror. She adjusts and primps her hair and applies more makeup as if she is going out for the evening. Andrew is waiting for her explosive temper to hit, and when it did, it was like no other he has ever experienced. She becomes a banshee woman again! She begins yelling and screaming so violently that she even spits on the windshield.

She is so angry with Andrew, but her hatred for Ethan has hit a new height.

"It is all Ethan's fault. He's the one who has caused all this mess. He is so damn self-righteousness. I want him dead, Andrew. I don't care what YOU have to do to accomplish it, but I want him DEAD!!! DO YOU HEAR ME ANDREW? I WANT HIM DEAD. WHATEVER IT TAKES, WHATEVER THE COSTS!! HE MUST DIE AND SOON."

"Isabel, wanting Charley dead, has caused this whole situation. You always want everyone dead and now your plans are now available for everyone to see," Andrew is yelling back at her. Isabel opens the car door once the car stops in the garage and they are walking into the kitchen. She is still shouting.

"Andrew, you're the one who wanted Charley dead. I never could comprehend why you wanted that damn winery, anyway. I only did what you didn't have the guts to do."

"You Isabel were the one who ordered the hit on Charley. Only you could have done it, and now there is evidence to prove it. I'm not going down with you. I refuse to go back to that jail!

"You have your black magic and friends in prominent places. You make this go away, Isabel!" In fact, your bodyguards Sid Jehu along with Paul Blumenthal have done so much killing for you I've lost count of just how many. I bet they are in the house right now, waiting for you. Why don't you just ask them to take care of this for you when we get there?" Andrew adds.

"If it weren't so obvious I would, but I can't and you know it."

"We wouldn't be in this mess if you didn't want that winery so badly! You make it right, Andrew, and do it

now! Do you hear me? Correct this problem permanently, NOW," screams Isabel.

Andrew retaliates with, **"Don't give me this innocent attitude of yours. You were the one who had Robert poisoned and made it look like a heart attack. What are you going to do when they find out you did the same thing to Ethan's wife Linda and talking about Linda, I bet if Ethan had her exhumed they will still find the chip you had implanted in her to have her be sterile?"**

"SHUT UP YOU IDIOT!! The walls always have ears!" Isabel screams.

"You promised we would never talk about it again, and now you bring it up. Just shut up. I never want to hear her name again. I told you that before, and I mean it!" Isabel retorts.

She is right. Unbeknownst to Isabel and Andrew, Ethan is waiting for them in the den. He is talking to Sid and Paul while he is petting the dogs. When he hears the poisonous venom, Andrew and she just spewed out of their mouths. Andrew's own words are almost more than Ethan can comprehend. Ethan's heart sinks. He can't believe what he just heard. Now anger builds and escalates inside of him. Anger such as he has never known before. His mind is racing.

Ethan suddenly remembers stories about the deaths, about his baby cousin, Isabel, and Andrew's youngest son. Andrew had turned away from his Christian upbringing when he married Isabel. He went to the wicked side of religion. His attitude over the years became more blatant, dishonest, rude, and conniving. Now he was wondering if the stories were true, that his cousin had resulted from being a sacrifice to Satan himself to get ahead in the corporate world. The disgust he feels is almost overwhelming. It appalls him, the thoughts he is thinking, but deep inside he knows he is right. Ethan doubles over, sick to his stomach. He wants to throw up, but he is so angry. Standing upright, he thinks about the here and now. He has to address what he just heard. Just then Isabel comes around the corner and is heading up the staircase. She is almost at the top of the landing when Ethan appears at the bottom of the stairs with his phone in his hand as he dials 911.

"911, what is your emergency?" the operator requests. Ethan doesn't hear her.

"ISABEL," Ethan demands. Startling Isabel by hearing Ethan's voice, Isabel pivots around to find him at the bottom of her stairs.

"What are you doing here, Ethan? Get the hell out of my house now!"

"Oh, I will leave after the police arrive, Isabel. I now know the truth about Linda! I beat myself up for all these years because I wasn't there for her when she needed me the most. Now I find out that you had planned it that way. **YOU MURDERED HER!!** I will make sure you will never see the light of day again outside of prison. You make me sick!" Ethan tells her as he stares directly into her evil black eyes.

Anger burns inside of him, yet he keeps himself under control. The courts would deal with her. He hears the operator talking and told her where he is and he wants to report a murder. He turns to leave the house, but she lunges at him, screaming and clawing at his face. Just then the security dogs come running through the house, but instead of attacking Ethan, they attack Isabel. She runs back up the upstairs; the dogs follow her, nipping and tearing at the bottom of her pants. The dogs are full of adrenalin, snarling. Suddenly one dog jumps up on her. Sid and Paul run up the stairs, trying to get the dogs off of her. She loses her footing. The men try to grab her but accidentally cause her to slam against the window, shattering it. Some of her blood splatters on the wall. In that split second, the men look at each other, knowing that she is the only who knows all the evil things they have done for her, decide to throw her out the window [(38)]. Isabel plummets out of the stained-glass window with the dogs jumping out the window, following her. Glass falls on top of her motionless body.

It happens so fast that Andrew did not have the time to call off the dogs.

Ethan, Andrew, Paul and Sid run out the door to the back patio. The dogs tear open Isabel's throat, blood pulsates from her carotid artery in her neck. The blood drains from her body so quickly there is nothing anyone could do. She is dead within moments. The four men come around the corner onto the patio where the dogs are attacking Isabel. Sid tries to get the dogs off of her and slips in all the blood and kicks Isabel in the face several times. The dogs are in a frenzy because of all the blood. They keep tearing at her face and thrashed at her neck until her head pops off her body. The dogs run with head dripping with blood, fighting to take possession of it. Her face is torn and unrecognizable.

Andrew falls to his knees and is begging Ethan for forgiveness; Ethan just walks away and then notices the 911 operator is still on the phone, recording what is happening. The scene quiets down the 911 operator calls out

Ethan's name, tells him the police are on their way. The operator inquirers is the mansion called Jezreel Mansion. Ethan confirms, yes it is correct.

Paul and Sid hear the police sirens in the distance, coming closer. "Sid, we have to get out of here. Ethan saw us throw her out the window." At that Paul and Sid ran to Paul's car and made it out of the gate just as the first police are arrived.

The police arrive, with all their sirens piercing and disrupting the serene neighborhood, just moments after the operator tells Ethan they are on their way. Andrew is shouting at the dogs and trying to pull them off his beloved dead wife's head. The dogs run off with it as the police cars skidded into the driveway. Andrew is covered in Isabel's blood, looking up in distress, and runs back into the house.

"What am I going to do; I can't go back to that jail again. Oh Isabel, tell me what to do, but you can't. You're dead. The dogs killed you. I can't live without you, my love. There is only one thing to do. I have to get my gun. Isabel: I'm coming to join you. Ethan, why did you have to be here! You should have stayed away from here like Isabel said." Andrew says out loud to himself.

"It's your entire fault my wife is dead. I can't go back to jail. Ah, there it is: my pistol. I know its Ethan's fault. He needs to die too because of Isabel. Isabel, he will not get away with your murder... Yes, he needs to die too! Isabel told me he has to die, and now I agree with her. He has to die!" Andrew rants as he reaches the back door.

"Ethan, it's your entire fault that my beloved Isabel is dead! Now you're going to die. Do you hear me? I'm not going back to that jail."

The dogs suddenly run back to Isabel's body. They are tearing at her torso in a wild frenzy again. One of the swat team throws out what he thinks is a smoke grenade, it is actually a real grenade, and it lands onto her torso. The dogs are running away and her torso blows up into a thousand pieces. Only her feet and hands are left behind.[39]

Andrew is out of his mind in shock. He raises the gun up to aim at Ethan and doesn't notice the police standing there. Suddenly he hears people from what seems like a far distance away telling him something, but he doesn't understand what they are saying. All Andrew knows is his Isabel is dead and Ethan needs to die for it.

He turns to look at who is talking to him, but everything is a blur.

"Where are all those lights coming from? Why are there were so many people in my backyard? Ethan, where did you go," he mumbles?

Suddenly he runs out to the perfectly manicured, thick hedges to find Ethan and sees someone grab Ethan from behind and pull him behind the side of the house. It is a police officer.

"Why are there so many people in my backyard? Did Isabel plan a party she forgot to tell me about again? No, she's dead. Ethan killed her. I have to find him and kill him too!"

"Why are the police here? Do they know he murdered Isabel? I have to kill him for Isabel." Andrew tells himself.

Andrew moves in the direction toward Ethan. He hears those voices again, but he has to focus on Ethan. He raises his gun as Ethan gets back into view again. Suddenly he hears a loud bang, then feels a hard pinch on his right side and a burning sensation coursing through the inside of his body and out through his left side.

"What just happened", he wonders to himself? He is falling to his knees and falls onto the grass next to Isabel. They're both laying there, one dead and the other one has a fatal bullet wound. Their blood is blending together. Andrew reaches over and tries to put his hand onto hers, but he couldn't quite reach her as the police arrive at his side.

"Help me. I can't reach her." He asks as he draws his last breath.

Epilogue

Ethan's Office

Ethan is sitting in the office, staring at Linda's picture. He is now the Chairman of the Board, and Peter Loy is the new CEO. He knows nothing could bring her back, yet he feels some peace that Linda did not die in vain. Her killer had almost gotten away with her murder. Isabel had used the same poison to kill Robert Hampton as she did for Linda. His thoughts wondered *how many others in her path she did the same thing to.*

Speaking out loud, *I know there is still an ongoing investigation on the employees which were kidnapped. What a web of deception for what money, power, control? All those lives ruined for just a few to get ahead on this life.* 'Jesus help all those people and their families to heal from this situation.'

One conversation Ethan had with the police after that horrible day with Andrew and Isabel was about Paul Blumenthal and Sid Jehu. He saw them help Isabel fall through the window. He knew if anyone besides Hiram knew about the evil things which Isabel had done to others; it is these 2 people he told Rocco and Gibbons.

Ethan suggests to the Detectives they use this information to take the Death Penalty off the table if they will tell everything which Isabel had them do for her. "Hopefully it will bring some closure to someone's family."

He feels better about starting the process of restoring The Brotherhood Winery to its rightful owners and vows to restore the damages Andrew had caused the company. He could not bring Charley back, but he could restore the family business and make the financial arrangements to make it thrive to levels above and beyond the call of duty. It is his pleasure to make things right.

Ethan took Athea and Jo out of their boarding schools and brought them home for the funerals. He wants them to live with him and know how much he loves them. Unfortunately, they never made it home. There was a terrible car accident coming from the airport. An over the road truck, Jehu International Trucking, lost control after a tire blew out. The limo they were in went right under the truck. It took off the top of the car, along with Jo's head and a piece of metal sticking out of his chest.

Athea survived the accident but has permanent brain damage. She had to be admitted into Bellevue Hospital for the criminally insane. She had become a danger to herself and to others when she tried to kill Ethan and anyone else who came near her.

The Prayer

This prayer is from 'The American Awakening' by TommieZito.com

My name is Vonnie.

I've got to tell you 2 things real quick, that God loves you and has an awesome plan for your life. I've got to ask you a real quick question: If you were to die today, do you know for sure, without a shadow of a doubt, that you would go straight to heaven?

No or I think so:

Great! Let me tell you 3 things the Bible says real quickly.

1. It says, "For all have sinned and come short of the Glory of God.

2. It says, "The wages of sin is death, but the FREE gift of God is eternal life through Jesus Christ."

3. It says that, "WHO SO EVER calls upon the Name of the Lord will be saved, and you're a who so ever." Right? Of course you are – we all are. I'm going to say a quick prayer for you.

Lord, I pray that you bless (your name) and his/her family with long and healthy lives. Make yourself so real to him/her, and if (your name) has never received Jesus Christ as his /her Lord and Savior, I pray that he/she would do so right now (your name). If you would like to receive this free gift, Jesus Christ as your Lord and Savior, just say this with me:

Say this prayer out loud. Let the Lord hear your voice:

> JESUS, COME INTO MY HEART. FORGIVE ME OF MY SINS. WASH ME. CHANGE ME AND SET ME FREE. LET ME NEVER BE THE SAME AGAIN. JESUS, I BELIEVE YOU DIED FOR ME. HELP ME TO LIVE FOR YOU AND FULFILL EVERYTHING YOU HAVE CALLED ME TO DO. I THANK YOU THAT I'M NOW FORGIVEN AND ON MY WAY TO HEAVEN, IN JESUS' NAME Amen.

I have the best news anyone will ever tell you. As a minister of the Gospel of Jesus Christ, I tell you today that all your sins are forgiven you right now! And you can know for sure that you're on your way to Heaven. Remember, when you make a mistake, don't run from God, run to Him, because He loves you and He does have an awesome plan for your life!

Now find a church you will be fed the Bible scriptures. This church can be a house church, a brick and mortar building, or an online church. Ask Jesus to help you and you will find love and support with other Christians. Learning and reading the Bible are your lifelines. You might want to start with the book of John in the New Testament. There is a scripture in the Bible which Jesus had written just for you. Your mission is to find it and share what you learn with others. Bring to others the free gift which Jesus just gave you.

DEAR HOLY SPIRIT AS THEY READ THEIR BIBLES HELP THEM TO UNDERSTAND WHAT THEY ARE READING. GUIDE THEM TO WHAT THEY NEED TO LEARN WHICH WILL GIVE THEM HOPE, LOVE, AND JOY IN THEIR LIVES. In Jesus' name Amen.

References

(1) Bible, New American Standard Version, I Kings 16:28-30 King Omri and King Ahab, Retrieved on April 25, 2017 from https://www.biblegateway.com/versions/New-American-Standard-Bible-NASB/

(2) The Brotherhood Winery, Retrieved on May 27, 2012 f rom www.brotherhoodwinery.com

https://wwwlfdtool.com/catalog/indexc.html#/

(3) Bible, New American Standard Version, I Kings 16:31, King Ethbaal Retrieved on April 25, 2017 from https://www.biblegateway.com/versions/New-American-Standard-Bible-NASB/

(4) Bible, New International Version, Exodus 20:1-17. The 10 Commandments Retrieved on April 25, 2017 from https://www.biblegateway.com/passage/?search=Exodus+20%3A1-17&version=NIV

(5) Bible, New International Version Ephesians 6:2-3 Retrieved on April 25, 2017 from https://www.biblegateway.com/passage/?search=Ephesians+6%3A2-3&version=NIV

(6) Bible, New American Standard Version Isaiah 44:2 3, Retrieved on April 25, 2017 from https://www.biblegateway.com/passage/?search=ISA+44%3A2+&version=NASB

(7) Bible, New American Standard Version Matthew, 5:27-28. You shall not commit Adultery. Retrieved on April 25, 2017 from https://www.biblegateway.com/passage/?search=Matt+5%3A27-28&version=NASB

(8) Bible, New International Version (NIV) Malachi 3:6-10 Retrieved on April 25, 2017

from https://www.biblegateway.com/passage/?search=Malachi+3%3A1-10&version=NIV

(9) Bible, New American Standard Version Revelations 21:8, Retrieved on April 25, 2017 from https://www.biblegateway.com/passage/?search=Rev+21%3A8&version=NASB

(10) Bible, New American Standard Version, Matthew 6:24 Retrieved on April 25, 2017 https://www.biblegateway.com/passage/?search=Matthew+6%3A24+&version=NASB

(11) Bible, New American Standard Version 1 Kings 18:28-42 Retrieved on April 25, 2017 https://www.biblegateway.com/passage/?search=1+Kings+18%3A28-42++&version=NASB

(12) Bible, New American Standard Version Exodus 22:18 42 Retrieved on April 25, 2017 https://www.biblegateway.com/passage/?search=Exodus+22%3A18+-++42++&version=NASB

(13) Bible, New American Standard Bible (NASB). Deuteronomy 18:9-22. Retrieved on April 25, 2017 https://www.biblegateway.com/passage/?search=Deuteronomy+18%3A9-22&version=NASB

(14) Bible, New American Standard Version 1 Chronicles 10:13 42 Retrieved on April 25, 2017 https://www.biblegateway.com/passage/?search=1+Chronicles+10%3A13+-++42++&version=NASB

(15) Bible, New American Standard Version Galatians 5:14 Retrieved on April 25, 2017 https://www.biblegateway.com/passage/?search=gal+5%3A14+&version=NASB

(16) Bible, New American Standard Version Galatians 5:17-23 Retrieved on April 25, 2017 https://www.biblegateway.com/passage/?search=gal+5%3A17-23&version=NASB

(17) Bibile, New American Standard Version, 2 Corinthians 12:2 Third Heaven, Retrieved on April 25, 2017 from https://www.biblegateway.com/passage/?search=2+Corinthians+12%3A2&version=NASB

(18) Bible, New American Standard Version. 2 Peter 2:4. Cast fallen angels into Hell. Retrieved on April 25, 2017 from https://www.biblegateway.com/passage/?search=2+Peter+2%3A4+&version=NASB

(18) Bible, New American Standard Version Isaiah 14:12 Lucifer declares he will be god Retrieve on April 25, 2017 from https://www.biblegateway.com/passage/?search=Isa+14%3A12+&version=NASB

(19) Bible, New American Standard Version Matthew 12:24-30 Rulers of the Demons. Retrieve on April 25, 2017 from https://www.biblegateway.com/passage/?search=Matt=12%3A24-30+&version=NASB

(20) Bible, New American Standard Version Revelations 12:9, 20:2 Dragon, Retrieve on April 25, 2017 from https://www.biblegateway.com/passage/?search=Rev+12%3A9+&version=NASB

https://www.biblegateway.com/passage/?search=Rev+20%3A2+&version=NASB

(21) Bible, New American Standard Version. Matthew 13:19 Wicked One. Retrieved on April 25 2017 from https://www.biblegateway.com/passage/?search=Matt+13%3A19&version=NASB

(22) 99 Names of Allah, Retrieved on April 25, 2017 from https://www.google.com/search?q=99+names+of+Allah&oq=99+names+of+Allah& aqs=chrome..69i57.16991j0j4&sourceid=chrome&ie=UTF-8

(23) Buddha, Retrieved on April 25, 2017 from https://kadampanewyork.org/

buddha-shakyamuni?gclid=EAIaIQobChMI
2tSExYSo5QIVyICfCh08iwudEAAYASAAEgI6DfD_BwE

(24) Buddha, Retrieved on April 25, 2017 from https://www.google.com/search?q=who+was+budda&oq=who+was+budda&aqs=chrome..69i57.4684j0j1&sourceid=chrome&ie=UTF-8

(25) Bible, New American Standard Version. 2 Corinthians 4:4 god of this World Retrieved on April 25, 2017 fromhttps://www.biblegateway.com/passage/?search=2+Corinthians+4&version=NASB

(26) Bible,, New American Standard Version. 2 Corinthians 11:14 Satan disguises as light Retrieved on April 25, 2017 from https://www.biblegateway.com/passage/?search=2+Corinthians+11%3A14&version=NASB

(27) Bible, New American Standard Version. Luke 10:18. Jesus saw Satan Fall. Retrieved on April 25, 2017 from https://www.biblegateway.com/passage/?search=Luke+10%3A18&version=NASB

(28) Bible, King James Version Jude 1:6 Retrieved on April 25, 2017 from https://www.biblegateway.com/passage/?search=jude+1%3A6&version=KJV

(29) Bible, New American Standard Version 2 Peter 2:4-5 Fallen Angels Retrieved on April 25, 2017 from https://www.biblegateway.com/passage/?search=2+Peter+2%3A4-5&version=NASB

(30) Bible,, New American Standard Version Genesis, 1 God spoke and created the Heavens and the Earth, Retrieved on April 25, 2017 from https://www.biblegateway.com/passage/?search=gen+1&version=NASB

(30) Bibile,, New American Standard Version. Psalms 33:6-10 God spoke and created the Heavens and the Earth, Retrieved on April 25, 2017 from https://www.biblegateway.com/passage/?search=Psalms+33%3A6-9&version=NASB

(31) Digital Tattoo, Retrieved January 5, 2020 from https://digitaltattoo.ubc.ca/abouttheproject/

(32) Digital Tattoo purpose, Retrieved June 6, 2020 from https://savedmag.com/bill-gates-quantum-dot-digital-tattoo-implant-to-track-covid-19-vaccine-compliance/

(33) CHRISPR-CAS9 Gene Knockout Kits, Retrieved June 6, 2020 from. https://www.ncbi.nlm.nih.gov/pmc/articles/PMC6528186/

(34) Biometrics,, | Definition of Biometrics by Merriam-Webster, retrieved July 6, 2019. from https://www.merriam-webster.com/dictionary/biometrics

Definition of biometrics. 1 : biometry. 2 : the measurement and analysis of unique physical or behavioral characteristics (such as fingerprint or voice patterns) especially as a means of verifying personal identity.

(35). Sidroth.org/tomhorn, Retrieved on June 6, 2020 from https://sidroth.org/television/tv-archives/tom-horn-sharon-gilbert/?src=banner_disc Retrieved on July 9, 2019

(36) Trans-Humanism, Retrieved on April 24, 2020 from. https://www.britannica.com/topic/transhumanism

(37). Miranda Rights. Retrieved on April 27, 2020 from andresmejerlaw.com

(38) Bible, New American Standard Version. 2 Kings 9 Jehu becomes King. Retrieved on

April 25, 2017 from Retrieved on April 25, 2017 from https://www.biblegateway.com/passage/?search=2+Kings+9&version=NASB

(39) Bible, New American Standard Version, 2 Kings 10:1-30 Jehu destroys Jezebel and Ahab's sons. Retrieved on April 25, 2017 from https://www.biblegateway.com/passage/?search=1.%092+Kings+10+1%3A10&version=NASB

(40) Bible, New American Standard Version, Revelations 4, Throne Room, Retrieved on April 25, 2017 from https://www.biblegateway.com/passage/?search=Rev+4&version=NASB

(41) Bible, New American Standard Version Revelations 20 2-5 God reigns forever. Retrieved on April 25, 2017 from https://www.biblegateway.com/passage/?search=Revelation+20%3A2-5&version=NASB

REMEMBER;

DO TO OTHERS
WHAT YOU WANT DONE TO YOU

About the Author

Vonnie Bittner was born and raised in Williamsport, PA. She was married for 28 years and is where she raised her 3 daughters. She moved to Northeast PA after her youngest daughter went to college and to help with her grandchildren. She moved 4 years later to the Tampa area to assist with her Mother's care till her passing. She moved back to the Northeast 5 years later for her Father's failing health. She still resides in Northeast PA today.

She went to college at the age of 46. Life had a way of getting into her plans but she persevered to completing her BS/PSY and graduated at the age of 55. Her last class was a creative writing class where she wrote a short story and was strongly encouraged to write it as a novel. This is the novel written for your enjoyment. She retired from being a Life Coach/Caregiver to devote more time on her writings and crafts. Watch for her next book in the series of Ancient to Modern Times

CPSIA information can be obtained
at www.ICGtesting.com
Printed in the USA
LVHW010738021121
702214LV00009B/281